HARLAN COBEN

SECONDS AWAY

A Mickey Bolitar Novel

Indigo

First published in Great Britain in 2012 by Orion Books and Indigo
Paperback edition first published in Great Britain in 2013
by Orion Books and Indigo
imprints of The Orion Publishing Group Ltd
Orion House, 5 Upper Saint Martin's Lane
London WC2H 9EA
An Hachette UK Company

1 3 5 7 9 10 8 6 4 2

A CIP catalogue record for this book is
available from the British Library.

ISBN: 978 1 78062 021 3

Printed in Great Britain by CPI Group (UK) Ltd, Croydon CR0 4YY

The Orion Publishing Group's policy is to use papers that
are natural, renewable and recyclable products and made
from wood grown in sustainable forests. The logging and
manufacturing processes are expected to conform to the
environmental regulations of the country of origin.

For my godson
Henry Armstrong

Praise for *Shelter*

'A powerhouse thriller with a heart that beats like a triphammer
. . . *Shelter* will make your heart race long after the last page.
Harlan Coben has created a hero worth following to hell and
back'   Eoin Colfer

'A suspenseful, well-executed spinoff . . . Coben's semi-noir style
translates well to YA, and the supporting cast is thoroughly
entertaining'   *Publishers Weekly*

'The suspense never lets up. The ending will leave you breathless.
I can't wait for Mickey Bolitar's next adventure'   Rick Riordan

'A gripping tale'   *Daily Mirror*

'As in all great thrillers, Coben piles mystery on top of mystery
until the suspense is almost unbearable. So many twists and
shocks, I wanted to scream. But I had to keep reading instead'
R. L. Stine

'One of the acknowledged masters of the modern thriller'
Irish Independent

'A spellbinding novel of mystery and intrigue, adolescence and
adulthood, crime and punishment from a writer who's at the
very top of his game'   Ridley Pearson

Also by Harlan Coben

CHAPTER 1

There are moments in your life that change everything.

I don't mean little things like, say, what cereal turns out to be your favorite or whether you get into any AP classes or what girl you fall in love with or where you wind up living for the next twenty years. I mean total change. One second your world is one thing, the next—snap!—it is completely altered. All the rules, all the things you accepted about reality, are turned around.

Like, up becomes down. Left becomes right.

Death becomes life.

I stared at the photograph, realizing that we are always just seconds away from life-snapping change. What I was seeing with my own two eyes made no sense, so I blinked a few times and looked again—as if I expected the image to change. It didn't.

The picture was an old black-and-white. Doing a little quick math in my head, I realized that it had to have been taken nearly seventy years ago.

"This can't be," I said.

I wasn't talking to myself, just in case you think I'm nuts. (Which you will think soon enough.) I was talking to the Bat Lady. She stood a few feet away from me in her white gown and said nothing. Her long gray hair looked as though it were moving even when it was standing still. Her skin was wrinkled and crinkly, like old paper someone had folded and unfolded too many times.

Even if you don't know *this* Bat Lady, you know *a* Bat Lady. She's the creepy old lady who lives in the creepy old house down the block. Every town has one. You hear tales in the school yard about all the horrible things she'll do to you if she ever catches you. As a little kid, you stay far away. As a bigger kid—in my case, a sophomore in high school—well, you still stay far away because, even though you know it's nonsense and you're too old for that kind of thing, the house still scares you just enough.

Yet here I was, in her inner lair, staring at a photograph that I knew couldn't be what I thought it was.

"Who is this guy?" I asked her.

Her voice creaked like the old floorboards beneath our feet. "The Butcher of Lodz," she whispered.

The man in the picture wore a Waffen-SS uniform from World War II. He was, in short, a sadistic Nazi who, according to the Bat Lady, murdered many, including her own father.

"And this picture was taken when?" I asked.

The Bat Lady seemed puzzled by the question. "I'm not sure. Probably around 1942 or 1943."

I looked at the man in the photograph again. My head spun. Nothing made sense. I tried to ground myself in what I knew for certain: My name, I knew, was Mickey Bolitar. Good start. I'm the son of Brad (deceased) and Kitty (in rehab) Bolitar, and now I'm the ward of my uncle Myron Bolitar (whom I tolerate). I go to Kasselton High School, the new kid trying to fit in, and based on this photograph, I am either delusional or completely insane.

"What's wrong, Mickey?" Bat Lady asked me.

"What's wrong?" I repeated. "You're kidding, right?"

"I don't understand."

"This"—I pointed to the photograph—"is the Butcher of Lodz?"

"Yes."

"And you think he died at the end of World War Two?"

"That's what I was told," she said. "Mickey? Do you know something?"

I flashed back to the first time I had seen the Bat Lady. I had been walking to my new school when she suddenly appeared in the doorway of this decrepit house. I almost screamed out loud. She raised a ghostly hand toward me and said five words that struck me in the chest like a body blow:

3

Mickey—I had no idea how she knew my name—*your father isn't dead*.

That was what had started me down this crazy road that now led to . . . to this picture.

I looked up from the photograph. "Why did you tell me that?"

"Tell you what?"

"That my father isn't dead. Why did you say that to me?"

She was silent.

"Because I was there," I said, my voice trembling. "I saw him die with my own two eyes. Why would you say something like that?"

"Tell me," she said in that creaky old voice. "Tell me what you remember."

"Are you for real?"

The old woman silently rolled up her sleeve and showed me the tattoo that marked her as a survivor of the Auschwitz death camp.

"I told you how my father died," she said. "Now it's your turn. Tell me what happened."

A chill ran down my spine. I looked around the dark room. A vinyl record spun on an old turntable, scratching out a song called "Time Stands Still" by HorsePower. My mom had been a HorsePower fan. She had even partied with the group back in her celebrity days, before I came along and washed all her dreams away. On the Bat Lady's mantel was that cursed picture, the one of the five hippies from the

4

sixties wearing tie-dyed T-shirts with that butterfly on the chest.

"Tell me," Bat Lady said again.

I closed my eyes and took a deep breath. It was so hard to go back there—and yet it seemed as though I did it every night.

"We were driving to San Diego, just my dad and me. The radio was on. We were laughing." That's what I remember best from, well, before. The way he laughed.

"Okay," she said. "Then what happened?"

"An SUV crossed the divider and crashed head on into us. Boom, like that." I stopped for a moment. I could almost feel it, the horrible jarring, the strain against the seat belt, the whiplash into sudden darkness. "The car flipped over. When I woke up, I was trapped. Some firefighters were trying to free me."

"And your father?"

I looked at her. "You knew my father, didn't you? My uncle told me that my father visited this house when he was a kid."

She ignored the question. "Your father," she repeated. "What happened to him in the accident?"

"You know what happened."

"Tell me."

I could see him in my mind's eye. "Dad was lying on his back. His eyes were closed. Blood was pooling around his head."

My heart began to tumble.

Bat Lady reached a bony hand toward me. "It's okay."

"No," I snapped, anger entering my voice now, "it's not okay. It isn't even close to okay. Because, see, there was a paramedic working on my dad. He had sandy hair and green eyes, and eventually this paramedic looked up at me, and when our eyes met, he shook his head. Just once. And I knew. His expression said it all. It was over. My dad was dead. The last thing I saw was my father on a gurney, and that paramedic with the sandy-blond hair and green eyes wheeling him away."

Bat Lady said nothing.

"And this"—I held up the old black-and-white photograph, my voice choking, the tears coming faster now—"this isn't a photograph of some old Nazi. It's a photograph of that paramedic."

Bat Lady's face, already the whitest shade of pale, seemed to grow even paler. "I don't understand."

"Neither do I. Your Butcher of Lodz? He was the paramedic who wheeled away my dad."

Her response surprised me. "I'm tired, Mickey. You must go now."

"You're kidding me, right? Who is this guy? Why did he take my father?"

Her hand fluttered up toward her mouth. "Sometimes, we want something to be so badly, we make it so. Do you understand?"

"I don't *want* this to be a picture of the paramedic. It just is."

She shook her head, her waist-length hair flying in the breeze. "Memory is so unreliable. You will learn that as you get older."

"Are you saying I'm wrong?"

"If the Butcher had somehow lived, he'd be nearly ninety years old. That's old for a paramedic."

"Whoa, I didn't say he was ninety. He's the same age as this guy."

Bat Lady just looked at me as though the crazy shoe was on the other foot now. I realized how it all sounded now—like the ravings of a lunatic. The song ended and another began. She took a step back, her ripped white gown dragging across the old wood floor. Her gaze hardened on me.

"What?" I said.

"It is time for you to leave. And you may not see me for a while."

"I don't get it."

"You've made a mistake," she said to me.

Tears started forming in the corners of my eyes. "You think I could ever forget that face? The way he looked at me before he wheeled away my father?"

Her voice had steel in it now. "Get out, Mickey."

"I'm not going—"

"Get out!"

CHAPTER 2

An hour later I sat in my backyard—or really, my uncle Myron's backyard—and filled in Ema. As always, Ema was dressed entirely in a shade of black that matched her hair. She wore black eye makeup. There was a silver skull-and-crossbones ring on her middle finger and more earrings than I could count.

Ema's natural disposition leaned toward the sullen side, but right now she stared at me as though I had suddenly sprouted a third arm.

"You just left?" Ema said.

"What was I supposed to do?" I countered. "Beat the information out of an old woman?"

"I don't know. But how could you just leave?"

"She went upstairs. What was I going to do, follow her?

Suppose—I don't know—suppose she started undressing or something."

"Ugh," Ema said, "that's just gross."

"See?"

Ema wasn't even fifteen but she sported a fair amount of tattoos. She was maybe five-four and what most in our society would call on the large side. When we met only a few weeks ago, she sat by herself for lunch at the outcast table. She claimed to prefer it.

Ema stared at the old black-and-white photograph. "Mickey?"

"Yeah?"

"You can't really believe that this is the same guy."

"I know it sounds crazy, but . . ." I stopped.

Ema had this way about her. Her outward shell, the one she showed pretty much the entire world, was defensive and surly. Ema was not what one would call conventionally beautiful, but when she looked at me like she did now with her big brown eyes, with all the concentration and caring emanating from her face, there was something almost celestial about her.

"Go on," she said.

"The accident," I began. "It was the worst moment of my life, times ten. My father . . ." The memories flooded me. I was an only child. The three of us lived overseas for pretty much my entire life, blissfully trekking through the most obscure corners of the world. I thought that we were carefree nomads, international bohemians who worked for various charities. I didn't realize how much more there was to it.

"It's okay," Ema said.

But it was hard to reveal more. When you travel that much, you don't get to make many (or really, any) friends. It was one of the reasons I wanted so much to settle down, why my father ultimately quit his job and moved us to California and signed me up for a real school and, well, died. So you see, what happened after we returned to the United States—my father's death, my mother's downward spiral—was my fault. No matter how you wanted to slice it, it was on me.

"If you don't want to tell me . . . ," Ema began.

"No, I do."

Again she gave me the big eyes, the ones that seemed so focused, so understanding and kind.

"The accident," I said. "It took away everything. It killed my dad. It shattered my mom."

I didn't bother going into what it had done to me—how I knew that I would never get over it. That wasn't relevant here. I was trying to figure out how to transition this back to the paramedic and the man in the photograph.

My words came slower now. "When you experience something like that, when something happens so suddenly and destroys everything in your life . . . you remember everything about it. Every single detail. Does that make sense?"

"Sure."

"So that paramedic? He was the first one to let me know that my dad was gone. You don't forget what that guy looks like. You just don't."

We sat there another minute in silence. I looked at the basketball rim. Uncle Myron had gotten a new one when he knew that I'd be living with him. We both found solace in it, in basketball, in the slow dribble, in the fadeaway jumper, in the way the ball goes swish through the hoop. Basketball is the one thing I have in common with the uncle I'm forced to live with and I can't quite forgive.

I can't forgive him. And, I guess, I can't forgive me either.

Maybe that was something else Uncle Myron and I had in common.

"Don't bite my head off, okay?" Ema said.

"Okay."

"I understand everything you said. You know that. And, well, this past week has been absolutely loony. I know that too. But can we just look at this rationally for a second?"

"No," I said.

"Huh?"

"I know how this looks rationally. It looks like I should be locked in a padded room."

Ema smiled. "Well, yeah, there's that. But just so we cover all the bases, let's go through it step by step, okay? Just to make sure I have this straight."

I nodded grudgingly.

"One"—she held up a finger with pinot noir nail polish—"you're walking to school last week and you go past the creepy Bat Lady's house and even though you don't know her, have never seen her before, she tells you that your father is alive."

"Right."

"Spooky, right? I mean, how did she even know who you were or that your father was killed—and what would possess her to say such a thing?"

"I have no idea," I said.

"Neither do I. So let's move to two." Ema held up a second finger, the one with the skull ring and canary-yellow polish. "A week later, after we go through hell and back, Bat Lady tells you that her real name is Lizzy Sobek, the famous Holocaust heroine no one has seen since the end of World War Two. Then she hands you a photograph of this old Nazi who killed her father. And you think it's the same guy who took your dad away on a stretcher." Ema spread her hands. "That about sum it up?"

"Pretty much."

"Okay, good, we're getting somewhere now."

"We are?"

She shushed me with a hand gesture. "Let's skip for a moment the fact that somehow the guy hasn't aged a day in seventy years."

"Okay."

"Here's the other thing: You always describe the paramedic as having sandy-blond hair and green eyes."

"Right."

"That's what you remember best about him, right? The green eyes. I think you said they had yellow circles around the pupils or something."

"Right, so?"

"But, Mickey?" Ema tilted her head. Her voice was gentler now. "This photograph is in black and white."

I said nothing.

"You can't see any colors. How could you tell, for example, that his eyes are green? You can't, can you?"

"I guess not," I heard myself say.

"So let's put it plainly," Ema said. "What scenario is more likely? That the Butcher of Lodz has a passing resemblance to a paramedic and you imagined more—or that a ninety-year-old Nazi is now a young paramedic working in California?"

She had a point, of course. I knew that I wasn't thinking straight. In the past week I'd been beaten up and nearly killed. I had seen a man shot in the head, and I was forced to stand by helplessly while Ema had come within seconds of having her throat slashed.

And that wasn't even mentioning the really stunning part.

Ema stood, brushed herself off, and started to walk away. "Time for me to go."

"Where?"

13

"I'll see you tomorrow."

She did this all the time—just disappeared like this. "Let me walk you," I said.

Ema put her hands on her hips and frowned at me.

"It's getting late. It might not be safe."

"You're kidding me, right? What am I, four years old?"

But that wasn't it. For some reason, Ema wouldn't show me where she lived. She always just vanished into the woods. We had quickly become close, yes, maybe the closest friends either of us had ever had, but we both still had our secrets.

Ema stopped when she reached the end of the yard. "Mickey?"

"What?"

"About the photograph."

"Yes?"

She took her time before she said, "I don't think you're crazy."

I waited for her to say more. She didn't.

"So what then?" I asked. "If I'm not crazy, what am I? Falsely hopeful?"

Ema considered that. "Probably. But there is another side to this whole thing."

"What's that?"

"Maybe I'm crazy too," she said, "but I believe you."

I stood and walked toward her. I'm six-four, so I towered over her. We made, I'm sure, an odd pair.

She looked up at me and said, "I don't know how or why,

14

and, yeah, I know all the arguments against it. But I believe you."

I was so grateful, I wanted to cry.

"The question is, what are we going to do about it?" Ema asked.

I arched an eyebrow. "We?"

"Sure."

"Not this time, Ema. I've put you in enough danger."

She frowned again. "Could you be more patronizing?"

"I have to handle this on my own."

"No, Mickey, you don't. Whatever this is, whatever is going on here with you and the Bat Lady, I'm part of it."

I wasn't sure what to say to that, so I settled for, "Let's sleep on it and talk in the morning, okay?"

She turned and started back through the yard. "You know what's funny?"

"What?"

"This all started with a crazy old lady telling you that your father was still alive. But now, well, I'm not so sure she's crazy."

Ema disappeared into the night. I picked up the basketball, lost in the—and, yes, I know how this will sound—Zen-like quality of shooting. After all that had happened, I longed for a little peace and quiet.

But I wouldn't get it.

I thought that it was bad then, but soon I would learn just how bad it could get.

CHAPTER 3

I was just about to take a jump shot when I heard Uncle Myron's car pull up.

Myron Bolitar was something of a sports legend in this town. He held every basketball scoring record, won two NCAA Final Four titles in college, and was drafted in the first round by the Boston Celtics. A sudden knee injury ended his NBA career before it really began.

I'd always heard my dad—Myron's younger brother—talk about how devastating that had been for my uncle. My dad had loved and hero-worshipped Myron—until my mother became pregnant with me. To put it mildly, Myron did not approve of my mother. He let that fact be known with, I guess, very colorful language. The two brothers fought over it, leading to Myron actually punching my father in the face.

They never saw or spoke to each other again.

Now, of course, it was too late.

I know Myron feels bad about this. I know that it breaks his heart and that he wants to make amends through me. What he doesn't get is, it isn't my place to forgive him. In my eyes, he was the guy who pushed my parents down a road that would eventually lead to Dad's death and Mom's drug addiction.

"Hey," Myron said.

"Hey."

"Did you get something to eat?" he asked me.

I nodded and took a shot. Myron grabbed the rebound and threw the ball back to me. The basketball court meant a lot to both of us. We both got that. It was neutral territory, a no-fight zone, our own small land of truce. I took another shot and winced. Myron spotted it.

"Tryouts are in two weeks, right?" he asked.

He was talking about the high school basketball team. My hope, I confess, was that I'd break those old records of his.

I shook my head. "They were moved up."

"So when are they?"

"Monday."

"Whoa, soon. Are you excited?"

I was, of course. Very. But I just shrugged and took another shot.

"You're only a sophomore," Myron said. "They don't take many sophomores on the varsity."

"You started as a sophomore, didn't you?"

"Touché." Myron threw me another pass and changed the subject. "Still sore from last night?" he asked.

"Yes."

"Anything more than that?"

"What do you mean?"

"I'm wondering whether we should take you to a doctor."

I shook my head. "Just sore."

"Do you want to talk about what happened?"

I did not.

"Seems to me you put yourself and others in danger," Uncle Myron said.

I was debating on how to tap-dance around the truth. Myron knew some of it. The police knew some of it. But I couldn't tell them all of it. They'd probably never believe it anyway. Heck, I didn't believe it.

"There are always consequences to being a hero, Mickey," Uncle Myron said in a soft voice. "Even when you're sure you're doing the right thing. I've learned that the hard way."

We looked at each other. Myron was about to say something more when his cell phone buzzed. He looked at the caller ID, and something close to shock crossed his face.

"Sorry," he said to me, "but I need to take this."

He stepped away, deeper into the yard. He hunched over and started talking.

You put yourself and others in danger . . .

I could take the risks—that would be on me—but what

about my friends? What about the "others"? I stepped away in the opposite direction and took out my cell phone.

Four of us had gone into that evil nightclub to rescue Ashley: Ema and I, of course—and then there had been Spoon and Rachel. Spoon, like Ema and me, was an outcast. Rachel was anything but.

I needed to check up on them.

I texted Spoon first and got the following auto-answer. Spoon: **I cannot reply at this time. Due to recent events I am grounded until the age of 34.**

And then, because he was Spoon, he added: **Abraham Lincoln's mother died of milk poisoning at age 34.**

I couldn't help but smile. Spoon had "borrowed" his father's custodial truck in order to help us. His parents were the most caring and overprotective in our little group, so I'd figured that he'd get in the most trouble. Luckily, Spoon was, if nothing else, resourceful. He'd be okay.

I texted the fourth and final member of the gang— Rachel Caldwell. How to describe Rachel . . . ? I will make it simple: Rachel was, for lack of a better phrase, the hottest girl in school. By definition, I guess, every school has one, and, yes, she was much more than super-attractive, so please don't label me a sexist pig too quickly. The bravery and resourcefulness she'd demonstrated in that horrible place was mind-boggling.

But still, if I am being totally honest here, her hotness

was the first thing to pop into my—and almost everyone in school's—head.

How Rachel ended up joining forces with the looked-down-upon new kid (me), the self-defined goth-emo "fat girl" (Ema), and the janitor's nerdy kid (Spoon) was still something of a mystery.

I thought hard about what to text Rachel. I admit it—I got nervous and doofy around her. My palms started to sweat. I know that I should have been mature and above it. Most of the time I am. Or maybe not. Anyway, after long consideration about what exactly I should text, I put my fingers to the keypad and went with this charming opener: **U OK?**

As you can see, I'm very smooth with the ladies.

I waited for Rachel's response. None came. When Uncle Myron finished his phone call, he stumbled toward me in something of a daze.

Borrowing from my clever text to Rachel, I asked, "You okay?"

"Fine," Myron said. "Who was that?"

My uncle's voice was distant. "A close friend I haven't heard from in a while."

"What did he want?"

Myron just stared off.

"Hello?" I said.

"He needs a favor. A strange one." Myron checked his watch. "I have to run out. I should be back in an hour."

Well, that was weird. My phone buzzed. I checked my

caller ID, and when I saw Rachel's name, my pulse did a little two-step. I slid away from my uncle and opened Rachel's message. It read: **Can't talk now. Can I call you later?**

I immediately texted back **Sure** and then wondered whether that sounded too anxious or whether I should have waited, oh, eight seconds to make it look like I wasn't just standing around waiting for her text.

Pathetic, right?

Uncle Myron hurried off to his car. I headed into the kitchen and grabbed a snack. I pictured Rachel at home, texting me. I had only been to Rachel's house once. Yesterday. It was a big sprawling estate with a gate at the front of the driveway. It also looked empty and like a really lonely place to live.

The local newspaper, the *West Essex Tribune,* was on the kitchen table. The front-page story for the third straight issue involved the big-time actress Angelica Wyatt's visit to our little town. Rumor had it that not only was Angelica Wyatt filming a movie here but that, per the headline:

LOCAL TEENS TO BE USED AS EXTRAS!

Everyone at Kasselton High was excited about this possibility. The boys in my school, many of whom still had that controversial poster of Angelica Wyatt in a wet bikini on their walls, were particularly thrilled.

I, on the other hand, had more important things to occupy my time.

I pushed the paper to the side and took out the photograph of the Butcher of Lodz. I put it on the table and stared hard at it. Then I closed my eyes, imprinting the picture in my mind like a sunspot. I made myself go back to that California highway, to the accident, to being trapped in the car, to seeing my dying father, to looking into those green eyes with the yellow rings as they snuffed out all hope.

In my mind's eye, I locked in on the paramedic's face. Then I tried to superimpose this image in my head onto the one I'd created by staring at that photograph.

It was the same man.

But that was impossible. So maybe the Butcher had a son who looked just like him. Or a grandson. Or maybe I was losing my mind.

I should go see the Bat Lady again. I should demand answers.

But I had to think about how to approach her. I had to think it through and consider every possibility and try to stay logical. Plus there was something else to consider.

There is an old saying, "Nothing is certain, except death and taxes."

Whoever said that forgot one: homework.

I debated asking Uncle Myron to write an excuse note for me:

Dear Mrs. Friedman:
Mickey's French Revolution assignment will be tardy because he was rescuing another student,

*watching a man get shot, getting the stuffing beaten
out of him, being grilled by the cops . . . oh, and
he saw a photograph of an old Nazi who disguised
himself as the California paramedic who told him
that his father was dead.*

Mickey will turn in the assignment next week.

Nah. I didn't think that would work. That, and I hate the
word *tardy*. How come you only use the word *tardy* when
it comes to school? And how come you don't just say *late*?

Man, I needed sleep.

My bedroom had been, for too many years, Uncle Myron's bedroom. It was located in the basement and would be
considered "retro" if it wasn't completely lame. There was a
vinyl beanbag chair and a lava lamp and even trophies that
dated back more than twenty years.

My partner for the French Revolution project was none
other than Rachel Caldwell. I hadn't known Rachel long,
but she hit me as one of those girls who always handed her
assignments in on time. You know the type. She comes in on
test day and swears she's going to fail and then she finishes
the test in record time, hands in her perfect paper, and spends
the rest of the class putting reinforcements in her notebook.

No way she'd let me be "tardy" with the assignment.

Fifteen minutes later, my cell phone rang. It was Rachel.

I hit the appropriate button and said, "Hello?"

"Hi."

23

"Hi."

Yep. Pretty dang smooth all the way around. I decided to go now with what was fast becoming my patented ice-breaker: "You okay?"

"I guess," she said.

Rachel sounded strangely distracted.

"Pretty wild night," I said.

"Mickey?"

"Yes?"

"Do you think . . . ?"

"What?"

"I don't know, Mickey. Is it over? It doesn't feel like it is."

I wasn't sure what to say to that. I had felt the same thing—like the bad was just beginning. I wanted to offer words of comfort, but I didn't want to lie.

"I don't know," I said. "I mean, it should be."

Silence.

I said, "We have that French Revolution project due tomorrow."

"Right."

More silence. I pictured her sitting alone in that empty mansion. I didn't like it.

"Should we get to it?" I said.

"Excuse me?"

"Should we try to do the assignment? I know it's late but I can come over or we can do it over the phone or . . ."

Then, through the earpiece, I heard a noise in the background.

Rachel may have gasped. I wasn't sure. There was more noise.

"Rachel?" I said.

"I have to go, Mickey."

"What?"

"I can't talk now." Her voice took on a strange, firm tone. "I have to take care of something."

"What?"

"I'll see you at school in the morning." She hung up.

But Rachel was wrong. I wouldn't see her in the morning, because by then everything would be different.

CHAPTER 4

It began with a hard knock on the door.

I had been dreaming about my mother and father. We were somewhere I'd never been in real life—my mother, the legendary Kitty Bolitar, was playing tennis.

Before she got pregnant, my seventeen-year-old mother was the top-ranked amateur female tennis player in the world. She quit tennis to have me. And she never played again.

Weird, right?

In the dream, Mom is on center court playing in some big-time match. The crowd is huge. I sit in the stands next to my dad, but he doesn't see me. Dad just gazes lovingly at my mother on the court. They had been so happy, my parents. Most adult couples with kids, well, they aren't like that. Sure, they eat together and go to the movies and all that, but they seem to rarely make eye contact. They just occupy the same space, but maybe there's a comfort in that, I don't know.

But it was different with my parents. They never took their eyes off each other, as though no one else existed, as though they'd just fallen in love that very morning, as though they were ready to sprint across a field of daisies and embrace with some corny music playing in the background.

Yes, as their son, I can tell you that it was mortifying.

I always assumed I'd find love like that. But now I don't want it. It isn't healthy. It makes you too dependent. You smile when they smile. You laugh when they laugh. But when they stop laughing, so do you.

And when they die, a part of you dies too.

That's what happened to my mother.

In my dream, my mother hits a cross-court winner with a whiplike forehand.

The crowd screams.

A voice says, "Game, set, match . . . Kitty Bolitar!"

My mom flings her racket in the air. The crowd rises to its feet. My dad stands and claps and has tears in his eyes. I try to stand and clap too, but I can't. It's as though I'm glued to the chair. I look up at my father. He smiles down at me, but suddenly he starts floating away.

"Dad?"

I struggle, but I still can't get up. He's floating toward the sky. My mom joins him. They both wave for me to follow them. Mom calls out to me.

"Hurry, Mickey!"

But I still can't move.

"Wait!" I shout.

But they keep floating away. I put both hands on the arm-rests and try to will myself up. But I'm trapped. My parents are still in sight, but they are so far away now.

I will never reach them. I take a deep breath and try one more time to stand.

That is when I realize that I'm being held down.

There is a hand on my shoulder. The hand is strong. It locks me in place.

"Let me go!"

But the hand's grip tightens. I spin all the way around and there, standing over me, with that same hope-crushing expression on his face, is the green-eyed, sandy-blond paramedic.

More knocks on the door.

The paramedic vanished. So did my parents.

I was back in my basement bedroom. My heart pounded. I sucked down air and tried to calm myself. The knocking grew louder.

Why hadn't Myron answered?

I rolled out of bed and climbed the steps.

More impatient knocks.

"I'm coming," I shouted.

Where was Myron?

I reached the front door. I knew I should have asked who

it was, but I just opened it. Two policemen in full uniform stood there.

I took a step back.

"Mickey Bolitar?"

"Yes."

"I'm Officer McDonald. This is Officer Ball."

"Is something wrong?" I asked.

"There's been a shooting. We need you to come with us."

CHAPTER 5

For a moment I couldn't speak. When I found my voice, I said, "My uncle?"

The one named Ball said, "Excuse me?"

"Myron Bolitar. My uncle. Was he the one who was shot?"

Ball looked at McDonald. Then he turned to me and said, "No."

"Then who?"

"We aren't at liberty to discuss the case with you, son."

"I need to ask my uncle."

"Pardon?"

I started up the stairs. The two officers stepped inside too.

"Myron?" I called out.

No answer.

I entered his bedroom. Myron's bed was empty. I checked

his bedside clock. It was seven A.M. I guessed that Myron had woken up earlier and left without telling me. That wasn't like him.

I came back down the stairs.

"Are you ready to come with us?" Ball asked.

"Am I a suspect?"

"How old are you, son?"

"Almost sixteen."

"You really need to come with us."

I didn't know what to do, but really, what choice did I have?

"Let me throw on some clothes," I said.

I hurried down to the basement. My cell phone was blinking. I checked for messages. There were two. The first was from Ema. She had sent it at 4:17 A.M. Did that girl ever sleep?

Ema: **we need to find the paramedic who wheeled away your dad. I have an idea.**

Man, I wanted to know what it was, but it would have to wait.

The second text was from Myron: **Had to leave early and didn't want to wake you. Have a good day.**

Terrific. I tried to call Myron's cell, but it went straight into voice mail. When the beep sounded, I said, "The cops are here. They want to take me . . ." I stopped. Where did they want to take me anyway? "To the station, I guess. They won't tell me what's going on. Call me when you get this, okay?"

31

I hung up.

Ball yelled down the stairs, "Son, we really need to hurry."

I threw on some clothes and headed back up. Two minutes later, I sat in the back of a police cruiser as we pulled down the street.

"Where are you taking me?" I asked.

McDonald drove. Ball sat next to him. Neither replied.

"I asked—"

"It would be best if you were just patient."

I didn't like this.

"Who was shot?" I asked.

McDonald turned around. He narrowed his eyes. "How did you know someone was shot?"

I didn't like his tone.

"Uh, you told me," I said. "When I opened the door."

"I said this was about a shooting. I didn't say someone was shot."

I was going to make a dumb wisecrack—something about how I must be clairvoyant—but fear was starting to take over. I stayed quiet. Up ahead I could see the Kasselton police station. I remembered my last visit there, two nights ago, and now I also recalled that Police Chief Taylor hated Myron and thus by extension me.

But the squad car drove straight past the station.

"Where are we going?" I asked.

"I think you've asked enough questions. Just hang on."

CHAPTER 6

Fifteen minutes later, I sat in what had to be an interrogation room in a Newark police station. A small woman came in and sat across from me. She wore a tasteful suit, and her hair was pinned up in a bun. I guessed she was about thirty.

She stuck out her hand and I shook it. "I'm homicide county investigator Anne Marie Dunleavy," she said.

Homicide?

"Uh, I'm Mickey Bolitar," I said.

"Thanks for coming in to talk to us."

She took out a pen and made a production out of clicking the top. The door opened behind her. When I looked toward it, my heart sank. Chief Taylor stomped into the room as though the floor had offended him. He wore his police uniform and, despite being indoors and in fairly dim light, aviator sunglasses.

I waited for Chief Taylor to say something sarcastic to me. He didn't. He crossed his arms and leaned against the wall. I looked back toward Dunleavy.

"I'm underage, you know," I said.

"Yes, we know. Why?"

"Are you allowed to question me without my guardian present?"

She flashed a quick smile, but there was no warmth in it. "You watch too much TV. If you were a suspect in a crime, it might be different. As it is, we just need to ask you some questions. Is that okay?"

I wasn't sure what to say, but I settled for, "I guess so."

"Who is your legal guardian?"

"My mother."

Uncle Myron had wanted to be, but that had been part of the deal. I would live with him under the condition that my mother, despite being in rehab, remained my sole legal guardian.

"If you insist, we can call her."

"No," I said quickly. That would be the last thing Mom's already fragile psyche would need. "It's fine, don't worry about it."

"Do you know why you're here?" she asked.

I was going to say that it had something to do with a "shoot-ing," but that assumption hadn't helped much in the car.

"No."

"No idea at all?"

So much for that play. "Well, the officer said it had something to do with a shooting."

"It does. In fact, two people were shot."

"Who?"

"Is there anything you can tell us about it?"

"About what?"

"About the shooting?"

"I don't even know who was shot."

Dunleavy looked at me skeptically. "Really?"

"Really."

"You have no idea?"

Chief Taylor remained silent. I didn't like that. I looked at him and even from this distance I could see my reflection in his sunglasses.

"Of course I have no idea," I said. "Who was shot?"

She changed the subject. "Can you tell us where you were last night?"

I didn't like where this was going. I risked another glance at Chief Taylor. He stood with his arms crossed.

"I was home."

"When you say home—"

"The house where you picked me up."

"You're staying with your uncle, is that right? Myron Bolitar?"

At the mention of my uncle, Chief Taylor winced a little.

"I am, yes."

She nodded and wrote something down. "So tell me what you did last night."

"I did some homework. Watched some TV. Read a book."

"Was your uncle home?"

"No, he was out."

"Where?"

"He didn't say."

"And when did he come home?"

"I don't know. I fell asleep."

"What time would this have been?"

"What time did I fall asleep?"

"Yes."

"Around eleven," I said.

Dunleavy jotted that down too. "And your uncle still wasn't home?"

"I don't think so. I don't know for sure. My bedroom is in the basement and I had the door closed."

"Doesn't he check on you when he comes home?"

"Usually, yes."

"But not last night."

"Unless he came down while I was sleeping."

She made another note.

"What else did you do last night?"

"That's it."

She finally glanced behind her at Chief Taylor. Chief Taylor recrossed his arms and gave me a tough-guy stare.

"What?" I said.

"Did you talk or text with anyone?" Dunleavy asked.

"Yes."

"Which one?"

"Both."

Chief Taylor spoke for the first time. "And yet you didn't mention that, did you, Mickey?"

"Excuse me?"

"Investigator Dunleavy asked what you did last night. You gave her some song and dance about homework and TV—but you said nothing about texting and talking. That seems kind of suspicious, don't you think?"

"I also made a peanut butter and jelly sandwich," I said. "I took a shower. The shampoo I used was Pert."

Chief Taylor didn't like that. "A wise guy, just like his uncle. Are you being a wise guy with an officer of the law, Mickey?"

I was. I could be stupid with my mouth sometimes, but I'm usually not suicidal. So I stopped.

Dunleavy put a hand on Chief Taylor's arm. "I think he was trying to make a point, Chief. Weren't you, Mickey?"

Maybe I did indeed watch too much TV, but even if I hadn't, this felt a whole lot like a good-cop bad-cop routine. Chief Taylor gave me one more hard frown and went back to the wall. He leaned against it as though it might fall without him.

"Let's start with your talks," Dunleavy said. "Did you talk to someone in person or via the phone or what?"

I swallowed. What was going on here? "Via the phone."

"And with whom did you speak?"

"Just a friend."

"Her name?"

Her. Interesting. How did she know it wasn't a "his"?

"Her name," I said, "is Rachel Caldwell."

She was staring hard down at the paper, but I saw something I didn't like in the way her body sort of jerked at the sound of Rachel's name.

My blood went cold.

"Oh no . . . ," I heard myself say.

"Did Ms. Caldwell call you or did you call her?"

"Is it Rachel? Is she okay?"

"Mickey—"

"What happened?"

"Yo, kid."

I glared into Chief Taylor's sunglasses, again seeing my own reflection.

"Pipe down. You're here to answer our questions, not the other way around. Got it?"

I said nothing.

"Got it?" he repeated.

Not. One. Word.

"Mickey?" Dunleavy cleared her throat. She had the pen ready. "Did you call Ms. Caldwell or did she call you?"

My head spun. I tried to put it together. What was going on? Suddenly Rachel's words came back to me:

I have to take care of something.

What had she meant by that?

"Mickey?"

I found my voice. "Um, Rachel called me."

"Just like that?"

"Well, no. I had texted her first. Then she called me back."

I quickly filled her in on the brief text exchange. I also told her that I had texted Spoon, but they had no interest in that. Whatever had happened . . .

. . . shooting . . . two people shot . . . homicide . . .

. . . involved Rachel.

"So after your texts, Ms. Caldwell called you back?"

"Yes."

"Do you know what time this was?"

"Maybe nine."

"The phone records tell us it was 9:17 P.M."

They had already checked the phone records.

"That sounds right," I said.

"So what did you two talk about?"

"I was just checking in on her. We had an ordeal on Wednesday. You probably know about that."

They said nothing.

"So I was making sure that she was okay, saying hi, that kind of thing. We also have a project due in school. I thought we could talk about that."

"Did you?"

"Did I what?"

"Did you talk about the project?"

"Not really, no."

"How long have you known Rachel Caldwell?"

"Not long. I just started at the school—"

Chief Taylor jumped back in. "We didn't ask when you started at the school. We asked—"

"I don't know exactly. I don't think we talked before maybe a week ago."

"Not a long time."

"Yes, not a long time." I was getting scared—and when I get scared, I have a habit of getting angry and even sarcastic. So I added, "See, that's what I meant when you asked, 'How long have you known Rachel Caldwell?' and I replied, 'Not long.' Sorry I didn't make that clear."

They didn't like that. Neither did I.

"And yet you were both here in Newark on Wednesday," Dunleavy said. "Involved in that mess at the Plan B nightclub, is that correct?"

"It is."

"Interesting. Have you met Rachel Caldwell's father?"

That question threw me. "No."

"How about her mother?"

"No."

"Any family member?"

"No. Please. What's going on? Is Rachel okay?"

"Tell us about your phone conversation with Rachel Caldwell."

"I already did."

"From the beginning. Word for word."

"I don't understand. Why do you need to know word for word?"

"Because," Homicide Investigator Dunleavy said, "right after you finished talking to her, someone shot Rachel Caldwell in the head."

CHAPTER 7

I couldn't move.

The door to the interrogation room opened. A young officer leaned in and said, "Chief Taylor? Call for you." With one last hard glare, Taylor left me alone with Dunleavy.

I swallowed. "Is Rachel . . . ?"

For a moment she said nothing. Homicide. She said that she was from homicide. I took Latin. *Homo* meant "human being," *cidium*, "to kill." Murder.

I don't cry much. Almost never, in fact. My dad and Uncle Myron were the kind of guys who cry at sentimental TV commercials. Not me. I shut it down. But right then I could feel tears pushing their way into my eyes.

"She's alive," Dunleavy said.

I almost fainted from relief. I started to ask more, but Dunleavy put up her hand to stop me.

"I'm not at liberty to discuss her condition, Mickey. What I need you to do is to help me find the person who did this to her. Do you understand?"

I did. So I told her everything I remembered about the phone conversation, brief as it was. I thought about the bad guys we had helped arrest. Hadn't Uncle Myron warned me? You don't just catch bad guys and move on. Actions had consequences.

Had someone taken revenge out on Rachel?

"Tell me more about Rachel," she said.

"Like what?"

"Let's start with her social life. Is she popular?"

"Very."

"What kids does she hang out with?"

"I don't really know. Like I said, I'm new to the school."

Dunleavy glanced behind her at the door, as if she expected it might open. It didn't. Then she said, "How about Rachel's boyfriend, Troy Taylor? What's he like?"

Even with all this danger and fear, I could still feel my cheeks redden at the name of the chief's son. Troy Taylor was a senior, captain of the basketball team, and he had made it his mission to make my life hell.

"I don't think they go out anymore," I said, trying hard not to grit my teeth.

"No?"

"No."

"You okay, Mickey?"

My hands had tightened up into fists. "Fine."

Dunleavy tilted her head. "Are you her boyfriend now?"

"No."

"Because you look a little jealous."

"I'm not," I half snapped. "What does any of this have to do with what happened to Rachel?"

"I understand you assaulted Troy Taylor."

That surprised me. "I didn't assault him. It was self-defense."

"I see. But there was an altercation?"

"Not really. Maybe a quick one—"

"And was this altercation over Rachel Caldwell?"

"No. He took my friend Ema's laptop and—"

"And you hit him."

"No. That's not how it went."

"I see," she said in a way that suggested that she clearly didn't. "According to Chief Taylor, you've had a number of run-ins with the law."

"That's not true."

"No?" She looked down at a slip of paper. "It says here you were arrested for trespassing—"

"And released," I said. That had been at Bat Lady's house. "I was knocking on a door, that's all."

She kept reading. "You also operated a motor vehicle without a valid driver's license. You operated a motor vehicle while underage. Then there's breaking and entering, and using a fake ID to enter a drinking establishment and nightclub."

I decided to keep my mouth shut. I could explain it all, but she'd never get it. Heck, I didn't even get it.

"Do you have anything to say for yourself, Mickey?"

"Where's Rachel?"

She shook her head. Once again the door behind her opened. Officer Ball came into the room, and so did my uncle Myron. Myron gave Dunleavy a quick glance and rushed toward me.

"Are you okay?" Myron asked.

"I'm fine," I said.

Uncle Myron straightened up and faced Dunleavy. Though he didn't really practice law—Myron was an agent for athletes and entertainers—he was officially an attorney. He cleared his throat and said, "What's going on here?"

She smiled at him. "We're done here. Your nephew is free to go."

She started to rise.

"Investigator Dunleavy?" I said.

She stopped.

"Who was killed?"

Her eyes narrowed. "How do you know—?"

Now it was my turn to hold up the hand. "You said two people were shot. You also said you were a *homicide* detective. That means someone was killed, right?"

45

"Not always," she said, but her voice was soft.

Myron stood next to me. We both just watched her.

I said, "But in this case?"

She took her time, looking down, gathering her paper. But then she said, "The gunman also shot Rachel's mother. And, yes, she's dead."

CHAPTER 8

What do you do after getting news about a friend being shot and her mother being murdered?

In my case, you go to school.

Myron asked me a hundred questions, making sure I was fine, but in the end, what was I going to do—take what my classmates call "a mental health day"? I checked my phone and saw two texts from Ema. The first one had been sent early in the morning: **I found something about your dad's paramedic that makes no sense.**

Normally, I'd be all over that, but about an hour later, Ema's next point was much more urgent: **OMG! RUMOR THAT RACHEL WAS SHOT! WHERE ARE YOU?**

The mood at school was both somber and surreal. There were counselors on hand for kids who were having trouble dealing with the news of the shooting. Some students were openly weeping in the hallways—the ones you'd expect to get overly emotional. It didn't matter if they knew Rachel well or not, but, hey, people react differently to tragedy and it wasn't fair to judge.

Rumors were flying all over the place, but nobody seemed to know how seriously Rachel was injured. Two days ago, Rachel had told me that her parents were divorced and that her mother lived in Florida. She hadn't mentioned anything about her mom visiting.

So what was Rachel's mother doing in New Jersey?

I found Ema sitting alone in the cafeteria. Some would say that we sit at the outcast or "loser" table. That may be, but to me the cafeteria is more like a sports stadium. The so-called cool kids get the boxes and suites while the rest of us sit in the bleachers—but I always have more fun when I sit in the bleachers.

"Wow," I said to Ema.

"Yeah. Where were you this morning?"

I told her about the police asking me questions. As I did, I spotted Troy Taylor out of the corner of my eye. Troy sat, to keep within my sports metaphor, in the "owner's luxury box." Our fellow students came up to him to pay their respects or offer condolences.

I looked over at his table and frowned. "They weren't even dating."

Ema gave me the flat eyes.

"What?" I said.

"That's what matters to you now? Troy Taylor's past with Rachel?"

She had a point.

"And just for the record, Rachel didn't sit here. She sat with them." Ema pointed toward Troy's table. "Once she graced us with her presence to unload some baked goods. That's all."

"She helped us," I said.

"Whatever." Ema waved her hand dismissively. Her dark nail polish was chipped.

We ate in silence for a few moments.

"Mickey?"

"What?"

"Do you think the shooting is connected to what happened at the nightclub? I mean, are we in danger too?"

"I don't know. But we should probably be more careful."

"How?"

She looked at me with a mix of curiosity and hope. I flashed back to Wednesday, to the knife against her throat, how close Ema came to dying. My heart crumbled anew. I was about to offer up some lame statement about not worrying, that we'd come up with some answer, but I was mercifully interrupted.

"Hello, comrades. Even on this terrible day, it gives me great pleasure to see you."

It was Spoon. He always held his tray close to him, afraid

that someone would intentionally knock it out of his hands. This was our table in the farthest corner of the "bleachers"—Ema, Spoon, and yours truly. Spoon put down his tray and pushed up his glasses. His eyes were red, but he wasn't crying.

"So," Spoon said, "do we take on the case?"

Ema frowned. "What are you talking about?"

"Rachel was shot."

"We know," Ema said.

He looked at her, then at me, then at her again. "So it's agreed then?"

Ema again asked, "What are you talking about?"

"Rachel. She's part of our group."

"No, Spoon," Ema said, pointing toward the table of varsity jackets and cheerleader sweaters. "She's part of that group."

Spoon shook his head. "You know better."

That silenced Ema.

"We have to act," Spoon said.

"Act how?" I asked.

"What do you mean how?" He stuck out his chest. "We need to find out who shot her. This is too important. We cannot rest until we find out who committed this terrible deed. We should make a pact—we do not quit until we know the truth and Rachel is safe."

Ema sighed. "Ready to rescue the pretty girl, I see."

Spoon wiggled his eyebrows. "I'm a hero to all the babes."

He turned to me. "What do you say, Mickey?"

"We don't even know where she is," I said.

Spoon smiled. "I do."

That got our attention. Ema and I leaned forward. Spoon just smiled. We waited. Spoon smiled some more.

Finally I said, "Talk, Spoon."

"Right, sorry. My father. You know he's the head custodian at this school, right?"

"Of course we know," Ema snapped. "Get on with it."

"Ah," Spoon said, raising his namesake in the air, "but do you know about the custodial network?"

"The what?"

"The custodial network. It's probably too intricate to explain in detail, so let me give you the basics: Janitors talk to one another. They are the eyes and ears of any establishment. See?"

Spoon stopped and waited for a reply.

I said, "No."

Spoon sighed. "Another janitor in the custodial network is friendly with my father. This particular janitor—his name is Mr. Tansmore—works at Saint Barnabas Hospital in Livingston, New Jersey. He told my dad that's where Rachel is currently residing."

"Did he say how bad her injuries were?" I asked.

"Negative. But he did say she had a gunshot wound. Here's what I suggest: We go to the hospital after school and visit her."

51

I looked back at Troy Taylor. He was studiously ignoring me, but his best buddy, Buck, was giving me the stink-eye. Buck pounded his fist into his palm and mouthed the words *Dead man* in my direction.

I reacted by yawning back at him, patting my mouth in full pantomime.

"Tired?" Spoon asked.

"No. That was directed at Buck."

Spoon frowned. "Buck's tired?"

Yep, Spoon could be maddening.

"Just forget it, Spoon."

"Forgotten," Spoon said. Then he leaned in and said, "Well?"

"Well what?" Ema replied, clearly irritated.

"Do we go to the hospital after school? Do we try to figure out what happened to our fallen comrade?"

"Are you out of your mind?" Ema said. "You don't just waltz into a hospital and visit a shooting victim. You don't even know if she's allowed visitors or wants visitors—and if she did, she'd probably want her close friends, not us. On top of that, the police, including Troy's father, are working on the case. Real, live law enforcement officers."

Spoon wiggled his eyebrows again. "The police weren't the ones who brought down Buddy Ray at the Plan B nightclub. We were."

"And we were almost killed," Ema said.

"Fear not, fair maiden." Spoon slid his chair closer to her. "I saved you once. I can do it again."

"Don't make me punch you," Ema said.

I said nothing.

Ema looked at me. "You're not seriously considering this, are you?"

"I don't know," I said. "Suppose we can help."

"You're kidding, right?"

"We may be in danger too," I said. "We can't just stay on the sidelines. You said it yourself. We're all a part of this."

"No, I said you and I are a part of this. And I was talking about that paramedic and the Butcher of Lodz and maybe Bat Lady. I wasn't talking about Rachel Caldwell." Ema rose. "I gotta go to class."

"What? Lunch isn't even over yet."

"It is for me. I got things to do."

She started to walk away.

Spoon said, "What's up with her?"

"Got me."

"Women." Spoon nudged me with his elbow. "Am I right, Mickey?"

"As rain, Spoon."

"Right as rain," Spoon said. "While no one is sure, the expression probably derives from our days as an agrarian society. See, most agriculture relied on rain since other means of irrigation were not yet available—rain was, well, right.

53

Others though believe it's just a good alliterative, what with the two *r*s . . ."

I was no longer listening because I was watching Ema. When she walked past the "luxury box" table, Troy Taylor, who was supposedly mourning his injured girlfriend, cupped his hands around his mouth and said, "Hey, Ema. Mooo!"

Troy started laughing. So did a couple of his buddies.

Buck, also known as Mr. Follower, said, "Yeah, Ema. Moooooo!"

Someone else at the table joined in as Troy accepted high fives.

I stood up, feeling the anger rise. I started to move toward Troy and Buck. My hands clenched into fists, readying to do battle. But when Ema turned and looked back at me, I pulled up. There was something in her eyes, some sort of defiance and sadness.

Our eyes locked. I saw something there, but I really couldn't say what exactly. It moved and confused me at the same time.

Ema mouthed the word *Don't*.

I stood there for another second, but now I knew. I had to sit back down.

Ema turned and walked away, ignoring the cruel cackling behind her. I thought about that look in her eyes, the hurt, and something told me that it had nothing to do with Troy or his immature name-calling.

"Mickey?"

"Yes, Spoon."

"Contrary to popular belief, cows do not have four stomachs. They have four digestive compartments."

"Thanks for clearing that up for me," I said.

CHAPTER 9

There was still ten minutes until lunch ended. I headed outside to shoot some baskets. The same two flyers were posted everywhere. The first—the one most of the students were getting all excited about—had a surprisingly sexy photograph of Angelica Wyatt on it:

AUDITIONS FOR EXTRAS
TWO DAYS ONLY!
MAYBE YOU'LL MEET ANGELICA WYATT!
Be a Star—Even for a Few Seconds!

Pass, I thought.

Plus all my attention—all my focus—was locked in laser-like on the second flyer:

BASKETBALL TRYOUTS MONDAY!
3PM
MEET in GYM 1
Juniors and Seniors ONLY will try out for Varsity
Freshmen and Sophomores will try out for JV

Funny. Despite what happened the past few days, I still cared about basketball. I guessed that I would start off trying out for JV, but at the risk of sounding immodest, I didn't plan on staying there very long.

I took a few shots by myself. I didn't want anyone at my new high school to see me play before tryouts. Don't ask me why. I traveled almost every afternoon to play pickup games in a tough section of Newark. That was where I'd been honing my game.

As I mentioned before, my uncle Myron was a great player—the leading scorer in this school's history, a first-team collegiate All-American, a first-round NBA draft pick by the Boston Celtics.

But according to my father, I was better.

We would see. That was the beauty of basketball. It wasn't about talk. It was about what happened on the court.

I was about to head back inside when I saw the now-familiar black car with the tinted windows pull up. I stopped and waited. That car. That car with the weird license plate. The car that had been following me since this all began.

57

The car that held that mysterious bald guy. The car that had taken me yesterday to see Bat Lady.

It was back.

I waited for the bald guy with the freshly shaved head to get out. He didn't. The bell would ring in another minute or two. What did they want now?

I started toward the black car. When I got closer, the back door opened. I slid inside. The bald guy was there. The divider was up so once again I couldn't see who was driving.

"Hello, Mickey," Shaved Head said.

I had had enough of him and his sudden appearances. "Would you mind telling me your name?"

"How are you feeling?" he asked me.

"Fantastic. Who are you?"

"We understand Rachel was shot."

I waited for him to say more. He didn't. I studied his face. He was younger than I'd first thought. Thirty, thirty-five at the most. He had strong hands and sharp cheekbones, and he spoke with an accent I usually associated with snooty prep schools.

"Wait a second," I said. "Is Rachel getting shot related to you guys?"

"You guys?" he said.

"The Abeona Shelter."

I had recently learned that my parents were not merely fun-loving nomads who traveled the world and did the occasional good deed. They ran covert operations to rescue children in danger as members of a clandestine organization called the Abeona Shelter.

Abeona was the Roman goddess who protected children. The organization's secret symbol was the Tisiphone Abeona—a rather exotic butterfly with what looked like eyes on both wings.

I found the butterfly in that photograph of the hippies at Bat Lady's house. I found another in one of Ema's tattoos. And I found yet another at my father's gravesite.

Bat Lady seemed to be the leader. Shaved Head worked for the organization too. And now, it seemed, the Abeona Shelter had recruited my friends and me. Two days ago, we rescued a girl from a terrible fate. But it hadn't been easy.

"It seems apparent," Shaved Head said, "that you've become very fond of Rachel Caldwell."

"So?"

"So how fond?"

"What are you talking about?"

"Has she given you anything?"

I made a face. "Like what?"

"A gift. A package. Anything."

"No. Why would she do that?"

Shaved Head said nothing.

"What's going on here?" I asked. "Why was Rachel shot?"

"I don't know."

"I don't believe you," I said.

"Believe what you will. These are the risks we all take."

"What are you talking about?"

"You take risks. She warned you about that." She. He meant the Bat Lady. "But you can walk at any time."

"I don't understand. Why were we chosen to join you?"

He shrugged and looked out the window past me. "Why are any of us chosen?"

"That's deep, really, but you're avoiding the question. Spoon, Ema, Rachel, me—why us?"

"Why you?" He continued to look out the window. His jaw clenched and for a moment, he looked totally lost. Then he added something that surprised me: "Why me?"

The bell rang. He opened the door.

"Hurry back to class," he said. "You don't want to be late. And, Mickey?"

"What?"

"Whatever you do, don't talk to your uncle about us."

CHAPTER 10

Giggles from random classmates accompanied Spoon as he approached my locker at the end of the school day.

I just stared at him for a moment. Then I said, "What are you wearing?"

Spoon frowned. "What does it look like?"

"It looks like surgical scrubs."

"Exactly," Spoon said. He smiled widely. "It's the perfect disguise to get us into the hospital. I can pretend to be a doctor, see?"

I'm tall—six-four—and I weigh about two hundred pounds. Spoon was small in pretty much every way. He was the kind of thin that looked too fragile, like a strong wind might snap a bone. His glasses were never quite on straight and looked too big for his face.

I can easily pass for older than sixteen. Spoon could still

buy movie tickets as a "child under twelve" without making the cashier bat an eye.

"So are we going to see Rachel?" Spoon asked.

"Yes," I said.

He grinned. "You can call me Dr. Spoon. You know, to keep us in character." He glanced left and then right. "Where's Ema?"

I'd been wondering the same thing. I scanned the corridor in search of her. Nope. I had sent her a text to meet up here so we could all take the bus together, but she hadn't replied.

"I don't know," I said.

"So it's just you and me?"

"I guess. Wait, I thought you were grounded."

"Yes, but today I have a meeting of the MILF club."

I stopped. "Uh, excuse me?"

"Musicals I Love Foundation. I don't like to brag, but I'm founder and president of the club."

Oh boy. "You might want to change the name."

"Why?"

"Forget it."

He rubbed his chin. "I guess I can raise it at the next meeting."

"How many other members are there?" I asked.

Spoon looked confused. "There's supposed to be other members?"

I closed my locker.

"You want to join?" Spoon asked. "You can run for vice

president. I love musicals, don't you? Next week, Dad's taking the whole club to see the new Frank Wildhorn musical. Do you know who he is? *Jekyll and Hyde? The Scarlet Pimpernel?* I love the song 'This Is the Moment,' don't you?"

He actually started singing it.

"Yeah," I said, so he'd stop. "I love it."

I quickly sent Ema another text—**PLEASE COME WITH US.** No response.

I took another look down the corridor and sighed. "I guess it's just you and me."

"Shrek and Donkey!" Spoon shouted.

"Uh, yeah."

"Better yet"—Spoon snapped his fingers—"Don Quixote and Sancho Panza! Do you know who they are? Forget the book, I'm talking about the musical. *Man of La Mancha?* You're the brave Don Quixote and I'm his squire sidekick, Sancho. By the way, the play won the Tony for Best Musical in 1966, but you probably knew that, right?"

I didn't know about the Tony Award in 1966—who did?—but weirdly enough, I did know the musical and the story. For once, a Spoon analogy made perfect sense: Don Quixote had been delusional and, well, insane.

I took one more look down the hall for Ema. Nothing.

"Come on," I said.

Dr. Spoon and I walked toward the bus stop at Northfield Avenue. When we made the turn, I almost cried out in relief. There, waiting at the stop with an impatient frown, was Ema.

I ran up to her and gave her a hug. "Ema!" She seemed surprised by the hug. Then again, so was I.

"You came!" I said.

"Of course I came. If you two do this yourself, you'll just mess it up."

Spoon came over and became the third guy in the hug. When we all let go, Ema looked at Spoon's outfit, then looked at me. I just shrugged.

Spoon spread his arms. "You like it? Sexy, right? Like that TV character."

"Dr. McNightmare," Ema said.

While we rode the bus, I filled Ema and Spoon in on my meeting with Shaved Head in the black car. They listened in silence. When we got to Saint Barnabas Medical Center, we tried the direct route: just walk in. That, not surprisingly, did not work. There was a front desk that demanded both a picture ID and a reason for being there, several security guards, and even a metal detector.

Ema frowned. "Who wants to sneak into a hospital anyway?"

"People steal medical supplies," Spoon said. "They try to steal computers or medications or records—"

"I was asking a rhetorical question, Spoon."

"Oh."

She looked at him again. "Wait, is that a stethoscope around your neck?"

"Why, yes," Spoon said, rather pleased with himself. "Part of my disguise."

"Where did you get . . . ?" Ema looked over at me. I just shook my head as if to say, *It's not worth it*. She stopped.

"So now what?" I asked.

Spoon said, "Follow me."

So we did. We walked back outside and around the back. There was a big metal door that only opened from the inside. Spoon knocked on it three times, stopped, knocked two more times. We waited. Spoon raised his eyebrows, then gave the door two more knocks.

A man wearing a green janitorial jumpsuit opened the door. He looked out at us with a scowl. "What do you want?"

"Mr. Tansmore? It's me. Arthur." Then Spoon actually took the stethoscope off his neck, like maybe Mr. Tansmore wasn't able to see him through this clever disguise. "Arthur Spindel."

I'd forgotten that Spoon's real name was Arthur, even though I'd only given him that nickname a few days ago.

"Oh, hello, Arthur," Mr. Tansmore said. He looked out to make sure no one else was in the area. Then he said, "Come on in. Quickly."

We did.

"See?" Spoon whispered to me. "The custodial network."

Mr. Tansmore led us down into the basement. When we reached the bottom step, he turned and said, "You're not up to no good, are you, Arthur?"

65

"No, sir."

Tansmore didn't like it, but he didn't seem all that interested either. "If you get caught—"

"We never heard of you," Spoon said. "Don't worry."

"Okay. Wait here five minutes, then do whatever it is you need to do."

"Thank you," Spoon said.

"Right. Make sure your dad knows—"

"It's already taken care of," Spoon said.

I looked at Ema. She shrugged. We do that a lot around Spoon.

Spoon asked, "Do you know anything new about Rachel Caldwell's condition?"

Tansmore just shook his head.

"How about what room she's in?"

"I don't know." Mr. Tansmore had a deep voice. "She's under eighteen, right?"

"Right."

"So she'll be in the pediatric wing. Probably on the fifth or sixth floor. I got to get back to work."

He left us alone in the basement.

"What was that stuff about making sure your dad knows and it's taken care of?" I asked.

"Part of the custodial network," Spoon explained in a whisper. "But I'm sworn to secrecy."

Whatever. Spoon timed the five minutes on his watch.

Then he led us out of the basement. When we got to the first floor, Ema asked, "Now what?"

Spoon considered this. "We need to find a computer terminal."

This wasn't easy. The first floor was mostly administrative offices, but they were all either occupied or with someone nearby. It wasn't as though we could walk in and start using one.

"Maybe we should go to the fifth floor of the pediatric wing," Spoon suggested.

Sounded like a plan. Not much of one, but I wasn't sure what else we could do here. We took the elevator up, made a left, then a right, and entered the pediatric wing. The contrast was somewhat startling. The main part of the hospital was decorated in drab beiges and grays, which fit the mood. The pediatric wing was in bright colors, like one of those kiddie party places or a particularly cheery preschool classroom.

I understood the goal, but something about it came across as fake—as a lie even. This was a hospital. The kids in here were sick. You couldn't mask that with bright colors.

You also couldn't mask the smell. Sure, they had some heavy cherry air freshener, but underneath that, you could still smell, well, hospital. I hated that smell.

We started down the corridor. Most of the doors to the patient rooms were closed. When a door was opened, we tried to peek in, but you really couldn't see enough to tell who was inside.

"This is pointless," Ema said.

I agreed.

"We need to get hold of a computer," Spoon said.

But I could see that it wasn't going to happen. All the terminals were in plain view with strict security on them. There were all kinds of password and ID features too, trying to protect patient privacy.

This wasn't going to be easy.

We kept walking. One of the nurses eyed us. We must have made some sight. I was dressed normally enough, I guess, with blue jeans and a sweatshirt. Ema was all in black, pasty makeup, silver jewelry, a plethora of tattoos. Dr. Spoon was, well, you know.

"What are we looking for?" Ema whispered to me.

I didn't have a clue, so we kept walking.

There was a big art project, I guessed, going on. Every door had a different little-kid drawing on it. Some doors had five or six. There were drawings of elephants and tigers and assorted animals. There were drawings of castles and mountains and trees. The ones that moved me were the drawings of a house—always rectangular with a triangle roof—complete with a stick-figure family on the green lawn. There was always a bright sun in the corner with a smiley face.

Whoever drew those, I surmised, missed their homes and families.

I was looking at the drawings, my eyes skipping from door to door, when I saw something that made me freeze.

Ema looked at my face and said, "What's wrong?"

For a moment, I just stared at the door. Ema slowly turned and followed my gaze. A gasp escaped her lips.

This door had only one drawing on it. There was only one subject. There was no background, no trees or high mountains, no stick-figure family or smiling sun in the corner.

There was only a butterfly.

"What the . . . ?" Ema turned back to me.

There was no question about it. It was the same butterfly as I'd seen at Bat Lady's, at my father's grave, in one of Ema's tattoos. The Tisiphone Abeona. Except, for some reason, the eyes were purple.

I suddenly felt a deep chill.

"Mickey?"

I didn't know what to say.

"I don't get it," Ema said.

"Neither do I, but we have to find a way into that room."

The door was right by the nurses' station in the Intensive Care Unit. It was, in short, under constant watch. I looked around and figured, what the heck. I might as well try the direct route.

"You two wait out of sight," I said.

"What's your plan?" Ema asked.

"I'm going to just walk in the door."

Ema made a face.

"It's worth a shot," I said.

Ema and Spoon moved to the end of the corridor where no one could see them. I walked casually toward the butterfly door. I was Mr. Relaxed, Mr. Cool. I almost started whistling, that's how nonchalant I was about the whole thing.

"And where do you think you're going?"

The nurse stared at me, her arms crossed. She frowned like that librarian who doesn't believe your story about why you're returning the book late.

"Oh, hi," I said, pointing at the door. "I'm visiting my friend."

"Not in that room you're not. Who are you?"

"Wait," I said, dramatically snapping my fingers and then hitting myself on the side of the head. "Is this the fifth floor? I'm supposed to be on six. Sorry."

Before the nurse could say another word, I hurried away. I met up with Ema and Spoon down the corridor.

Ema said, "Wow, you're smooth."

"Do we need sarcasm right now?"

"Need? No. But that doesn't mean we can't enjoy a little."

"Maybe," Spoon said, "I can go in, what with my clever disguise and all. I can just pretend I'm a doctor."

Ema said, "Spoon, that's a great idea."

I looked at her, confused.

"Well, it's a great idea," Ema said. "But let's make a few adjustments."

CHAPTER 11

The nurses' station was in the middle of two corridors. There were rooms on both sides of the station. Three minutes after my attempt to enter the butterfly room, Spoon sprinted up the opposite corner to the nurse who had stopped me from entering.

"Nurse! I need a crash cart, stat!"

"Huh?"

"Stat," Spoon said. "It means quickly."

"I know what it means but—"

"Nurse, do you know the origin of the term? *Stat* is actually short for *statim*, which is the Latin term for 'immediately.'"

The nurse squinted at him. "How old are you?"

"Twenty-seven."

Another frown.

"Okay, I'm fourteen. But I'm one of those genius kids you read about."

"Uh-huh. And how come your scrubs have 'Dr. Feelgood' embroidered on the pocket?"

"That's my name! Do you have a problem with it?" He arched an eyebrow. "By the way, you're very attractive."

"Excuse me?"

"We doctors always hit on the nurses, didn't you know that? I bet you're very flattered right now." Spoon flexed an arm with about as much thickness and tone as washed-up seaweed. "Do you want to feel my muscle?"

Two more nurses stepped over. "Is this kid giving you trouble?" one asked.

"That's Dr. Kid to you, Nurse." Again he arched an eyebrow. "By the way, you're very attractive."

I was right near the butterfly door now. All eyes were trained on Spoon. I was just about to reach for the door when one of the nurses, maybe sensing something, started turning back toward me.

Oh, this wasn't good.

I was going to duck . . . but what good would that do? I was right out in the open. The nurse's eyes were almost on me when Ema shouted, "Kevin! Where are you? Kevin!"

The nurse swiveled her head back toward the voice as Ema hurried over to Spoon.

Time to move.

I opened the door with the butterfly on it and stepped into the dark. As the door closed behind me, I heard Ema going on, "Kevin, you were supposed to stay in the psych ward. I'm so sorry, this is my brother and he wandered off. I'll take it from here . . ."

Her voice—all voices—fell away as the door closed behind me.

I was turning toward the bed when I heard someone say, "Mickey? How did you get in here?"

There, sitting up in the bed, was Rachel.

CHAPTER 12

I hurried to her bedside. There was a bandage on the side of Rachel's head, but she looked relatively okay. There wasn't a ton of tubes snaking out of her or anything like that. Her sleeves were pulled up. My gaze was drawn to that old, horrible burn mark on her inner arm—the one flaw that seemed to enhance the rest of the physical perfection. Rachel's eyes were wet from what looked like tears.

I wanted to hug her or do something, but instead I stood by her bedside and waited.

"How did you get in?" Rachel asked.

"Spoon is causing a diversion."

She tried to smile, but broke into a sob instead. "My mom . . ."

I moved closer to the bed and sat on the edge. I took her hand. "I heard. I'm so sorry."

Rachel's head fell back on the pillow. She blinked and stared up at the ceiling. "It's my fault."

"You can't blame yourself."

"You don't understand," she said in a small voice. "I got her killed."

I froze. Rachel started to cry again.

"What do you mean?" I asked.

She just shook her head.

"Rachel?"

"You need to leave."

I ignored that. "What do you mean, you got her killed?"

She shook her head again. "I don't want to put you in danger too."

"Don't worry about me, okay? Just tell me what's going on. Are you okay?"

The door behind me started to open.

I have fast reflexes. That, I know, was a genetic thing. When your mother was one of the greatest tennis prodigies of her era and your uncle was a professional-level basketball player, that had to help. I didn't hesitate. The moment I heard the door opening, I dived down and slid underneath Rachel's bed.

Someone said, "Hello, Rachel."

My stomach dropped when I recognized the voice.

I could hear Rachel adjusting herself on the bed. "Chief Taylor?"

"It's been a long time," Chief Taylor said, which, I thought, was sort of an odd thing to say to a teenage shooting victim. I could see his brown shoes move toward the bed. "How are you feeling, Rachel?"

There was something in Chief Taylor's voice—a strange sort of tension. He was trying to sound like the confident cop, but something felt off.

"Fine, thank you."

Rachel's voice too. There was a strain there, a friction, something playing under their casual words.

"The doctors tell me you were very lucky."

"Oh yes, very," Rachel said—and I heard a tinge of anger in her tone. "My mother is dead. I feel so blessed."

"I didn't mean that," Taylor said, ever the idiot. "I meant your physical health. It seems the bullet grazed your skull, but didn't penetrate."

Rachel did not speak.

"I'm very sorry for your loss," Chief Taylor said in a voice that didn't sound sorry.

"Thank you," Rachel said in a voice that didn't sound very grateful.

What was going on here?

"Did you know I was first on the scene?" Taylor asked.

"I didn't, no."

"Yep. I called the ambulance for you."

Silence.

"What do you remember about the shooting?" Taylor asked.

"Nothing," Rachel said.

"You don't remember being shot?"

"No."

"What do you remember?"

"Chief Taylor?"

"Yes."

Rachel yawned. "I'm not feeling very well right now."

"But you just said you were feeling fine."

"I'm still on some medications. I'm feeling very drowsy. Could you come back another time?"

There was a long pause. Then Chief Taylor said, "Of course, Rachel. I understand. Maybe we can talk later."

"Sure."

I watched his brown shoes head away from the bed. They stopped at the door. "One more thing," he said.

Rachel waited.

"A homicide investigator named Anne Marie Dunleavy will be coming by to interview you. Don't feel obligated to talk to her before we speak again, okay?"

Huh?

"If you do talk to her," he continued, "well, you just said you don't remember anything. It's okay to tell her that."

Double huh?

Chief Taylor opened the door to head out, but there was a nurse at the door.

"We need to roll her down for X-rays," the nurse said.

"I'll hold the door for you," Taylor said.

I was trapped.

As the nurse came in, I stayed where I was. So did Chief Taylor. From the bed I could hear the nurse pull a lever and then those sidebars came up.

They were going to wheel her out in this bed.

There was no way I wouldn't be exposed.

I looked left and right. Nothing. I could try to commando crawl, but where would I go? Taylor would see me in an instant. The nurse was positioned to roll the bed. Chief Taylor was holding open up the door.

There was nowhere for me to hide.

"Wait . . . ," Rachel said weakly.

"For what, dear?"

"I'd like to use the bathroom first."

Ah, Rachel! Good thinking.

"There's one where we're going," the nurse said in a voice that was not going to be denied. She started to push. "It will be easier to go there."

"But—"

The nurse started pushing the bed. I did the only thing I could. There were bars under the bed. I grabbed them and pulled myself up. I pressed my feet against the underside and lifted my entire body off the floor.

The nurse stopped, probably because of the additional weight. "Is the brake still on the wheels?"

I held on as she checked. Have you ever done that exercise called the plank, the one where you hold your body in an upper push-up until your entire core starts to quiver? Well, that was sort of what I was doing, except upside down. I felt like a bat or something.

I didn't know how long I could hang on.

The nurse wheeled the bed right past Chief Taylor's shoes.

My fingers were starting to tire. My stomach was turning to jelly.

The nurse started down the corridor. I watched the distance between us and Taylor's shoes increase. I wondered whether Rachel had figured out what I was doing and I guessed that maybe she had. When we reached the elevator, I couldn't hold on any longer. I let go, collapsing back to the floor.

"Nurse?" Rachel said.

"Yes?"

"Could you get me my stuffed bunny?"

"Pardon me?"

"I'm really sorry. Kirbie—that's my bunny's name—is in my room. I'm . . . I'm scared to go anywhere without her. Please?"

The nurse sighed.

"Please?" Rachel said again.

"Okay, dear. Just wait here."

As soon as the nurse moved away, I slid out from under the bed. "You have a stuffed bunny?"

"Of course not. Get out of here before she gets back."

"I want to know—"

79

"Another time, Mickey, okay? Just go."

The elevator doors opened beside me. I stepped inside and pressed the button. I watched as the doors started to close. Rachel tried to smile at me, but it wouldn't hold. And then, maybe half a second before the doors shut all the way, I saw someone else behind her.

It was Chief Taylor. And he was staring straight at me.

"Hold that elevator!"

But I didn't let my fast reflexes work this time. The doors closed all the way. There was a small delay, as if the doors might open again and let Chief Taylor in. But they didn't.

I headed down to the lobby and walk-sprinted out the door.

CHAPTER 13

I caught up with Spoon and Ema in the parking lot.

"Keep moving," I said. "Chief Taylor might be on to us."

We hurried down the block and back onto Northfield Avenue. There was a dry cleaner located on the corner. We ducked behind the building.

"Was Rachel in that room?" Ema asked.

I nodded and told them everything that had happened.

"So," Ema said, "somehow Abeona is involved in this too?"

"Seems so," I said.

Spoon was silent. He looked a little lost. I worried about him. He hadn't asked for any of this. True, none of us had, but he seemed a little more like a babe in the woods. Our friendship, if that was what this was, started only a few days ago when he walked up to me in the cafeteria and offered me, well, his spoon. That was how our relationship, not to mention his nickname, started.

"So what do you think we should do?" Ema asked me.

"I hate to interject," Spoon said, finally speaking, "but the Musicals I Love Foundation meeting would definitely be over by now. My parents will be expecting me."

"Musicals I Love Foundation?" Ema repeated.

I gave her a don't-ask headshake.

When the bus showed up, we hopped on and started back for home. We got off where we had begun, on the corner of Kasselton Avenue and Northfield. I figured that I'd walk home via Bat Lady's house and stop by to see her. But I didn't know what to say. I was exhausted and scared and confused.

As we neared Bat Lady's street, my cell phone trilled. It was Uncle Myron. I was going to ignore it, but that wouldn't do any good. "Hello?" I said.

"I figured you'd be home by now," Myron said.

"I'm on my way."

"Do you want me to pick you up?"

"No, I'm good."

"But you're on your way?"

"Yes."

"Good," Myron said. "I need to talk to you about something."

I switched hands. I could see Bat Lady's creepy house now. "Is everything okay?"

"Everything's fine," he said.

"Okay then. I'll be home soon."

I hung up. Bat Lady's house looked, as always, haunted. The wind had picked up and for a moment, I almost thought the gusts would topple it. There was a bent willow tree in the front yard and, I knew, woods in the back. Night had started to fall.

Ema and Spoon stayed on the sidewalk across the street. As I approached, I noticed that no lights were on. Not one. Strange. Usually the Bat Lady had a light on in her bedroom. But not tonight. I knocked on the door, feeling the porch beneath my feet shake. One of the columns had already collapsed.

There was no answer.

I walked back over to Ema and Spoon. We started down the street in silence. Suddenly—yet as always—Ema said, "I'll see you guys later."

She veered toward the woods without another word.

I wanted to ask where she was going or if I could accompany her, but I had been through that before. She would only get upset with me. I watched until she vanished into the thickness.

Unsure what to do, I let my curiosity get the better of me. I knew that it was probably wrong, that it was some kind of breach in our trust and friendship. As I said before, we are all entitled to our secrets. But I asked anyway.

"Spoon?"

"Yeah?"

I could still back off, but I didn't. "What's Ema's deal?"

"What do you mean?"

I gestured toward where she'd just disappeared. "Where does Ema live, who are her parents, that kind of thing."

Spoon pushed the glasses up his nose. He seemed lost in thought.

"Spoon?"

"No one really talks to me directly. So this is all stuff I've overheard."

I thought about that, about this town, about what it has done to him. Spoon wasn't so much actively bullied or picked on as he was ignored. Week after week, month after month, year after year—ignored or worse. He had found an escape by pouring himself into things that don't turn away from you—musical theater, books, random facts, his imagination. He was like a sponge, absorbing all of this information and goodness, but he didn't really have anyone to wring himself out on, as it were.

Except now, I guessed, he had me.

"Well," I said, "you're a great overhearer."

Was that even a word?

Spoon smiled. "Really? You think so?"

"Sure. So tell me. What have you overheard about Ema?"

He made a face as though he was mulling that one over.

"No one seems to know much," Spoon said in a faraway voice. "But . . . there are stories."

"Like?"

"You know her real name is Emma, not Ema, right?"

I did. It seemed that Buck had helped give her that nickname in Spanish class, noticing that her real name was Emma and that she was kind of emo.

"She moved into town three years ago. I've never been invited to her house. Big surprise, right? But it isn't just me. I don't know anyone who has. Rumor has it, she lives in a cabin in the woods, you know, and her dad does something illegal. Like making moonshine or something."

I frowned. "Making moonshine?"

"Moonshine is a slang term for an illegally produced distilled beverage. There are other terms for it. Hooch, Devil's Brew, White Lightning—"

"I know, I know," I said, putting a hand up to slow him down. "It just sounds kind of weird."

Spoon's eyes were wide now. "They also say her dad's an alcoholic. And he hits her a lot. They say she's got all those tattoos to cover up her bruises."

Could that be true? I didn't know what to say, but it suddenly felt like something heavy was sitting on my chest.

"I Googled her once," Spoon said. "Emma Beaumont. But there was nothing relevant. In fact, there is no listing of a Beaumont in town."

"Nothing at all?"

"Nothing," Spoon said. "In short, I don't know what Ema's 'deal' is. But I like her a lot, don't you?"

"I do," I said. And then, corny as it sounded, I added, "I like you a lot too."

My words startled him. Spoon looked up at me, blinked a few times, and then puffed out his chest. "I like you a lot too."

Spoon and I both just stood there, saying nothing.

"We're having a moment, aren't we, Mickey?"

"Right," I said, "and now I think it's time to end it."

"Agreed," Spoon said. Then: "Mickey?"

"Yes?"

"Don't you think it's time you told me all about Abeona?"

He had a point. He had more than earned his stripes. "Yeah, Spoon. Maybe we should talk."

"As we walk," he said. "I have to get home, remember?"

"Right. The Musicals I Love Foundation meeting is over."

"Exactly. Do you want to be vice president?"

"Sure, why not?" I said. "It'll look good on my college applications. One thing, though."

"Yes?"

I threw my arm around him. "We need to work on a name change. . . ."

CHAPTER 14

I didn't know what to do with what I'd just learned.

Ema was my best friend. I know that might sound pathetic—we had only known each other a few weeks—but it was the truth. We were more than that, really, though I couldn't quite figure out what that meant yet.

But if she was in danger. If someone was hurting her . . .

She had told me to butt out.

But could I?

From three houses away, I spotted Uncle Myron standing in the front doorway. For a moment, I just stood there and watched him. I tried to sort out my feelings for him, but they were all over the place.

Myron saw me and raised his hand in a wave. I waved back and hurried over to him.

"Are you okay?" he asked. "How are you feeling?"

I knew that he meant well, but I wished he'd stop it. "I'm good."

"The news reports say Rachel's wounds are not life threatening."

"Yeah, that's what they said in school," I lied.

"Do you have a lot of homework?"

"Some."

"Come on," Myron said, starting for the car. "I want to show you something."

"What?"

"It's a surprise." He started toward his car. I followed. "And it might explain why I won't be around much the next couple of weeks."

Not be around much? That would be welcome. Don't get me wrong. I understood why I had to stay with Uncle Myron. He was trying. I was trying. But I wanted my mother back. Dad, well, Dad was dead. Dead is dead. But Mom was just . . . broken, I guess. When something is broken, it can be fixed, right?

I flashed back to that photograph of the Nazi who looked like Dad's paramedic. For a second, just a second, I debated telling Myron about it. But what would he do? He would think I was crazy. And even if he didn't, well, did I want him involved in this? Did I trust him enough to share? Hadn't even Shaved Head warned me not to?

Good questions.

I slid into the passenger seat. Myron drove a Ford Taurus.

We spent the first two minutes sitting in uncomfortable silence. I'm okay with uncomfortable silence. Uncle Myron is not.

"Soooo," Myron said, stretching the word out, "how was school today?"

Really? I thought, holding back the sigh. "It was okay."

"I'm so glad you have Mrs. Friedman. She was my favorite teacher back in the day."

"Yep."

"She brings history to life, you know?"

"I know."

I looked out the window.

"Basketball tryouts start Monday, right?"

Let it go, I thought. "Yep."

"Good luck with that."

"Thanks."

As we drove past the Coddington Rehab Center, I could feel Myron tense up. He hit the accelerator a little bit harder, trying to be subtle. I got it. My mom was inside there. After her most recent relapse—and, yes, it was a bad one—I was told that I couldn't visit her for at least another two weeks. I didn't like it. I thought that maybe their "cure" was too cruel. But I would listen. Still I looked out the window and imagined what was going on up that little hill. My mother was going through withdrawal now. I pictured her alone in some dark room, doubled over in pain as the poison left her veins.

"She'll be okay," Myron said.

Like I was in the mood for platitudes. I changed subjects.

"Where are we going?" I asked.

"Just wait one more minute. You'll see."

He turned down a side road. Up ahead I could see a driveway with a dark ornate gate, like something you'd see in some scary old movie. Two stone lions guarded the entrance. Myron pulled up and stopped the car. He leaned out the window and waved to the guard. With a slow creak, the gates swung open.

"Are we still in Kasselton?" I asked.

"On the border, yes."

I expected to see a house right away, but the driveway winded up a hill. I don't know how long the ride was but I'd guess that it was nearly half a mile from the entrance until I saw the . . . well, "house" really wouldn't do. Neither would "mansion." It was more like a dark castle, a nightmare version of the one in Disney World. There were towers and spires, and it had an almost fortresslike feel.

"A famous mobster lived here for nearly fifty years," Myron said. "When your dad and I were kids, well, there were all kinds of rumors about this place."

"Like?"

Myron shrugged. "Just stories. Like with Bat Lady's house. Probably nothing to them."

He should only know.

"So who lives here now?" I asked.

"You'll see."

We stopped the car. There was a moat around the castle.

I don't think I'd ever seen that before. A burly bodyguard nodded at us. Myron nodded back. We crossed the bridge. Myron knocked.

A few seconds later, a man in black tails and slicked-back hair greeted us at the door. "Good evening, Mr. Bolitar."

He spoke with a thick British accent and looked like something you'd see on one of those boring British historical shows.

"Good evening, Niles."

Was this guy a butler?

"Meet my nephew, Mickey."

Niles smiled at me, but there wasn't much warmth there. "Charmed."

"Yeah," I said. "Charmed."

"You may wait in the drawing room," he said.

I don't know where the term *drawing room* comes from, though I bet Spoon could tell me. There were no crayons or sketch pads or anything like that. The chairs were covered in red velvet. I stayed standing because the furniture looked old and like it might snap if we sat. I noticed Myron stood too. There was an antique globe and lots of dark woods.

Niles came in holding two cans of Yoo-hoo. Myron smiled happily. Yoo-hoo, for those who don't know, is like a chocolate soda. Myron loves it. I think it tastes like dirt.

Myron took his and started to shake the can. Niles turned to me and I said, "No, thanks."

Niles left us alone. I turned to Myron. He was gazing at

his can of Yoo-hoo as if it were his new girlfriend. I cleared my throat.

"Well?" I said.

Myron gestured for us to sit. We did. Gingerly.

"So remember yesterday when my friend called?" Myron began.

"Yes."

"He asked me to do him a favor and watch out for someone."

I narrowed my eyes. "Watch out?"

"Yes."

"Like you're watching out for me?"

He swigged the Yoo-hoo. "Well, not quite."

And then she walked into the room.

Like calling this place a "house" was inadequate, saying she "walked" also seemed far too tame. Accurate, yes. I mean, she didn't do anything extraordinary. Not really. She didn't glide into the drawing room or ride in on a white horse or anything like that. But she might as well have.

She made an entrance and she made it just by entering.

I didn't say "wow" out loud, but I almost did.

We both quickly stood, not because we were being gentlemen, but because something about her entrance demanded it. There, in the flesh, was the talk of the town, the movie poster come to life, Angelica Wyatt.

"You must be Mickey," she said.

Angelica Wyatt was, in a word, stunning. She stepped

over to me and took my hand in hers. "Such a handsome young man."

I looked over at Myron, who was smiling like a dope, and I realized that I probably was too. "Uh, thanks."

Even with movie stars, I remain the essence of smooth.

"It's so nice to meet you," she said.

"Uh, same."

I had to stop wowing her like this.

"Let's sit," Angelica Wyatt said.

We did. Myron and I took the couch. Angelica Wyatt took the chair across from us. She crossed her legs, making an event of it. Her smile was enough to curl a man's toes.

"Thank you for loaning me your uncle," she said. "It seems that there are some who think I may need extra protection during this shoot."

I looked over at Myron. I didn't quite understand. Myron was an entertainment agent. How was he supposed to protect a famous actress?

Maybe, like my dad, Myron had some hidden talents too?

Angelica Wyatt seemed to be studying my face. "Your resemblance to your uncle is obvious," she said. "But I also see a lot of Kitty in there. You have her eyes."

At the mention of my mother, I could feel a lump form in my throat. "You know my mother?"

"I did," Angelica Wyatt explained. "Years ago. When she was a tennis prodigy and I, well, I guess you'd call me a young starlet."

I didn't know what to say.

"How is she?" Angelica Wyatt asked.

I glanced at Myron, but he turned away. So. He hadn't told her. "She's having a tough time right now," I said.

"I'm sorry to hear that," she said. "When I heard about your father . . ." She swallowed hard. "They were so close. I'm just so sorry."

"Did you know my father too?"

Now she was the one who glanced over at Myron. I could feel something weighing me down, crushing my heart in a hundred different ways.

"I did, yes."

"Can you tell me how?"

Myron squirmed a little. Angelica Wyatt looked away, and a small smile toyed with her lips. My mother was only thirty-three. I figured that Angelica Wyatt was maybe a year or two older.

"It was a fun time," Angelica Wyatt began. "Maybe too fun, if you know what I mean."

"I don't," I said.

"We were young celebrities, I guess you'd say. Your mother was getting a lot of attention for her tennis—not to mention her good looks. I was starring as the college-age daughter in a TV series." Her smile was wistful. "Your mother . . . she was so funny. She had this wonderful laugh, and this way about her. People were drawn to her. Everyone wanted to be near Kitty Hammer."

She stopped. Myron had his head down. I remembered my mother's laugh. It was a sound I had taken for granted, of course, and would now give anything to hear again.

"And my father?" I said.

"Well, he came along and changed everything."

"How?"

Angelica Wyatt considered that. "They say love is like a chemical reaction. Have you heard that?"

"I guess."

"That was what happened. It was like your mother was one person before they met and like that"—Angelica Wyatt snapped her fingers—"she was someone different." She smiled. "We were all so young. Too young, in fact. It was all too much, too fast."

"How so?" I asked.

"How old are you now, Mickey?"

"Almost sixteen."

"By the time your mother was sixteen, she was already on magazine covers. She was being touted as the next big thing in tennis. Gossip magazines wrote about her. And then, not too many months later, she would fall in love with your father."

We all stopped. The room was silent. Angelica Wyatt left out the big part of the story, of course—the elephant in the "drawing room," if you will.

Not too many months later, Kitty Hammer would be pregnant. With me. She would be forced to stop training at the peak of her career. She would never play again. She would lose everything.

Why?

Because she was pregnant, yes, but also because those closest to my parents were against the marriage. They would put pressure on the new couple. They would tell them that they were too young, that they were being foolish, that there were too many things they didn't know about each other. They would even say horrible, scandalous things about my mother in the hopes that my father would see the "light."

I turned and glared at Myron. The old anger resurfaced.

"Pardon me."

It was Niles the butler.

"Ms. Wyatt, you have a phone interview with *Variety*."

She sighed and rose. Myron and I did likewise. She took my hand in her hands and looked at me. There was something comforting in her eyes, something warm and genuine. "We'll talk again, okay?"

"I'd like that," I said.

And then she was gone.

CHAPTER 15

Again the car ride started in silence. Again Myron had to break it.

"So what time are basketball tryouts?"

"I don't get it," I said, trying to keep my temper in check. "Why you?"

"What?"

"Why would you be 'watching out'"—I made quote marks with my fingers—"for Angelica Wyatt?"

"It's how I land clients sometimes," he explained. "See, Angelica Wyatt is leaving her agency. I was hoping—"

"I thought you sold your company."

"I did," Myron said.

"So?"

"So it's complicated."

"I don't understand. You, what, get hired out as a bodyguard?"

"No."

"Then what?"

We hit a traffic light. Myron turned and met my eye. "I help people."

"Help people how?"

"I watch over them. I solve tricky problems. And sometimes . . ."

"Sometimes what?"

"Sometimes I rescue them."

Myron started driving.

"Is that what you think you're doing with me?" I asked. "Rescuing me?"

"No. You're family."

"So was your brother. Why didn't you rescue him?"

I saw the pain flash across his face. But I wasn't done.

"You could have, you know," I said, and it was like a dam broke. "You could have rescued both of them. Mom and Dad. Right from the start. You could have understood that they were young and scared. You could have accepted that they loved each other instead of trying to break them up. Mom could have delivered me and gone back to her tennis. She could have been the great star she was supposed to be. Mom and Dad wouldn't have had to run away—they could have raised me right here. I could have had a real relationship with my grandparents. You and I, we could have been uncle and nephew. We could have played ball together."

Myron stared straight ahead. A tear ran down his cheek. My eyes started to brim up too, but I'd be damned if I would let any tears escape.

I didn't let up. "And if you had done any of that, Mom wouldn't be a shell of herself sitting in rehab today. She'd be laughing that laugh. And Dad would be alive, and we'd all be hanging out. Do you ever think of that, Myron? Do you ever look back and wonder, what if you had believed in them?"

I felt suddenly spent and exhausted. I closed my eyes. My head dropped back on the neck rest.

A few moments later, Myron spoke in a soft, pained voice. "I do think about that. I think about it every day."

"So why, Myron? Why didn't you help?"

"Maybe you can learn from my mistakes."

"Learn what?"

"It's like I said before." Myron pulled into the driveway, his face darkening. "There are always consequences to being a hero. Especially when you're sure you're doing the right thing."

CHAPTER 16

When we got home, Myron and I went our separate ways. I did homework with the television on, hoping to catch updates of the shooting at Rachel's house, but the cable news had no mentions of it.

I thought a lot about Rachel sitting in that hospital bed. I thought about Ema and the rumors Spoon had heard. I thought about my mother going through detox. I thought about my father dead and Bat Lady's cryptic words. I thought about Myron's warning about the dangers of being a hero.

I was going to go online and search for Rachel's name, but before I did, I flipped stations, figuring I'd check the local news. Channel Five ran its ominous nightly warning: "It's ten P.M., do you know where your children are?" before flashing to the news.

The anchorman had black hair that looked like a plastic

wig with wet paint and enough rouge on his cheeks to re-mind me of a visit to the Ringling Brothers and Barnum and Bailey Circus.

"The president visits troops overseas. A shooting in Kas-selton leaves a mother dead and a daughter hospitalized. And that soda you're drinking? It might be poisonous. We'll tell you all about the big soda scare and how to stay safe—after this commercial break."

I looked down at my glass of water. I was glad it wasn't soda.

When the waxy anchorman came back, he talked about the president and then he got to the "soda scare" story, which told how one person claimed to have found a worm in a cer-tain soda that he got in a fast-food restaurant in West Nyack and so the how-to-stay-safe warning seemed to be to check your soda if you bought it at a certain fast-food restaurant in West Nyack.

Finally: "A shooting in a ritzy neighborhood in Kasselton, New Jersey, last night left a mother dead and her daughter with a gunshot wound to the head." The screen now showed Rachel's house. "The shooting of Nora Caldwell and her daughter, Rachel, took place in this lavish mansion. Police believe that it may have been a break-in gone wrong, but they also say it is too early in their investigation to speculate."

So they knew nothing, I thought.

There were many things that were bothering me about the investigation. For one thing, I had been at Rachel's house the day before the shooting. She told me that her parents were divorced, that she lived with her father, who was mostly absent (traveling around with Trophy Wife #3), and that her mother lived in Florida. How come she didn't mention that her mother was up visiting and presumably staying in her ex-husband's house?

Did that make sense?

Had Rachel just thought that it wasn't important to tell me her mom was visiting—or was there something else there?

I didn't know. But something didn't sit right.

On top of that, what was up with Chief Taylor's weird hospital visit? I assumed that he must know Rachel via his son, Troy—I was trying not to grit my teeth as I thought about this—but what was up with him not wanting Rachel to talk to Homicide Investigator Dunleavy until she talked to him first? Was he afraid of what she'd say—or, more likely, was Chief Taylor just being a tool who wanted to know everything first?

I climbed into bed, thinking about the fact that both Rachel and I had lost a parent. It made you feel like you were always standing on shaky ground, like the earth could give way at any time and that you could fall and no one would be able to grab you.

I thought about Ema and the rumors. I wondered where she was right this very second, whether she was okay. I picked up my phone and texted her: **Just wanted to say good night.**

Two minutes later, Ema replied: **u can be such a big girl sometimes.**

I smiled and texted back: **OK. Good night.**

Ema: **I got some info on your Nazi paramedic.**

Me: **What?**

Ema: **let's meet before school bell Monday. I can show u then.**

CHAPTER 17

Ema was waiting in the back corner of the student parking lot when I arrived. These spaces were coveted, and I guess there was a time when students started throwing punches over them. Now the school wisely raised money by selling them. If you wanted a prime space for the school year, it cost a grand. What was most amazing to me was not only did the spots sell out in record time, but there was a waiting list.

I was carrying a gym bag with my basketball stuff in it. Today was the first day of tryouts. Despite all the other things that were going on in my life, I still had butterflies in my stomach over that.

I walked to school. So, I guessed, did Ema. I mean, I had never seen a parent drop her off. She usually just came out of the woods behind the field. As I approached, I couldn't help but notice that Ema looked somehow . . . different. I couldn't put my finger on it. She was still dressed in all black without a hint of color. The skin was still pallid, her lipstick choice today a slightly more venomous shade of red.

"What?" Ema said.

I shrugged. "You look different."

Her eyes narrowed. "Different how?"

I couldn't put my finger on it, but there was definitely something—something maybe about the tattoo on her arm . . . Whatever. Now was not the time. "Doesn't matter. You said you learned something about the Butcher of Lodz?"

Ema suddenly looked wary.

"What?" I said.

"You have to promise you won't ask about my sources."

I frowned. "You're kidding, right?"

"Yeah, right, because what joke could be funnier than that?" She bit down on her lower lip. "You have to promise me. You won't ask."

"I don't get it."

"Just promise, okay?"

"I don't even understand what I'm promising," I said, "but okay, I won't ask about your sources or whatever."

Ema hesitated, studying my face to make sure that my promise was legit. Then she said, "I did some Photoshopping with your picture of the Butcher. If I sent someone a picture of a guy in a Nazi uniform and asked if he worked as a paramedic, they'd think I was nuts."

I nodded. That made sense.

"So I used Photoshop to change his clothes into something more current. I also sent one photograph that was in the original black and white, and one that I colorized."

"Who did you send them to?"

Ema gave me a hard look.

"Oh, wait," I said. "Is that the source you're talking about? The one I'm not supposed to ask about?"

"Not really," Ema said. Again she hesitated. All around us, cliques were gathering. They were chatting or laughing or, like us, having serious talks. I wondered how many of them were talking about old Nazis from World War II. I doubted many were.

I sent the pictures to the director of Emergency Medical Services for San Diego," Ema said. "My source is the one who got me in touch with him. But that's not important."

"Okay," I said. "And what did the director tell you?"

"Hello, colleagues!"

I turned. It was Spoon. Ema did not look pleased.

Spoon pushed the glasses up his nose. "Am I late?"

"We just got started," I said.

We both turned back toward Ema. She looked even less pleased. "Wait."

"What?"

She pointed at Spoon. "What's he doing here?"

"He's part of this, Ema."

She looked at Spoon. Spoon wiggled his eyebrows and spread his arms.

"Like what you see?" Spoon asked.

Ema frowned. "Are you really wearing a pocket protector?"

"What, you want the pen to ruin my shirt?"

"*That* shirt? Yes."

"But green plaid is back."

"Okay," I said, stepping between them. "Can we get back to this?"

Ema's eyes locked on to mine.

"He's part of this," I said again.

She dropped her gaze. "Fine, whatever, it's your Nazi."

"Please continue," Spoon said.

Ema ignored him. "Anyway, I sent the pictures to the EMS office in San Diego. They would have been the ones to respond to any car accident in that area. I also gave them the date of your accident."

"One question," Spoon began, rubbing his chin. "Who's your source?"

Ema shot daggers at him with her eyes.

"Spoon," I said.

He looked at me. I shook my head for him to keep silent.

"So the photographs were sent down to human resources. They checked through their files. They showed the photograph to every employee they could find. Then, just to make sure, they sent me a link to a website with headshots of every licensed paramedic who has worked for the county for the past three years."

She swallowed, but I knew what she was about to say next.

"There is no record of him. No one recognizes him. According to the San Diego EMS office, this guy never worked for them."

Silence.

Then I said, "There are private ambulance companies, right? Maybe one of them . . ."

"It's possible," Ema said, "but they wouldn't be called to an accident scene on an interstate. That's the county's jurisdiction."

I tried to sort through what she was telling me. . . . But what had I expected her to find? That a ninety-year-old Nazi who looked about thirty had been working for the San Diego Emergency Medical Services? Still, at the very least, the sandy-blond paramedic *looked* like the Butcher of Lodz. Someone should have been able to find the guy, right? If they showed the picture around or looked through their records, wouldn't someone have come back and said, "Hey, this guy looks like . . ." well, whatever his name was?

I looked toward Ema. "So it's a dead end?"

She looked at me with those caring eyes of hers.

"I mean, who was the sandy-blond guy with the green eyes I saw that day? Who took my dad from the scene?"

Spoon stayed silent. Ema took a step toward me. She put her hand on my arm. "We just started investigating. This is just the first step."

Spoon nodded in agreement.

"There has to be an accident report," Spoon added. "The names of everyone involved would be on it. We should get a copy."

"Good idea, Spoon," Ema said.

He puffed out his chest. "I'm not just eye candy, you know."

We. They kept saying *we*. It felt ridiculous—*we* were just a bunch of dumb kids—and yet it also felt ridiculously comforting to have these two on my side.

Ema turned back to me. "I'll get my source on it."

"The source I shouldn't ask about?" I said.

"Right."

The bell rang. Students started to stream into the school. We said our good-byes and headed inside. My first three periods went by slowly and uneventfully. No boredom compares to school boredom. You stare at that clock and try to use any kind of mind-meld trick just to make the hands move faster. They never do.

I had Mrs. Friedman for period four today, my final class before lunch. I may have mentioned this before, but Mrs. Friedman was my favorite teacher. She had been teaching a long time—Uncle Myron was one of her former students— but she had not lost an iota of enthusiasm. I loved that about her because that enthusiasm was contagious. Nothing seemed to bore her. No question was unworthy of an answer. No moment was unworthy of study.

Mrs. Friedman lived in a happy snow globe of AP History.

But today even Mrs. Friedman seemed a little off her game. The smile was there, but it was nowhere near its normal wattage. Of course, I knew why. So, I assumed, did the rest of the class. Mrs. Friedman's eyes kept finding their way back to that empty desk.

Rachel's desk.

Rachel had first introduced herself to me here. Yep, that's right. The hottest girl in the school had smiled at me and struck up a conversation with yours truly in this very classroom. I had been both dumbstruck and rather pleased with myself. I had only been a student here a few short weeks, and I, a lowly new kid and sophomore, had already drawn the attention of *that* girl.

I must have been super cool and incredibly charming, right?

Nope. I soon learned that Rachel had ulterior motives for flirting with me.

In all that had happened, I had almost forgotten about that. Rachel had been deceptive at first. She may have had her reasons. But now that I thought about it, did I really, fully trust her—like I trusted Ema and Spoon? She had been part of our group that had taken down some very nasty bad guys. She had been brave and resourceful and put herself on the line.

But still, Rachel had first come to us from a dishonest place.

Could I just let that go? And what was with all that mysterious talk in her hospital room? What was with the Abeona butterfly on her door?

Was she still keeping secrets?

"For tomorrow," Mrs. Friedman said, toward the end of class, "please read chapter seventeen in your textbooks."

I opened mine up, checking to see how long chapter 17 was, and as I started thumbing through the pages, I spotted the header for chapter 36, something we wouldn't cover until the final quarter of the school year:

WORLD WAR II AND THE HOLOCAUST

The bell rang. I sat there for a second. Mrs. Friedman was an expert in World War II and the Holocaust. Maybe if I showed her that old black-and-white photograph . . . well, no. That might be too much. And what would be the point? But maybe if I asked her about the Butcher of Lodz, maybe she could cast some light on all this.

I couldn't imagine how, but what would be the harm?

Mrs. Friedman was at the blackboard, working the eraser. She was the only teacher I knew who still used a blackboard and chalk. She was old-school in every way, and I loved her for it.

"Mrs. Friedman?"

She turned and smiled at me. "Hello, Mr. Bolitar."

Mrs. Friedman always addresses us as "Mister" or "Miss." Again, with some teachers this would produce groans and eye rolls. Not with Mrs. Friedman.

I wasn't sure how to start, so I just dived in. "I wanted to ask you a history question."

She stood there, waiting. When I stayed silent a beat too long, she said, "Well, go on. I didn't think you'd want to ask me a math question."

"Right, of course."

"So what is it, Mr. Bolitar?"

I swallowed and said, "Do you know anything about the Butcher of Lodz?"

Mrs. Friedman's eyes popped open a bit wider. "Hans Zeidner? The Butcher of Lodz from World War Two?"

"Yes."

She seemed almost shaken just by his name. "I don't understand. Is this for another class?"

"No."

"What then?"

I wasn't sure how to answer. Mrs. Friedman was much shorter than I was, but I felt myself shrinking under her gaze. I stood there, trying to come up with something plausible. A second or two more passed and then Mrs. Friedman held up her hand as if she understood and I didn't need to go on.

"Lodz is in Poland," she explained. "There was a Jewish ghetto there in the 1940s. Hans Zeidner served as a Nazi officer there. He was Waffen-SS—they were the worst of the worst. Responsible for the brutal murder of millions. But the Butcher is probably better known for his time in Auschwitz."

Auschwitz. Just the word hushed the room.

"Do you know about Auschwitz?" Mrs. Friedman asked me.

"Yes."

She took off her reading glasses. "Tell me what you know," she said.

"Auschwitz was a notorious Nazi concentration camp," I said.

She nodded. "Most use that term. 'Concentration' camp. I prefer the more accurate one—extermination camp. Well over a million people were murdered there, ninety percent of whom were Jewish." She stopped. "The camp was run by Rudolph Hess, but the Butcher of Lodz was one of his more ruthless henchmen. Do you know the legend of Lizzy Sobek?"

Again, I wasn't sure how to answer that, so I went with something vague. "She was a little girl in the Holocaust, right?"

Mrs. Friedman nodded. "Lizzy Sobek was a thirteen-year-old girl from Lodz."

"Lodz. As in the Butcher?"

"Exactly."

"Did she live in that ghetto?"

"For a while," Mrs. Friedman said. She looked off, lost

for a moment, and I wondered where her mind was taking her. "Much of Lizzy Sobek's story, well, the documentation is sketchy. We don't know what exactly is true and what is legend."

I swallowed hard.

"Are you all right?" Mrs. Friedman asked.

"Fine."

"You look pale."

"This is tough stuff, that's all. But I want to hear it."

Mrs. Friedman studied my face. I don't know what exactly she was looking for—maybe why I was interested in something so grim, maybe why I seemed to have a personal connection to these people. "By all accounts, the Sobeks were a close-knit family. The father and mother were Samuel and Esther. The children were Emmanuel, age sixteen, and of course Lizzy, who was thirteen. They were Jewish and hid in the Lodz ghetto until the Butcher's men found them and transported them to Auschwitz. Her mother and brother were immediately killed in the gas chambers. Her father was put into a labor camp."

"And Lizzy?"

Mrs. Friedman shrugged. "Let me go on with what we do know first, okay?"

"Okay."

"Somehow Samuel Sobek escaped Auschwitz with about a dozen other prisoners. They tried to hide in the woods, but the Waffen-SS, led by the Butcher, eventually tracked them down. They didn't bother to return the prisoners to camp. They lined them up, gunned them down, and threw them in a hole in the ground. Just like that. Lizzy Sobek's father was one of those executed and dumped in a mass grave."

A chill filled the room. There was suddenly no sound, not anywhere. If my fellow classmates were still in the building, they were somewhere far away now.

"What about Lizzy?" I asked.

"Well," Mrs. Friedman said, walking toward the bookshelf, "that's the part that's harder to document. We have records of Lizzy Sobek entering Auschwitz with her family in September of 1942, but we have no records of what happened to her after that—only the legends."

"So," I said slowly, "what are the legends?"

"That Lizzy Sobek escaped Auschwitz too. That she somehow evaded capture and joined the resistance. That even as a young girl, she actually fought the Nazis. But the most renowned tale of Lizzy Sobek involves a rescue mission she supposedly led in southern Poland."

"What sort of rescue?"

Mrs. Friedman pulled a book off the shelf. "Somehow a group of resistance fighters were able to stop a train transporting Jews to Auschwitz. Not for long. Just for a few brief moments. They put downed tree trunks on the track. The guards had to jump down to remove them. But you see, on this train, there was one particular car that was carrying the children."

I froze when I heard that. Children. Lizzy Sobek had been trying to rescue children.

"Someone broke open the cargo door, and the children managed to escape into the woods. Over fifty of them. And they claim that the person who broke the door open—the person who led the raid—was a young girl."

"Lizzy Sobek," I said.

Mrs. Friedman nodded. She opened the book in her hand. I could only see part of the title—something about illustrations from the Holocaust—but she started paging through it quickly.

"Do you believe the legend?" I asked.

"There is evidence backing up the story," she said a little too carefully, like she was reading from a script she didn't fully believe. "We do know that the children were indeed rescued. We know that most claimed that the leader was a young girl matching Lizzy's description. But on the other hand, none of the children actually met or spoke to Lizzy Sobek. If the story is to be believed, she rescued them, led them up the hill, and then went on her way."

"Still," I said, "with so many witnesses . . ."

"Yes, there's that," Mrs. Friedman said. "But there are other issues that cast doubt on the story."

"Like?"

She was still leafing through the illustrations. "Like the witnesses were all children. They were young. They were scared. They were hungry. It was dark out."

"So it might not have been Lizzy Sobek that they saw."

Mrs. Friedman nodded, but I could see a shadow cross her face. "But there was something more."

"What?" I asked.

"It was February. In Poland. There was snow on the ground."

"So it was cold."

"Freezing."

"And you think that, what, affected their judgment?"

Mrs. Friedman stopped on a page. She took off her reading glasses and I could see tears in her eyes. "This," she said, pointing to the page, "was drawn by one of the children rescued that day."

She lifted the book and showed me the drawing. When I saw it, my heart stopped.

There were children running up a hillside in the night. They were running away from a train and into the woods. The central figure in the drawing was a lone girl standing on a hill, waiting for them. And surrounding the lone girl were dozens and dozens of . . .

"Butterflies," I said out loud.

CHAPTER 18

I stared at the drawing.

"According to the children," Mrs. Friedman said, "the butterflies guided the children to safety. Butterflies. In the middle of winter."

I stayed perfectly still.

Abeona, I thought, though I knew that it was impossible.

"Do you believe it, Mrs. Friedman?"

"Which part? That there were butterflies? In Poland, during the middle of winter? No, that's impossible."

"So the story about the rescue . . ."

"I don't know." Mrs. Friedman tilted her head. "There are many cases through history of mass delusions via mass hysteria—especially when it comes to children in harm's way. Much of what we view as 'unexplained' is actually psychological trauma. And butterflies are common in such delusions. We do know that the train was stopped and that these children were rescued."

"But we don't know about butterflies or Lizzy Sobek," I said.

I stared at the drawing, thinking that maybe I did.

"So the people who believe the legends," I began. "What do they think eventually happened to Lizzy Sobek?"

"That Lizzy Sobek continued to fight for the resistance. That she was killed in a later raid"—she looked up from the drawing—"by the Butcher of Lodz."

The same man who killed Lizzy's father. The same man who, what, never aged and bided his time for seventy years before wheeling away my father?

I was missing something.

"And what happened to the Butcher?"

"That's one of the great mysteries of World War Two," Mrs. Friedman said. "Nobody knows."

In the distance now I could hear students laughing, the sound echoing down the corridors. Here we were, discussing a man who'd murdered countless, and nearby, there was laughter.

"Some say the Butcher died during the war. Some say he escaped Allied forces and ran far away. Simon Wiesenthal and the Nazi hunters searched for him after the war—there were rumors he was in Argentina—but they never found him."

The bell rang, making me jump. We both stood there a

moment, but it was time to stop this, to leave this dark horrible past and somehow return to our regular high school life.

"You're okay, Mr. Bolitar?"

Still in a daze, I said, "I'm fine, thank you, Mrs. Friedman."

I stumbled out of the classroom and started down the hallway. When I got to the lunchroom, Ema could immediately see that something was wrong. Spoon, uh, couldn't. I filled them in on my conversation with Mrs. Friedman.

"So what do you think it all means?" Ema asked.

None of us had an answer. Spoon was eating a peanut butter and jelly sandwich with the crust cut off so neatly and with such perfect right angles that I wondered whether someone had used a protractor. He nudged me and changed subjects. "Are you going out for the basketball team today?"

Ema looked up and waited for my answer.

"Yes."

Something crossed her face. I wasn't sure what. She had known the answer. She knew how important basketball was to me. I had waited my whole life to stay in one place long enough to be on a team. It was one of the main reasons my family had returned to the United States. My parents wanted me to have a normal life for a little while, play on a high school basketball team, maybe get a scholarship to college. That had been the plan.

"You realize," Spoon said, swallowing down a bite of his sandwich, "that some of your games may interfere with your duties as our club's new vice president. There may be conflicts."

"Yeah, Spoon, that's a chance I'll just have to take."

That answer did not make him happy. "Are you implying that basketball is more important to you than the MILF club?"

Ema dropped her fork. "The what club?"

"We're changing the name," I explained.

The "luxury box" lunch table seemed in better spirits today. You could keep those guys down for only so long, I guess. Troy Taylor was showing off by spinning a basketball on his finger. He curled his arm behind his back and kept the ball spinning and then let it roll from one hand, across his chest, to the other. When he was done, everyone applauded. He bowed and looked across at me as if to gauge my reaction. I gave him nothing.

"Hey," Spoon said, "either one of you going to audition for that new Angelica Wyatt movie?"

"Pass," I said.

Ema frowned hard. "Of course not."

"I might," Spoon said, "except . . ."

"Except what?"

"Well, suppose Angelica Wyatt falls hard for me. How do I explain to her that I'm still underage?"

That was enough for Ema. She got up and left.

I managed to make it through the rest of the day and

headed into the boys' locker room to get dressed for tryouts. The place was packed. When I entered, Troy and Buck spotted me and started up with the death glares.

Boy, this was going to be fun.

I would again note that I had butterflies in my stomach, but after hearing about Lizzy Sobek, I figured that I better come up with a different metaphor. Let's just say I was nervous. Really, really nervous.

I threw on shorts and laced up my basketball shoes.

"Lame," I heard a voice say.

I turned. It was Buck. "Excuse me?"

"Your sneakers." He pointed at them. "Did you get them out of, like, some sales bin?"

Snort. Laugh. Snort.

"Um, yeah," I said.

While I didn't think that my reply was particularly clever, Buck seemed lost by it. "Well, they suck."

"Thanks." I pointed at his feet. "Yours are very pretty."

Buck bent in close to me, his mouth inches from mine. "Why don't you do everyone here a favor and go home?"

I leaned away. "And why don't you do everyone here a favor and carry breath mints?"

I hurried out to the gym before he could react. Dozens of kids were warming up, stretching, shooting around. I made my way to the basket farthest from the locker room. I stretched and took a few shots. But I was nervous. The shots clanged off the rim.

From across the court, I heard snickering. Then Buck yelled, "Nice bricks!"

Man, I had to relax.

A whistle blew. Someone shouted, "Everyone grab a seat on the bleachers." So we did. Troy and Buck sat in the first row, so I made my way to the back. Coach Grady came out, and the gym fell silent.

"Welcome, gentlemen, to basketball. My name is Coach Grady. I'm the head coach here at Kasselton. Next to me is Coach Stashower. He'll run JV."

Coach Grady wore gray sweatpants with elastic leg cuffs and a black hoodie with a hands-warmer pouch. His hair was thinning and the few remaining strands had been grown long and plastered down to his scalp.

"In a few minutes," he continued, "we are going to divide you up. The sophomores and freshmen are going to Gym Two." He pointed to the smaller gym adjacent to this one. "The seniors and juniors will stay here."

Coach Grady's voice echoed the way a voice always does in a high school gym. They are all the same. They all have that thick brick and wooden pullout benches and smell like old socks and disinfectant. I glanced around this place I so much wanted to call home. A big poster that read 1,000 POINT SCORERS snagged my eye. Eleven students in the history of this school had achieved that goal. Nine boys, two girls.

One player had even scored more than two thousand points.

Guess who?

Yep, Uncle Myron—the all-time leading scorer. My eyes traveled down the list. I stopped when I saw the name EDWARD TAYLOR—that was Troy's dad and, well, Chief Taylor. He was the second-leading scorer of all time with 1,758 points in his career. I looked down a few more names. There was TROY TAYLOR, the most recent entry, with 1,322 points and an asterisk, noting that Troy was still an active player and so that number would rise.

I sighed. It was like a list of my enemies. I was surprised the Butcher of Lodz hadn't scored a thousand points!

"As most of you know, we have a stellar group of seniors returning to this team. Last year, we even won the county championship for the first time in a decade." Coach Grady gestured toward the new COUNTY CHAMPIONS banner on the far wall. I counted six other county championships, the first in 1968.

"All five starters from that team are back with us this year," Coach Grady went on, "and when the season is over, we want to finally hang another state championship banner up on that wall."

Now he gestured to the two large STATE CHAMPIONSHIP banners that humbled the county ones. That's right—Kasselton High had won only two state championships in their history, both dating back about twenty-five years. I did the math, but I already knew what the answer was going to be. Guess who'd been on both teams? Come on, you'll never guess.

Dang, how did you know?

Uncle Myron. Long shadow much?

"That's our goal," Coach said. "A state championship. We will settle for nothing less."

That got applause, the most enthusiastic of which came from Troy and Buck and the rest of the returning players sitting in the front. The rest of us, now suddenly feeling like interlopers on the "chosen" seniors, were a tad more restrained.

"Now, before we break down and start tryouts, team captain Troy Taylor would like to address all of you. This is important stuff, so listen up. Troy?"

Troy rose slowly. He turned and stood in front of us and lowered his head, as though in prayer. For a few moments, he didn't move. What the heck was this? Troy seemed to be trying to summon some inner strength.

Or maybe he was working up to shouting "Ema! Moooo!" again.

Man, I did not like this guy.

Finally, Troy broke the silence. "As you know, this is a very hard time for Kasselton High and especially for me personally. A beautiful girl was shot and nearly killed."

Oh no, I thought. He isn't going there . . .

"A girl I care so much for. A girl who cheered for this team and, well, her lucky boyfriend . . ."

He was going there!

"A girl who has been such a big part of Troy Taylor's life . . ."

Wait, did he just refer to himself in the third person? I wanted to slap the side of his head. What a pompous gasbag. I looked at the faces of my fellow tryout-ees, figuring that they'd be bored or sneering. But that wasn't the case at all. They sat in rapt attention.

"Well, that special girl who stole my heart is lying in a hospital bed, clinging to life."

Troy paused now and I wondered when he'd hired an acting coach. I rolled my eyes at one of the other guys in the bleachers, but he just glared at me.

They were buying it!

"Despite her condition, Rachel and I have, of course, been in touch."

Huh? What a liar. Or . . . wait, hold up a sec . . .

"So I want you all to know. Rachel will pull through. She has promised me that. She has promised me that she will come back and put on her cheerleader uniform and cheer when Troy Taylor sinks his patented three-pointer . . ."

I wondered whether I had ever wanted to punch someone so badly in my entire life.

"So I want us all to keep Rachel in our thoughts. We are dedicating this season to her. All of our uniforms will have this on it."

Troy pointed to the right side of his chest where the initials RC—Rachel Caldwell—had been sewn onto his practice jersey.

You have to be kidding me.

"And I want you to wear these initials with pride. I want you to think of Rachel, in that hospital bed, and I want that to make you play even better, even harder . . ." Troy started to bite his lips as though fighting back tears. Buck rose to comfort him, but Troy shook him off and pointed to the sky.

"Take care of my Rachel, Big Guy. Bring her back to me."

There was a moment of silence—and then the guys sitting with me broke into thunderous applause. They start hooting and hollering and then they started up a "Troy! Troy! Troy!" chant. Troy actually raised his hand to acknowledge the ovation, like he'd just been introduced to present an Oscar. I sat there, thinking I might just vomit on the first day of tryouts.

Coach Grady blew his whistle. "Okay, that's enough," he said in a tone that maybe gave me hope *he* wasn't buying it. "Everyone take five laps. Then JV to Gym Two and let's start with layup drills."

CHAPTER 19

There is plenty I don't love about sports. I don't love how athletes are worshipped because they can, say, hurl a sphere with greater velocity or jam a ball through a metallic hoop with more proficiency than most. I don't love how important we make the games, comparing them to real battles and even wars. I don't love how it is all anyone in towns like Kasselton talks about. I don't love (hate, in fact) trash talk and excessive celebrating (as my father used to say, "Act like you've been there before"). I don't like the way spectators scream at referees and whine about coaches. I don't like the single-mindedness and selfishness that is inherent in all competitors, including me. And in a town like this, I don't like all the babble about becoming a pro athlete when your odds are eight times better of falling and dying in your bathroom (true!).

But there is plenty I do love. I love sportsmanship, as corny as that sounds. I love shaking hands after the game and giving an opponent a knowing nod. I love sharing a great moment with my teammates, the joy in that singular connection. I love the sweat. I love making the effort, even if it doesn't go my way. I love how you can be surrounded by a frenzy of activity—and yet still be completely alone. I love the sound of a ball dribbling off the gym floor. I love the escape you find only on a playing field. I love the purity of the game itself. I love the competition—and by that I mean "winning," not "beating," "besting," or "belittling" your opponent, though I get how that can all get confused. I love the randomness of the breaks. I love how you really don't know how that ball is going to bounce. And I love the honesty. I love the fact that even if your dad is your Little League coach and makes you pitcher or quarterback, eventually, if you don't have the talent, that fact will win out.

My point?

It took a while. I was nervous at first. I missed more shots than I normally do. My new potential teammates froze me out at first, because I was the new kid, an interloper, and I had already made enemies with guys like Troy and Buck. But once we started to scrimmage, once we began to sprint up and down and shed our nervous energy, once I moved into that magical "zone" where the rest of the world disappears—that place I love like no other—I began to make passes and shots that drew gasps.

Coach Stashower, a younger English teacher, said nothing for a while, but about an hour into practice, I saw him go into Gym 1 and talk to Coach Grady. Coach Grady stood in the doorway and watched for a while, his arms folded. I upped my game. I made two straight three-pointers and then I drove hard to the hoop and dished off to one of my teammates, who made the easy layup. I grabbed rebounds. I shut down my man on defense. I focused on the game and for a while I even forgot that the varsity coach was watching me.

But I knew.

That was what I meant by the honesty of the game. On the court, you can run but you can't hide. In that same vein, you can try to hold someone back but if he's got the goods, he will eventually break free. Coach Grady might have wanted it neat and simple and expected. He had his returning seniors all ready to go. But sports in general never fits into the neat and simple and expected. If it did, we wouldn't need to watch or even play, would we?

"Okay," Coach Stashower shouted, "that's it for today. Go shower up. Tryouts tomorrow are at five P.M. See you then."

As we began to disperse, lots of the guys came over and congratulated me. They asked me questions about where I'd learned to play, where I was from, what classes I was taking. I know I said I loved the postgame handshake. I do. I like the respect you give an opponent or a teammate. But I don't like the fact that because you happen to leap high or

demonstrate above-average coordination that people suddenly want to be your friend.

But, hey, that doesn't mean I didn't enjoy the attention.

Some people might call that hypocritical. I would probably agree.

The JV was finished before the varsity, so I was able to
shower and get dressed without running into Troy and Buck.
As I calmed down, I start thinking back on Troy's speech.
Maybe, awful as this sounded, he was being somewhat legit.
Maybe he and Rachel still had a relationship. They had
dated, right? So maybe they had started up again. Maybe
her brush with death had brought them back together.

I wished that the thought didn't turn my stomach so
much.

I dried off and let myself catch my breath for a second.
When I checked my phone, my heart sped up all over again.
There was a short text from Rachel: **Hey**

I smirked. Rachel must have gone to the Mickey Bolitar
School of Big Opening Lines. I checked the time on the text.
She had sent it an hour ago. I quickly typed a killer response:
Hey, you still there?

No reply. I put the phone down and dressed, staring at it,
waiting for it to vibrate. I was putting on my sneakers when
it did.

Rachel: **Yes. Where r u?**

Me: **Tryouts today.**

Rachel: **How did they go?**

Me: **Fine. Who cares? How are you??**

Rachel: **Better. Bullet skimmed my head but caused no damage. Being released tomorrow afternoon.**

Immature as this sounded, I wanted to ask her if she'd been in touch with Troy, but a) it wasn't my business; and b) could you imagine anything more petty? Plus his speech came back to me:

That special girl who stole my heart is lying in a hospital bed, clinging to life.

The one who was being released tomorrow? Liar!

Rachel: **Cand you stop by my house tomorrow after school?**

Okay, I admit it—I felt a swelling in my chest and there was a smile on my face. School ended at three. Tryouts started at five.

Me: **No problem.**

Rachel: **My dad will be home by 4. I don't want him to see you so we have to make it fast.**

I didn't know what to make of that.

Me: **Something wrong?**

Rachel: **Gotta go. Don't tell anyone I texted you. No one. See u tomorrow.**

I stared at the phone another minute or two and then finished getting dressed. When I got outside, Coach Stashower was waiting for me.

"You have a minute, Mickey?"

"Sure, Coach."

Coach Stashower had thick curly hair and wore a polo shirt with the Kasselton Camel, our school mascot, on it. We moved into the PE teachers' office and he closed the door.

"You're some player, Mickey," he said with something approaching awe.

Not sure what else to say, I went with, "Thank you."

"I mean, this is only one day." He cleared his throat, his voice more serious now. "Tryouts last the rest of the week. It may have been just a fluke."

I didn't say anything. I knew. He knew. Again, I don't say this to sound cocky or full of myself. I say it because I know. I hate when the gorgeous girl always pretends she has no idea she's pretty. It is dishonest. That kind of false modesty can be as annoying as bragging. So I didn't say anything— there was no need because it all gets said on the court—but Coach Stashower knew that it wasn't a fluke.

"Coach Grady is going to be working with the varsity for another hour, and he didn't want you to wait around for him. He also needs to think about some stuff." Coach Stashower stopped then, unsure how to continue. "Anyway, he asked if you can come to his office tomorrow at lunch. Can you make it?"

I tried very hard not to smile. "Yes, Coach."

"Okay then. Go home and get some rest."

CHAPTER 20

But I had no interest in rest. I was still flying high.

What I really wanted to do was play more basketball. I realize that this may sound obvious, but the more you play, the better you get. Plus I loved it.

I checked the clock. The pickup games down in Newark might still be going on. I could grab the next bus and be downtown in half an hour.

I texted Tyrell Waters, a junior at Newark's Weequahic High School, who lived on those courts: **Games still on?**

I realized that I probably wouldn't get an answer—Tyrell could be playing right now—but I got one immediately.

Tyrell: **Yep, come on down.**

I caught the bus at the Northfield Avenue stop. The bus was filled with weary housekeepers, nannies, and various domestics, who always gave this white boy curious looks.

The trip from the leafy suburb of Kasselton to the grimier streets of Newark was only seven miles in distance but much farther in pretty much every other way.

The pickup basketball games were played on cracked asphalt with rusted rims. I started coming down here about a month ago because this is where the best basketball is played. You can call me prejudiced for that, but again it's like that false modesty thing. If you want to get better—and keep your game under wraps until tryouts—these urban streets were the place to go.

Tyrell spotted me coming toward him. He waved and gave me a smile. "I sat out a game so we could be on the same team."

"Thanks."

I was pretty much the only guy from the well-to-do suburbs who made this trek on his own. When I first showed up, I had been greeted by plenty of doubt and even derision, but again that was the beauty of sports. Once we got on the court, corny as this might sound, all that stuff fell to the side. I've played basketball throughout the world, most of the time in countries where I didn't know the language. It didn't matter. You bond on the court. You all speak or at least understand the same language. The other nonsense just fades away.

"So what's going on?" Tyrell asked.

"First day of tryouts."

"How did it go?"

"Pretty well."

Tyrell smiled. "Yeah, I bet. Hey, Weequahic plays Kasselton this year. That should be a fun game."

"I look forward to it."

On the court, someone made a dunk to give his team the victory. There were always spectators at the pickup games. On the right, a group of homeless guys were cheering and jeering and placing "bottle bets" on the games. Various coaches and parents stood closer in, leaning against the fence, scrutinizing every move.

Pickup basketball is simple: winners stay on, losers sit. No one likes to sit, so the games become very competitive. Tyrell is a great point guard. He sees the entire court with just a quick glance. He fed me two down low, and we jumped out to a quick lead. We cruised from there. I don't remember how many games we played or how much time it took. It was all just a wonderful escape. For a little while I didn't think about my father or my mother or Rachel or any of it.

Darkness crept in, so someone turned on the floodlights. We kept playing. It was getting late, but I didn't really care. After we won the most recent game—Tyrell drove the length of the court for the final basket—I checked my phone. Uncle Myron had called three times and texted asking where I was. I figured it was best to call him back.

"Where are you?" he asked.

"I'm at the courts in Newark."

"Tryouts weren't enough today, huh?"

This was the one thing Myron totally got. "I just wanted to get a little more playing in," I said.

"So how did it go today?" "Fine."

He obviously wanted details, but like I said, it is always better to let your game do the talking. Myron probably understood that too.

"I'm going to be home late," Myron said. "Angelica is filming tonight and I need to be there. Will you be okay?"

Why did I feel such relief when I knew he wouldn't be around?

"I'll be fine, don't worry."

We said we'd stay in touch and hung up. Tyrell and I managed to scrape up enough players for one more game, but then it was pretty much over for the night. Guys said good-bye and drifted away until it was only Tyrell and me left. The two of us shot around and shared some laughs. I beat him in a game of horse by only one letter, and he immediately demanded a rematch. We started breaking out trick shots and then, because this was the other magic of sports, we started talking for real.

"My friend was shot," I told him. "Her mother was killed." Tyrell stopped. "For real?"

"Yes."

He asked for details. I told him about Rachel, about Ema and Spoon, about Troy's speech at practice, about everything that happened at the Plan B nightclub.

When I finished, Tyrell shook his head and said, "Man, you have a way of finding trouble."

"I like to think trouble finds me."

"And I like to think every girl in school wants my bod," Tyrell said. "Doesn't make it so. Anyway, my old man told me you were involved in all those arrests at that nightclub. He didn't know what to make of it either."

I should have figured as much. Tyrell's father worked as an investigator for Essex County.

"In fact, Dad probably would've been the one to interview you, except he's working on this big drug ring in your hometown."

As if on cue, we heard a voice say, "Good to see you guys working on your game."

Tyrell's father smiled as he approached. His jacket was off, so I could see the badge and gun hanging from his belt. Mr. Waters gave his son a hug. If Tyrell was embarrassed about it, he didn't show it. He hugged his father back, and I felt a pang of envy.

Mr. Waters turned to me. "Hello, Mickey."

"Hello, Mr. Waters."

"How are things?"

Last time I was down here, Mr. Waters had driven me home. He'd seen Shaved Head following me and had grown concerned. When we reached Myron's house, he gave me his card and told me to call in case of trouble.

"I'm fine."

He kept his eyes on me. I realized that he was a county investigator, probably working in the same division as Investigator Dunleavy. I wondered whether he knew that I'd been questioned about the shooting at the Caldwell house.

"What do you say I take you guys out for a quick bite and then I can drive Mickey home?"

"Thanks for the offer," I said, "but I can take the bus."

"It's no hassle. I have to be in Kasselton for a case anyway. It'll be good to have the company."

That was what he had said last time, but there had been something of an ulterior motive. Of course, the ulterior motive was that he'd been worried about me.

"It's late and I'm starving," Mr. Waters said. "What do you boys say?"

Tyrell turned to me. "Come on. You gotta eat, right?"

Hard to argue with that logic. We headed to Hobby's Deli and sat in the corner. All three of us ordered triple-decker sandwiches the approximate size of a catcher's mitt. It was the best sandwich I had ever eaten. On a scale of one to ten, if this was a ten, the next best sandwich I'd had was a three.

"Cops always know the best places to eat," Mr. Waters explained.

He asked us about our day, about our studies, about our basketball. He listened and I could see how much he was enjoying this. I was enjoying it too, but that pang never left.

He dropped Tyrell at their two-family house on Pomona Avenue. Tyrell kissed his father's cheek before he got out. Another pang.

Tyrell fist-bumped me and said, "Kick that Troy guy's ass."

"Will do."

Mr. Waters waited until Tyrell was inside before driving again. Neither one of us said anything for a few minutes. Then Mr. Waters broke the silence. "I hear you were questioned by my colleague Investigator Dunleavy."

Just as I'd suspected. "Yes, sir."

But hearing her name reminded me of something else—in Rachel's hospital room, hiding under the bed, Chief Taylor's voice . . .

A homicide detective named Anne Marie Dunleavy will be coming by to interview you. Don't feel obligated to talk to her before we speak again, okay?

What had that been about?

"Everything okay, Mickey?"

"Fine, yes. I'm a friend of Rachel Caldwell's, that's all."

"I see."

"She and I talked on the phone before the shooting," I said.

Mr. Waters nodded, both hands on the wheel, his eyes straight ahead. "It's a terrible thing. What happened to her mother. Gunned down like that."

I said nothing.

"Did you know her?" he asked.

"Rachel's mother?"

"Yes."

"No, we never met."

"How's Rachel holding up?" he asked.

I squirmed in my seat. I didn't want to tell him that I'd sneaked into the hospital, but I didn't want to lie either. "She seems better."

"That's good. How about Henry?"

"Who?"

"Henry Caldwell. Her father." We hit a traffic light and came to a stop. Mr. Waters turned and met my eye. "How's he doing?"

"I don't know Mr. Caldwell."

"No?" Mr. Waters arched an eyebrow. "I just figured, you being such good friends with Rachel and all, that you'd have met one of her parents."

"I haven't," I said softly. "And I don't really know her all that well."

"But you talked on the phone right before the shooting."

This was sounding less and less like a casual conversation. "We were partners on a history project," I said.

He waited. When I didn't add anything else, Mr. Waters said, "And you two were both involved in that mess at the Plan B nightclub."

"Yes," I said.

We pulled up to Myron's house. Mr. Waters turned off the engine. "Mickey?"

"Yes?"

"Are you sure there's nothing you need to tell me?"

"I don't know what you mean."

"No? First, you have some weird bald dude following you in a black car. Then you get involved in a big-time arrest at an adult nightclub. And now, well, this shooting in your hometown."

I liked Mr. Waters. I really did. I also thought that he probably had my best interests in mind. But I didn't know what to say or even where to start. Too much had gone on in the past week, and I had been warned by Bat Lady not to tell anyone. Even if I defied her, what exactly would I say?

"Mickey?"

"I really don't know anything more," I said.

He rubbed his face for a moment. "You still have my card?"

"Yes."

"Put my number on your speed dial. I have a feeling you're going to need it."

CHAPTER 21

I didn't have homework, so I went online and did an image search for both Hans Zeidner and the Butcher of Lodz. Plenty of terrifying photographs from the Lodz ghetto popped up. They were all in stark black and white. I would say that they were like something out of a nightmare, but I don't even think my worst dreams could compete with this. Many of the photos featured frightened and starving children. I thought about Lizzy Sobek. I wondered what her life in that ghetto must have been like.

There was only one photograph that may have been the Butcher of Lodz.

It was, I thought, the most horrible photograph I had ever seen. It had been taken in November 1941 in the Baluty Marketplace in Lodz. Eighteen Jews were executed by hanging in that one day for trying to escape. In this photograph you could see three of them dangling by the neck from what looked like a child's swing set. In the background, you could see the crowd somberly gathered—even children—forced to watch as a warning. And there, standing right next to the dead bodies, with his back to the camera, was a man in a Waffen-SS uniform.

It was suddenly hard to breathe.

I shut down the computer. That had been it—there had been no photographs of the Butcher's face.

So how had Bat Lady gotten one?

It always came back to her, didn't it? Bat Lady had started me down this road the first time I saw her, opening up that door, stepping out with her long gray hair and white gown, pointing that bony finger at me . . .

Mickey? Your father isn't dead. He is very much alive. . . .

Hold the phone.

I remembered something else now. When I'd seen Ema earlier today, she somehow looked different to me. I couldn't put my finger on it, but now . . .

I grabbed my cell phone and texted Ema. I just said **R u there?** in case, I don't know, someone else was home and he checked her texts and got angry if it was someone asking more personal questions.

Ema replied quickly: **what's up?**

Me: **Going to Bat Lady's house. Wanna come?**

Ema: **can't.**

That was odd. Usually Ema could get out at all hours.

I typed: **Everything OK?**

Ema: **fine. let's go after school tomorrow.**

I was about to tell her about Rachel getting out of the hospital, but then I remembered how Rachel had insisted: **Don't tell anyone I texted you. No one.**

Could she have meant Ema too? I don't know, but the words *no one* seemed pretty clear.

To Ema, I typed in: **Can't.**

I was going to ask her about what I noticed, about what struck me as different with her appearance, but I wanted to check it out in person. It could wait.

Still thinking about the rumors Spoon had heard, I added: **R you OK?**

Ema: **fine. u?**

Me: **Fine.**

There was a pause and then Ema wrote: **this is an awesome text exchange.**

I laughed out loud.

Ema: **r u going to Bat Lady's tonight without me?**

I thought about it, but not for very long. I couldn't just sit here. I had to act: **Yes.**

There was a pause and then Ema wrote: **b careful. I've got a bad feeling.**

CHAPTER 22

Nobody knows when the Bat Lady first moved to town.

I'm sure that there were housing records and someone could probably figure it out, but if you ask anyone in Kasselton, they will tell you that she has always been in that dark, dilapidated house. Even Uncle Myron remembers the creepy old Bat Lady from his childhood. He told me that kids used to hurry past her house, even way back when he was a kid. He told me that one day, when my own father was twelve or thirteen, he had gone into Bat Lady's house on a dare . . .

. . . and that when my father came out, he was never the same.

I believed that. I had also gone into that house. I had also met Bat Lady. And now I'm not sure that I will ever be the same again.

The rumors that struck fear into the children about Bat

Lady were, I knew, completely bogus. Legend had it that she kidnapped children. Some nights, the locals say, if you walked past her house slowly, you could actually hear their cries. Some claimed to see them, dozens of children locked up in her house, ready to be . . . well, what? Killed, abused, eaten . . .

Or maybe, just maybe, they were rescued.

It was pitch-black by the time I made it to Bat Lady's house. The wind howled. It always seemed to pick up when you crossed her property. I'm sure that was just in my mind (and the minds of pretty much everyone else who walked past here), but the willow tree swayed and even from where I stood on the sidewalk, I could hear the porch creak.

All the lights were out, except for a lone lamp in the upstairs bedroom. That was a good sign. Last time I had stopped by, when no one answered the door, the light had been off.

Bat Lady must be back.

The night was silent, almost too quiet, as I approached the house. I knocked on the door. The sound echoed. I felt a chill. I listened for movement. Nothing. I knocked again and pressed my ear against the door. Silence. And then, suddenly, the silence was broken.

By music.

I jumped back. I remembered now that old record player, the one that played vinyls, in her living room. It was hard to picture a weird old lady listening to the albums I'd found stacked there: the Who's *My Generation*, the Beach Boys' *Pet Sounds*, the Beatles' *Abbey Road*, and the album that was currently playing, the one she always seemed to play, *Aspect of Juno* by HorsePower.

I knocked again. "Open up!"

Still no answer, just the sound of Gabriel Wire, the lead singer of HorsePower, telling me that "time stands still."

Like hell it does.

I started pounding on the door. No answer. I wasn't sure what to do. I couldn't keep pounding—the last thing I needed was to draw attention to myself—but I wasn't about to leave either.

I tried to look in the window, but they were boarded up in the front. Still, I could see through a sliver into the living room, to where that record player was. It was dark. I kept my eye there for a second.

Then a shadow walked by.

"Hello! Open up!"

I went back to the door and knocked some more. I was tempted to knock the door down, but then I remembered the garage. When I was last inside the house—when Shaved Head brought me to meet Bat Lady and talk face-to-face—he had parked in the garage and taken me via an underground tunnel.

Maybe I could get in that way.

I started toward the back. Bat Lady's house is set right up against the woods. I don't mean that the woods are off her backyard—I mean that the house literally sits against the trees, as if the very structure was a part of the forest. I quickly tried the back door, but the new lock held.

I took the small flashlight out of my pocket. It was extra creepy back there. I practically swam through a thick haze of trees until I reached the garage. I knew that inside there was a trapdoor that led to a tunnel. But the garage door was locked. So now what?

I can't say exactly why, but I headed to the lush garden behind the garage. Something, I don't know what, drew me there. Ema and I had found it during our last night visit here. I had no idea how Bat Lady kept her plants looking so lively this time of the year, but that was the least of my concerns. There was a path in the middle of the garden. I knew what was at the end of it.

I lifted my flashlight. It found the tombstone in the back. I read the now-familiar words:

LET US LABOR TO MAKE THE HEART GROW LARGER,
AS WE BECOME OLDER,
AS SPREADING OAK GIVES MORE SHELTER.
HERE LIES E.S.
A CHILDHOOD LOST FOR CHILDREN
A30432

I had figured that E.S. stood for Elizabeth "Lizzy" Sobek, but now I realized that it could just as easily be her brother,

Emmanuel, or her mother, Esther, though they had died in Poland more than half a century ago; so really, how could they "lie" here?

But that wasn't the main point.

No, Mrs. Friedman, Lizzy Sobek hadn't been killed by the Butcher of Lodz. Lizzy Sobek had survived the war and been, well, a hippie at some point and now everyone in town knew her as the Bat Lady, the creepy old lady who lived in the creepy old house.

I wondered what Mrs. Friedman would do if she learned that Lizzy "Butterfly" Sobek, the legendary resistance fighter who lost her family at Auschwitz, lived less than a quarter of a mile from Kasselton High School.

I moved toward the tombstone. In the background, one HorsePower song faded away and another began. I knew what was on the back of the tombstone—that same Abeona butterfly with its animal eyes on the wings. I had seen it here during my previous visit, but again something had drawn me here, so I had to play it out.

My footsteps echoed in the dark. I got my beam ready, aimed it at the spot, and gasped out loud. The butterfly was there, but someone had crossed it out. Someone had spray-painted a giant X across it.

I spun back to the house, and this time I could hear mocking laughter.

The sound ran down my spine.

Go home, Mickey, I told myself.

There was danger. You could feel it. Danger had a certain quality to it. You could almost reach out and touch it. I knew that I should go. I knew that I should regroup and think this out. But there was no way I was going to, not because I was particularly brave or, in this case, foolhardy, and not because I wanted to be as dumb as those teenagers who go into the serial killer's house in horror movies.

I just didn't want whatever was haunting me to escape again. If it got the better of me, okay, I could live (or die) with that. But I needed answers and I wasn't about to let the person who might be able to answer them slip through my fingers again.

I ran to the back door and knocked. Dumb. Nobody had responded before. What did I think would be different now?

I cupped my hands around my eyes and peered into the kitchen through the back window. Dark. But then I saw a shadow cross in the distance. Someone had streaked by and was heading up the stairs.

Why?

I tried picturing Bat Lady moving as fast as that shadow. I couldn't imagine it.

Someone else was in that house. Someone else had spray-painted an X onto the tombstone. Someone else had turned on the music and mocked me with a laugh.

I ran around to the front and looked up into Bat Lady's bedroom window with the light. I tilted my head, trying to get an angle, trying to see something—a shadow maybe, a silhouette, anything—and as I did, someone turned off the light.

Total darkness.

Oh no.

I didn't know what to do. I debated kicking in the door, but then what? This was probably nothing—a visitor or maybe even Bat Lady herself turning the lights down before heading to sleep. Still, my heart was pounding against my chest. I had to do something.

I was just debating my next move when the light in the window came back on. I moved back onto the grass so I could get a better look. I cupped my hands into a megaphone and called out, "Hello?" I didn't know what to call her. Her identity was a secret, so calling out to "Miss Sobek" wouldn't work. I wasn't sure yelling "Bat Lady" was the way to go either.

"Hello? Can you hear me?"

Nothing.

"It's Mickey. Hello? Can you open the door? Please?"

I saw something in the window move. A hand pushed the thin gauzelike curtain to the side and then a face peered out.

I screamed out loud this time.

There, from that upstairs window, the Butcher of Lodz was staring down at me.

CHAPTER 23

I couldn't breathe.

There was no question about it this time: It was the same guy in the old photograph—and he hadn't aged a day.

For a few seconds, my brain just shut down. I didn't wonder how this could possibly be. I didn't wonder whether I was dreaming. I didn't think about running after him or calling out or doing anything. I just stood there, frozen, looking up into those green eyes with the yellow rings, the same eyes I'd seen the day my father died.

When he ducked away from the window, my brain unlocked. For a single second, no longer, I stared up at the window and considered the possibility that my mind was playing tricks on me.

No friggin' way.

I ran back to the door and this time I didn't hesitate. I

lowered my shoulder and rammed into it. The door didn't give way so much as shatter, the wood breaking into splinters. I fought through them, pulling myself through the opening. I stood in the front foyer. The living room was on my left. The record player was still on. On the fireplace, I saw that same old picture of the hippies with the butterfly T-shirts.

I heard a noise above me.

He was still upstairs.

Okay, now what?

I could wait right here, couldn't I? He would have to come down these stairs. I could just stand here and wait and demand answers.

Would that really work?

I didn't know, but a thought occurred to me. I needed help, and one person immediately came to mind: Uncle Myron.

That surprised me, but then again, who else did I have? Ema and Spoon couldn't really come to my aid here. If I called Mr. Waters, well, I'd just broken into a house, hadn't I? I could get arrested.

Another noise from upstairs.

I grabbed my phone and hit Myron's number. Two rings later, he answered. "Mickey?"

My voice was a whisper. "I'm at Bat Lady's house."

"What? Why?"

"Can't explain. Please get over here. I need help."

I expected more questions. I didn't get them. Instead Myron said, "It'll take me fifteen minutes."

I hung up.

Now what?

Wait. Stand by the stairs and wait. Either Myron would get here in time and we could go upstairs together or the Butcher would have to come down.

But suppose Bat Lady was up there. Suppose he had attacked her or worse.

What if, right at this very moment, he was strangling her or something. Was I just going to stay down here and let that happen?

I stared at that old staircase. It didn't even look as though it could hold my weight. I was still debating what to do when a sound made up my mind for me.

From upstairs, I heard a window creak open.

Was the Butcher trying to sneak out?

Uh-uh, no way. No way was I going to let this guy get away when I had him trapped.

I ran up the stairs. Part of my brain told me to slow down, to be careful, to not underestimate my opponent. I was young, yes, but I had been trained all over the world how to fight.

So what was my training telling me now?

It didn't matter, because when I reached the upstairs hall-way, what I saw stopped me as if my feet had suddenly been nailed to the floor.

What the . . . ?

I don't know what I expected. I guess I figured that the

155

upstairs would be, well, like the downstairs—dark, dingy, maybe some old wallpaper, antique sconce lighting on the walls. But that wasn't what I saw.

I saw photographs. Hundreds. No. Thousands. Thousands and thousands of photographs.

The hallway was completely blanketed with pictures of children and teenagers. They were everywhere, on every available space, not just encasing both walls from top to bottom but even glued onto the ceiling overhead.

I reached my hand out and touched them. There were photos on top of photos. Layers and layers of photos—I couldn't say how deep. The photos were all various sizes. Some were black and white, some color, some fading, some vibrant. Some were smiling, some were grim. The children were of every race, creed, nationality, and even era.

Both bedroom doors were open and maybe that explained it, but there seemed to be a wind effect going through that corridor. A few of the portraits started peeling off, falling down around my feet. One was of a little boy, no more than eight or nine, with curly hair and sad eyes. The boy somehow looked familiar to me.

Something in his face . . .

Another photograph gently landed next to it. Then another. I looked down and saw a photograph at my feet that almost made me scream out loud.

It was a school portrait of Ashley—my former girlfriend who we all rescued down at the Plan B Go-Go Lounge.

I stared down at her pretty face, lost for a second, confused.

A sound at the end of the corridor knocked me out of my stupor. No time to worry about a bunch of pictures. Not right now anyway, because down the hall, at the end of this row of photographs, was the door leading to Bat Lady's bedroom.

He—the Butcher, the Paramedic, whoever—was in that room.

I headed for it now. The portraits were still peeling off the walls and ceiling, almost like they were shedding. Several landed on my face. I raised my hand as a shield, got to the door, debated how to enter, and then just threw open the door.

The room was empty.

There was no more wind because someone had just closed the window. And either that someone had to still be in this room or he had gone out the window.

I hurried over, closing the door behind me. If he had managed to jump out, he couldn't have gotten far. Not yet. He'd still be in the yard. I looked out the window.

Nothing.

Cold dread spread through me. Nothing. That meant he was still in here, still in this very room. I slowly turned away from the window.

The room had wallpaper that was either yellow or aged, I couldn't tell which. On the bedside table were two photographs. One was an old sepia-tone picture I had seen before—the Sobek family before the start of World War II. Samuel, Esther, Emmanuel, and little Lizzy. The other photo was in fading color—it was Bat Lady, looking to be in her fifties or sixties maybe, standing by a tree with that same sad-eyed, curly-haired boy whose picture I'd just seen in the corridor.

I kept very still and strained to pick up any sound.

Where was the Butcher hiding?

I stood right next to the bed and for a moment, I wondered whether he was hiding underneath it. I glanced down at my feet, just starting to think that it would be too obvious a hiding spot, when two hands shot out from under the bed, grabbed my ankles, and pulled hard.

I let out a scream and lost my balance. My elbow banged against the night table, knocking down the lamp, plunging the room into total darkness as I landed hard against the wood floor.

The hands kept pulling, dragging me under the bed.

In a frenzied panic, I started to kick, hoping to land something or maybe free my ankles. But he held on. I couldn't see a thing. I could just feel myself slowly being sucked down.

I was three-quarters of the way under the bed.

What was he trying to do anyway?

I didn't know and I didn't care. I wanted to be free. I kicked and bucked and screamed until finally one ankle, and then the other, slipped free. I scuttled across the floor and into the far corner. I huddled there, knees to chest, and waited.

I wasn't sure about my next move. My eyes had not started to adjust to the darkness from the shattered lamp. I had my hands up in a defensive position. My adversary was still in the room, but I didn't know where. I had to be prepared. Again I tried to stay still and listen, but my breathing was too loud now.

Then the bedroom door quickly opened and closed.

I got up and ran toward it. I fumbled for the doorknob, turned it . . .

The knob didn't move.

I twisted it harder, but the knob wouldn't budge. From behind the door I heard a sound like crinkling. I sniffed and smelled something that made my eyes widen. I reared back and once again used my shoulder. Nothing. I took a step back and rammed the door once again.

It gave way. I stumbled and fell into the middle of that corridor with all those photographs.

And they were on fire.

The fire raged, the flames quickly dancing up the walls and onto the ceiling, the photo paper working like kerosene. The portraits crinkled, peeled, and blackened, filling the corridor with smoke. The flames quickly flanked me, blocking my way back into the bedroom. I used the crook of my elbow to cover my mouth and searched for a way out.

I was surrounded by walls of flame.

I remembered a tip from a fire safety talk when I was in fourth grade: Stay low and crawl. I did that, but I wasn't sure it was going to do much good. The flames were everywhere, the heat unbearable. The smoke was starting to choke me. My path back to the bedroom had been swallowed up by the flames—the same with the path forward to the staircase.

With the flames creeping closer, I saw an opening on my right.

A doorway.

I rolled into what I guessed was a spare bedroom. I couldn't see much—I was still keeping low and the smoke was thick—but I could see that unlike the rest of the house, this one was brightly painted in red, yellow, and blue. My eyes started watering from the smoke. I tried to hold my breath and crawled some more. My hand hit something . . . squishy maybe? Rubbery? I heard a squeak and looked down.

It was a rubber duck. The floor was covered with toys.

I had no time to even register confusion. The fire roared into the room as though it were following me. I rolled onto my back and kicked away as the flames hungrily licked at my feet. My back hit a wall.

I was trapped.

In seconds, the flames would swallow me whole. I wish that I could tell you what I thought about at that moment, with death surrounding me. I don't think my life flashed before my eyes. I don't even think that I pictured my mother in rehab or my father at the accident or any of that. Fear—pure fear—pushed out all thoughts but one.

I had to find a way out of there.

I managed to open my watery eyes. The flames were moving closer. I looked up, and through the thickening smoke, I saw a window.

I read somewhere that no computer can compete with the human brain for speed of certain calculations. So what happened next took maybe a tenth of a second, probably less. My brain flashed to the front of the Bat Lady's house—the street view, if you will—and it quickly figured out the placement of the second-floor windows. I realized where I was, how high, and that if I got out that window, I'd be on the porch roof over the front door.

With the flames almost upon me, I jumped to the window and pulled it up.

It didn't move.

I could see there was no lock on it. The window was stuck.

No time to think or try anything else. I leaned hard with my back into the glass. I could feel the window shatter and give way as I fell outside. The oxygen fed the fire, but I kept myself flat on the roof. The flames shot over me.

The roof was pitched and I started to slide down it. Using my hands to find the edge, I let myself go with gravity. As I started to fall, I twisted my body so that my feet were beneath me. I landed hard on the front yard and tucked into a roll. I stood up and looked back at the house.

It was completely engulfed in flames.

In the distance I heard sirens. I had no idea what to do here. I turned to my left, saw nothing, turned to my right, and there, staring up at the flames, was the Butcher.

For a moment I just stared at him, unable to move. I was okay, physically. There may have been a scrape or minor burn, but I knew that I'd be fine. Maybe I was catching my breath. Maybe I was simply too stunned. But I stood there, no more than fifty feet from the man who had taken my father away and just tried to kill me, and I didn't move.

The sirens sounded again, and just like that, the Butcher turned and ran away.

That snapped me out of my haze. Again I thought: Uh-uh, no way. No way was he getting away from me. The Butcher may be fast, but I was faster and I had desire on my side. There was no way he was getting away with this.

I thought the Butcher would head for the woods, but instead he headed for the neighbor's backyard. There was no hesitation on my part. Not anymore. I sprinted with everything I had toward him. We ran through one backyard, then another, then a third.

I was closing the gap.

Behind me I heard voices. Someone yelled, "Stop!" I didn't. I figured that I'd obey when the Butcher did. He leapt over a hedge. I leapt it too.

Only ten feet separated us when he finally veered into

the woods. It wouldn't do him any good. I was there. I was going to catch up to him and take him down and . . .

I went down hard.

Someone had tackled me. He was straddling me.

"Stop! Police!"

I looked up into the face of Chief Taylor!

"Don't move!" he shouted.

"Let me go! You gotta go after him!"

But Chief Taylor wouldn't listen to me. "I said, 'Don't move.' Lie flat on the ground and put your hands on your head."

"He's getting away!"

"Now!"

Taylor started to flip me onto my stomach. I let him roll me and just kept going with it, throwing him off me. I jumped back to my feet.

"We can't let him go!" I shouted, turning back toward the woods.

But by now another officer was there. And another. One went for my legs, the other hit me high. I fell back to the ground. Taylor stood over me, his face red with rage. He reared back his foot as if to kick me, and then I heard another voice shout, "Get away from him, Ed!"

It was Uncle Myron.

Taylor turned to the voice. I tried to get up, tried to keep running after the Butcher, because there was no time to explain, not really, and I figured that they'd follow me and I could explain later. I actually managed to shrug him off, but when I looked back at the woods, there was no one, not a sound. I hesitated, looking for him, giving the cops a fresh chance to grab me.

There was no point in struggling anymore.

The night fell silent. The Bat Lady's house burned down to the ground. And the Butcher was gone.

CHAPTER 24

I told anyone I could about the blond guy, but they weren't listening. Still red-faced, Chief Ed Taylor took out his handcuffs.

"You're under arrest," he said to me. "Turn around and put your hands behind your back."

He reached for my arm, but Uncle Myron stepped between us. "What's the charge?"

"You're kidding, right? How about arson, for starters?"

"You saw him start that fire?"

"No," Taylor said, "but he was running away."

"Maybe because, oh, I don't know, the fire could have burned him?" Myron snapped. "What did you want him to do—put it out?"

Taylor's hands tightened into fists. "Well, Bolitar, how about the rest of it—resisting arrest, assaulting a police officer—"

"You jumped him in the dark," Myron said. "And all he did was roll you off him. He never hit you. If you're embarrassed that a teenager got the better of you . . ."

Chief Taylor's face turned even redder. Oh, this wasn't helping.

"I'm bringing him in, Bolitar. Get out of my way."

"Where are you taking him?"

"To the station for initial booking, then a bail appearance down in Newark."

"Bail? Isn't that a little overkill, Ed?"

"He might be a flight risk."

"He's a kid, for crying out loud." Myron put his hand on my shoulder. "Don't say a word, Mickey, do you hear me? Not one word." He turned back to Taylor. "I will be following your vehicle. As his attorney I'm forbidding you from questioning him."

Taylor had his cuffs out. "Hands behind your back."

"Seriously, Ed?" Myron said.

"Procedure," Taylor replied. "Unless you think your nephew deserves special treatment."

"It's okay," I said, putting my hands behind my back. Chief Taylor cuffed me. One of his men guided me into the back of a squad car and sat next to me. Chief Taylor took the front seat.

I looked back at the burning house. I thought about those photographs—the one of Ashley, the one of that sad-eyed boy with the curly hair. I thought about all I had seen and heard there and wondered what it all meant. That house, I figured, had been the headquarters for the Abeona Shelter. Now it was gone, burned down by . . .

Who? The Butcher of Lodz? A man who would be ninety but still looked in his thirties? Did that make any sense?

And most of all, the question that kept coming back to me again and again: What had he done with my father?

"I can't believe it," Taylor said.

I looked toward the rearview mirror and met Chief Taylor's eyes. I wanted to ask what he was talking about, but I remembered what Myron had said about keeping quiet.

The cop next to me made it easier: "What can't you believe?"

"Bolitar. The kid's uncle."

"What about him?"

"He's following us in a stretch limo."

It wasn't easy to turn around with my hands cuffed, but I managed enough. Chief Taylor was right. We were indeed being followed by a big black limousine.

"So, Mickey," Chief Taylor said, "this is the second time I've caught you near that old house. You want to tell me why?"

"No, sir."

"Maybe you got a thing for old ladies," Chief Taylor said, and in his mocking voice I could hear the echo of his son's *Ema Moo!* "Is that it, Mickey? Do you dig grannies or something?"

I didn't rise to the bait. Even the cop next to me was frowning at this lame approach.

The Kasselton police station was located across the street from Kasselton High School. A few hours ago, I'd been quietly celebrating my basketball debut in a gymnasium a few yards from where I was now being brought in by cops. Life is definitely a series of thin lines.

Taylor slipped out of his seat and closed the door behind him. A few seconds later, the cop sitting next to me helped me out. The limousine was right behind us. The back door opened, and Myron stepped out.

"You have a limo now, Bolitar?" Chief Taylor said. He ran his hand along the roof of the stretch. "You must really think you're hot stuff."

"It isn't mine."

"No? Then whose is it?"

"Actually"—and now I thought I saw the smallest hint of a smile on Myron's face—"it belongs to Angelica Wyatt."

Taylor scoffed at that. "Sure, right, and I'm George Clooney."

The tinted back window slid down. When Angelica Wyatt stuck her gorgeous face out the window, smiled, and said, "Are you the town police chief? What a pleasure to meet you," I thought Taylor would have a stroke.

"Uh, Miss Wyatt . . . oh, my, is it really you? We're all big fans, aren't we, fellas?"

There were five cops surrounding the limousine now.

They all nodded like puppets. Angelica Wyatt awarded them with yet another smile. She said something else, I couldn't hear it, but some of the cops began to chuckle. I met Uncle Myron's eyes and he rolled them.

Angelica Wyatt made a comment about how handsome men in uniform were. I saw Chief Taylor pet down his hair and puff out his chest. Really? Are we men this easily taken? Then I thought about Rachel Caldwell. Hadn't she done something similar to me when we first met? Hadn't I fallen for it?

I bet Ema would have something cutting, funny, and true to say about this.

Myron and I stood away from the rest of them. My hands were still cuffed behind my back. Angelica Wyatt continued to talk to Chief Taylor. He continued to giggle like a schoolgirl.

"What's going on?" I asked Myron.

That small smile was back on his face. "Wait."

Three minutes later, Chief Taylor came over and unlocked my cuffs. He turned to Myron. "You're his legal guardian?"

"I am."

He wasn't. Not really. That was part of the deal. I would stay with him, but Mom remained my legal guardian. Still, with her in rehab, he was the closest thing to one.

"You have to come inside and sign some papers, promising that he will appear when we need him, that kind of thing."

Myron and I managed not to ask what happened to the bail hearing in Newark. We knew the answer: Angelica Wyatt.

"Go wait in the car," Myron said to me.

A chauffeur complete with a chauffeur cap opened the door for me. I got in and sat next to Angelica Wyatt. It was weird for me, so it must have been weird for her. She was a big-time movie star and being in her presence was, well, like being in the presence of a movie star, something big and grand and unreal. It wasn't her fault. I don't think it was my fault either. It was just weird. I wondered what it was like for her to deal with that every day. It gave you great powers—look at how it'd freed me—but it must also have been a strange burden.

"Are you okay?" she asked me.

"Yes, ma'am. Thanks for your help."

I had never been in the back of a stretch limousine. The seats were rich leather. There was a small TV set and heavy crystal glasses.

"What happened? Were you in the house?"

Once again I didn't want to lie—but I wasn't up for telling the truth either. I really didn't know this woman. "I thought I saw a fire, so I tried to help."

Angelica Wyatt looked skeptical. "By going in the house?"

"Yes. To, uh, see if anybody was home."

"Why didn't you just call the fire department?"

Oops.

"Why would you call your uncle and tell him you needed help?"

"Believe me, if I had anyone else to call . . ." I stopped, wishing I had just stayed quiet.

"Mickey?"

I turned toward her. She looked at me with those eyes that somehow felt both comforting and oddly familiar. I liked her eyes, not just because they were brown and beautiful, but because I sensed the warmth there.

"I know it's none of my business, but your uncle is trying."

I said nothing.

"He's a good man. You can trust him."

"No offense," I said, which is something you say when you're about to offend, "but you really don't know the situation."

"Yeah, Mickey, I do."

I thought about that. She had told me that she'd been my mom's friend back when she got pregnant with me.

"He made a mistake," Angelica Wyatt said to me. "You'll understand that one day. Life isn't like one of my movies. Kids think grown-ups have all the answers, when the only difference between kids and grown-ups is that grown-ups know that there are no easy answers."

"Again, no offense," I said, "but it's been a long time since I thought grown-ups had all the answers."

She almost smiled at that. "We mess up. That's my point, Mickey. We all mess up. We try our best and we love you so much, but we are such weak, imperfect creatures."

Angelica Wyatt looked down. Her face fell and for a moment, I thought that she was about to cry.

"Miss Wyatt?"

"We all make mistakes. Your uncle wasn't the only one."

The limousine door opened. Uncle Myron looked in and said, "Everything okay here?"

Now I could see why Angelica Wyatt was such a great actress. Her face brightened and you'd never know that a few seconds ago, she'd seemed completely crushed.

"Sure," she said, sliding over to make room for him. "Mickey and I were just chatting."

CHAPTER 25

As you can imagine, I got the first, second, third, and fourth degree from Myron. Despite Angelica Wyatt's pleading, I still didn't trust him. I knew that maybe I should. I knew that when the chips were down, I had indeed called him for help. But both Bat Lady and Shaved Head had warned me not to say anything to Myron.

Still, there was a moment I weakened and almost said something. But then Myron inadvertently gave me another reason to keep him in the dark.

"Your father went into that house when he was a kid," Myron reminded me. "He never told me what he saw."

Good point—and if my dad chose never to tell Uncle Myron, I figured, well, neither should I.

At some point, Myron threw up his hands and moved back into the den. I debated what to do at this point. I couldn't just let it go completely, because the truth was, I did need something from him. I approached the den and sat down on the couch. Myron had bought his childhood home from my grandparents a few years back. That meant that he and my dad grew up right here, and, yeah, that was kind of weird. The two brothers had spent hours in here watching television. It was strange to picture it, my dad as a kid, hanging in this room with Uncle Myron.

I wasn't sure how to broach the subject, so I started with familiar territory I knew would interest him. "Tryouts went well today," I said.

"Yeah?" As I predicted, this subject captured his interest. "Did you work out with the JV?"

I nodded. "But Coach Grady said he wants to see me tomorrow."

Myron grinned at that. "You think he wants to move you up?"

"I don't know," I said, though I suspected just that. So did Myron.

"But you played well?"

"I thought so, yeah."

"That's great."

Silence. Okay, enough with the warm-up.

"I have to ask you a favor," I said. "I know this will sound insane, but I need you to trust me on this."

Myron sat up and leaned forward. "What's up?"

"I want . . . I want to exhume my father's body."

My words hit him like a wet slap. "What?"

I started to backpedal. Man, I should have thought this out better. "I want his body moved out here," I lied. "So he can be buried closer to us."

Myron just looked at me. "For real?"

"Yes, of course."

"What else, Mickey?"

"Nothing."

Myron's voice was firmer. "What else, Mickey?"

How to put this . . . ? "I never saw him," I said slowly. "I . . . I need to know it's him in that box."

Myron took a second now. When he spoke again, his voice was softer. "You mean, like, you need closure?"

"Yeah," I said. "Closure."

"I don't think seeing his body now will help."

"Myron, listen to me, okay? Just . . . just listen."

Myron waited.

"I need to know that it's Dad in that coffin."

He looked confused. "What do you mean?"

I closed my eyes. "I asked you to just trust me on this. Please."

Myron studied my face for a few moments. I stared right back at him, my eyes unwavering. I expected more questions, but instead he surprised me.

"Okay," Myron said. "I'll look into the legal protocol tomorrow."

CHAPTER 26

I suddenly realized that I was both starving and exhausted. Uncle Myron ordered enough Chinese food for a family of twelve. I tried to eat in silence, but Myron had to remind me, like he always did, that this had been my father's favorite Chinese restaurant and that he had especially liked the shrimp in lobster sauce.

After I finished eating, I thought about calling Ema and filling her in on what happened, but it was late and I was just too tired. It could wait. After hearing Spoon's rumors about Ema's home life, I both wanted to keep reaching out and yet feared that it might cause some kind of blowback.

A text came in from Rachel: **We still on for tomorrow after school?**

Me: **Yes. How are you?**

Rachel: **Fine. Gotta go. Tomorrow.**

When the school bell rang at eight thirty the next morning, I was back in my homeroom. Funny how school could smooth the rough edges off everything, even all that I was going through. Back inside this plain brick edifice, life seemed normal. School was boring, sure, but it was also an anchor. The rest of my life might be flying off in every direction, but here everything was wonderfully normal and even mundane.

Lunchtime was usually spent with Ema and Spoon, but today I was supposed to meet with Coach Grady, the varsity basketball coach. Part of me was relieved about avoiding them. Don't get me wrong. I trusted them both with everything I had and owed them the complete truth, but Rachel had asked me not to say anything about going to see her after school. I couldn't just ignore that, could I?

In short, the best answer might also be the most cowardly: avoid.

As I headed for Coach Grady's office, I passed a somewhat familiar spot and felt a funny longing. It was Ashley's locker. Ashley had been sort of my girlfriend before she vanished. The Abeona Shelter—that is to say, Ema, Spoon, Rachel, and me—had saved her, I guess. The last time I saw her, she waved good-bye to me and left in a van driven by another member of Abeona.

Now, just a few days later, all signs of Ashley were gone. Her locker had a fresh lock on it. Some other kid had moved in, I guessed, and taken over her space. Ashley was gone as though she had never been there. I wondered where she was now. I wondered whether she was okay.

I knocked on Coach Grady's door.

"Come in."

This was not normally an office you wanted to visit. Mr. Grady was also the vice principal in charge of discipline. If you were called to his office, it was usually to get detention or be suspended.

Mr. Grady looked at me over half-moon reading glasses. "Close the door," he said.

I did. He invited me to sit. I looked around his office. There were no family photos, no trophies or photos of former basketball teams—nothing personal.

"So," he said, folding his hands and putting them on his desk, "how did you feel about tryouts yesterday?"

I wasn't sure how to answer that. "It was fun."

"You've clearly played basketball for a long time."

"Yes."

"I know you traveled around a lot in your youth, right?"

I nodded.

"Spent a lot of time overseas, played for a lot of different teams."

"Yes."

"What was the longest time you played with the same group of guys?"

"Two months," I said.

He made a face as though he had expected that answer.

"It's one of the reasons we moved back to the United States," I said. "See, my father wanted me to have that experience—to settle down and stay in the same place and play with a real high school team."

"Sort of like, oh, I don't know, the seniors on this team?"

I said nothing.

"This same group of boys has been playing basketball together since the fifth grade. They've won together on every level, and now, well, this is it for them. Next year they all go their separate ways."

There was nothing to add to that, so I stayed quiet.

"I also explained to you recently that I don't like having freshmen or sophomores play on the varsity team. In the dozen years I've been coaching here, I haven't had a sophomore on varsity yet, and this year, with five starters from last year's team returning . . ."

He stopped. This was not going the way I had hoped.

"But that said, I saw your uncle play when he was here. I know that he was a once-in-a-generation talent. After watching you yesterday, you may be that too. I don't know yet. I don't want to get ahead of myself. But my job as coach is to be fair and give everyone a chance. If what I saw yesterday was a fluke or maybe the competition wasn't that great, well, we will find out. But for now, I don't see how I cannot at least give you a shot at trying out for varsity."

I wanted to pump my fist and shout, "YES!" but I managed to keep my emotions in check. "Thank you, Coach."

"Don't thank me. You'll either earn it or you won't." He looked back down and started writing. "Varsity tryouts are at four thirty. I'll see you then."

I rose and started for the door.

"Mickey?"

I turned back.

"I know you've already had issues with some of the seniors. Guys like Troy and Buck."

"Yes, sir."

"They are a very tight group—Troy, Buck, Brandon, Alec. They won't be happy with this move. If you make the team, you'll be taking a spot from one of their closest friends."

I shrugged. "Not much I can do about that."

"Yes, Mickey, there is. We will need cohesion to be successful on the court. Try to remember that. Be the bigger man."

CHAPTER 27

When I got to the cafeteria, Ms. Owens, the teacher I liked least (which was a nice way of saying "did not like" or even "hated"), gave me the evil eye and said, "Hall pass?"

I gave it to her. Ms. Owens studied it as though I were a terrorist carrying a fake passport. After a few more long seconds, she grudgingly let me in. I headed over to my normal table. Spoon and Ema were already in place, though there were two chairs separating them.

"Where were you?" Ema asked.

"Mr. Grady wanted to see me."

"Are you in trouble?" Spoon asked.

"No. Just the opposite."

As I explained about getting a varsity tryout, I spotted Troy and Buck. They had changed tables so that they sat now only with boys—more specifically, only boys on the varsity basketball team. I wondered whether they knew that I would join them at tryouts today. My eyes stayed on the table a beat too long.

Spoon said, "Your future teammates."

"Yep."

"You know Buck and Troy, of course. Have you met any of the others?"

"No."

"Well, Troy is one captain. The other is Brandon Foley. He's at the end of the table. He's the tallest player on the team. Six foot eight."

I had seen Brandon Foley in the corridors, and I often heard his voice over the morning announcements.

"He's student council president," Spoon said.

"And," Ema added, "he's also Troy Taylor's best friend. They've lived on the same street since birth and started playing together when they were in diapers, which in their case might have been last year."

Terrific.

As I was looking over at the table, Brandon Foley turned and met my gaze. I expected the standard mocking glare, but Brandon didn't do that. He made sure that I was looking at him and then he nodded in a gentle, almost supportive way.

Troy was sitting next to him. He turned to see where his friend was looking, so I quickly diverted my gaze.

"You okay?" Ema asked.

"Fine, but I have really big news."

I told them about the fire at Bat Lady's house. They listened with their mouths agape. When I told them about the portraits in the corridor, Spoon spoke for the first time.

"Obvious," he said.

"What?"

"Those pictures. It was a gallery of the children the Abeona Shelter has saved."

I told them about getting arrested, about Uncle Myron showing up, and how Angelica Wyatt was the one who saved me from a night in prison. Ema seemed annoyed by this.

"Wait, how does your uncle know Angelica Wyatt?"

"She's smoking hot," Spoon added.

We looked at him.

"I'm talking about Angelica Wyatt," Spoon explained.

"Yeah," Ema said, "we got that." She turned back to me. "So?"

"I don't know. Myron is her bodyguard or something."

"I thought he was a sports agent."

"He is. I don't get it either, but Angelica Wyatt knew my mom too."

"What are you talking about?" There was a snap in Ema's voice now. "How would she have known your mother?"

"They were, like, celebrity friends when they were young. My mom was a big tennis star, Angelica was a young actress. I guess they hung out. What's the difference?"

Ema just frowned.

"I have a thought," Spoon said.

Ema gave him a withering look. "I can hardly wait to hear this."

"This sandy-blond guy. Let's call him the Butcher, okay?"

"What about him?"

Spoon pushed up his glasses. "He tried to kill you. Doesn't it make sense that maybe he also tried to kill Rachel?"

Silence.

"And if that's the case, wouldn't it follow that maybe, just maybe, he's trying to kill us all?"

More silence.

"I hate to admit it," Ema said, "but Spoon may have a point."

"Thank you. I'm not just eye candy for the ladies, you know."

"We are going to have to be extra careful," I said.

"Has anyone heard from Rachel since we sneaked into the hospital?" Spoon asked.

So here we were. I could lie to them or I could betray Rachel's confidence. I aimed for something in between. "I have," I said as, mercifully, the bell rang. "But for right now, I need to leave it at that."

"What's that supposed to mean?" Ema asked.

"Yeah," Spoon added. "Aren't we in this together?"

"Just . . . trust me here." I remembered my schedule—visit Rachel, basketball tryouts. Hmm. They were both still looking at me, waiting for more. "How about this? Let's meet right after basketball tryouts. I should be able to tell you more then."

CHAPTER 28

When the final bell rang, I got my backpack and prepared for the walk to Rachel's house. I was just closing my locker when I heard Mrs. Friedman say, "Mr. Bolitar? A word, please."

Some kids nearby said, "Oooo, you're in trouble."

Mature, right?

After I moved into her classroom, Mrs. Friedman closed the door behind us. "I found something you might find interesting," she said.

"Oh?"

"I have a colleague who works at the United States Holocaust Memorial Museum in Washington, DC. Have you ever been?"

"No, ma'am."

Her face looked so sad. "You should. Everyone should.

It is horrible and yet so necessary. You go into that museum one person, you come out another. At least, you do if you have a conscience. Anyway, I spoke to my colleague and I asked her about Hans Zeidner, the Butcher of Lodz."

I waited for her to say more. When she didn't, I said, "Thank you."

Mrs. Friedman pinned me down with her eyes. "Do you want to tell me why you're so interested in this subject?"

I almost did. I thought about all that I knew, about Lizzy Sobek being the Bat Lady and living so close to where we now stood. I thought about the Butcher and my father and the fire. But in the end, I knew that I shouldn't and couldn't.

"I can't," I said. "Not yet anyway."

I figured that there would be a follow-up question, but there wasn't. Instead Mrs. Friedman opened her desk drawer and said, "Here."

There was a photograph in her hand. I took it from her. It was another old black-and-white picture of a man wearing a Waffen-SS uniform. The man in the photograph had dark hair and a thin mustache. His nose was pointy and mouse-like. His eyes were two black marbles.

"Thank you," I said, looking up at her. "Who is this?"

Mrs. Friedman made a face. " 'Who is this?' "

"Yes. Who is the man in the photograph?"

"Who do you think?" Mrs. Friedman said. "It's Hans Zeidner. The Butcher of Lodz."

CHAPTER 29

Occam's Razor.

My father had often repeated that one to me. Occam's Razor states the following: "Other things being equal, a simpler explanation is better than a more complex one." Put more succinctly, the simplest answer was usually the best one.

So why hadn't I even considered the simple possibility that Bat Lady's photograph was merely Photoshopped?

As I walked to Rachel's house, my mind traveled between rage at Bat Lady and rage at myself—mostly at myself. How could I be so gullible? In this day and age when any idiot with a computer can alter an image, why had I jumped to the conclusion that a Nazi from World War II hadn't aged a day in nearly seventy years and now worked as a San Diego paramedic?

' What kind of naïve dope am I?

The sandy-blond paramedic with the green eyes was not the Butcher of Lodz. He was not ninety years old. He was not the same man who had tortured and killed scores in 1940s Poland, including Lizzy Sobek's father. Ema had simply Photoshopped the guy's face onto a modern photograph to send out to San Diego, right? Why couldn't someone do the opposite—take a picture of a guy in his thirties and superimpose it on an old black-and-white?

Someone—the Bat Lady or Shaved Head, I guessed—had fooled me with simple digital photography.

Why? And what could I do about it?

It would have to wait. Right now, I had to concentrate on Rachel. When I approached her house, I saw a police car pulling out. I ducked behind a tree. Chief Taylor was in the driver's seat. No one was with him. As he drove past, he looked distracted and . . . scared?

I didn't know what to make of that. I waited until the police car was out of sight before making my approach. The gate at the entrance to Rachel's driveway had closed after Chief Taylor drove out. I pressed an intercom button and looked up into the camera. Rachel said, "I'll buzz you in." She was waiting for me at the front door. Other than the bandage on the side of her head, you would never guess that she'd been shot. Of course, the bullet hadn't entered her skin, just skimming the scalp, but somehow that made it all the more poignant. Probably half an inch, no more, was the difference between minor injuries and death.

The thought made me want to hug her, but it didn't feel right.

"I'm so glad to see you're okay," I said.

Rachel gave me a tight smile and kissed my cheek. She wore a short-sleeved shirt so that the burn mark was visible. I had always wanted to ask her how that had happened because it still looked painful, but of course, now was not the time. The red in her eyes told me that she'd been crying recently and probably a lot.

"I'm so sorry about your mom."

"Thank you."

"Did I just see Chief Taylor drive out?"

Rachel nodded and frowned.

"What did he want?" I asked.

"I don't know. He's been talking to my father a lot. Every time I come near them, they tell me it's nothing. Oh, and Chief Taylor keeps asking me what I remember."

He had done that at the hospital too. "I guess that's normal. Him investigating what happened and all."

"I guess," Rachel said. But she didn't seem convinced. "It's just weird."

"Weird how?"

"He seems on edge or something."

Rachel shrugged and led me down the hall. We stopped at an open doorway with yellow crime-scene tape across it. This, I could see, was clearly where it had happened. There was still blood on the floor. I moved closer to Rachel. She began to shake. I put my arm around her and pulled her toward me.

"Why don't we go somewhere else?" I said as gently as I could.

"No, it's okay. I wanted to show this to you."

The house was silent.

"Who's home with you?" I asked.

"No one."

That surprised me. "Where are your father and stepmother?"

"My stepmother needed a vacation—thankfully. She's at a spa in Arizona. My father is at work." When she saw the concerned look on my face, she waved it away. "Believe me, it's better."

For a moment we both just stared at the blood on the floor. Rachel's eyes flooded with tears again. Not sure what to say, I went with, "Do you want to tell me what happened?"

"I got my mother killed," Rachel said. "It's as simple as that."

Now I *really* wasn't sure what to say. When I spoke again, I did so slowly and carefully. "I don't see how that could be true."

"I got her to come here. I put my mother right in the crossfire."

"What crossfire?"

Rachel shook her head. "It doesn't matter anymore."

"Of course it does. Someone tried to kill you—and last night . . ." I stopped.

"Last night what?"

"Last night, someone tried to kill me."

Her body stiffened. "What are you talking about?"

I told her about the Butcher and the fire at Bat Lady's house. Rachel stood there, stunned. "Is she okay?"

"Bat Lady? I don't know. I never saw her."

"I don't understand this," Rachel said.

We both looked back toward the room.

"Tell me what happened," I said.

"I don't remember all of it."

"Tell me what you do remember."

I turned toward Rachel. The lights were low, casting a shadow on her lovely face. I wanted so badly to reach out and touch her cheek and pull her close. I didn't. I stood and waited.

"I have to go back a little," Rachel said. "I have to explain why my mom was here in the first place."

"Okay. No rush."

"Well, yeah, there is." She almost smiled. "Don't you have tryouts?"

"There's time."

Rachel stared down at the bloodstain on the carpet. "I was angry at my mother for a very long time. I thought she abandoned me."

I looked down at the blood too.

"My mother left us when I was ten. My father told me she still loved me, but that she needed to"—Rachel made

191

quote marks with her fingers—"rest. I didn't know what that meant. I mean, in some ways I still don't. I just knew that she'd abandoned me. My parents got divorced, and I didn't see my mother for three years."

"Three years? Wow."

"I didn't even know where she was."

I thought about that. "The other day, you told me that your mother lived in Florida."

"That wasn't exactly true. I mean, she was in Florida, at least part of the time . . ." Rachel stopped and shook her head. "I'm telling this all wrong."

"It's okay," I said. "Take your time."

"Okay, so where was I? The divorce. The next time I saw my mother, I was thirteen years old. She just showed up after school one day. I mean, it was so surreal, you know? Mom was just standing there with the other mothers, smiling like . . . well, a crazy person. She looked horrible. She had too much bright red lipstick on, and her hair was all over the place. She wanted to drive me home, but I was actually scared of her. I called my dad. When he showed up, there was this big horrible scene. My mother went berserk. She started screaming at him, about how he had locked her up, how she knew the truth about him."

The temperature in the room felt like it dropped ten degrees.

"So what happened next?" I asked.

"My father got really quiet. He just stood there and let

her rant, until the police came. It was so horrible. Her lipstick was all smeared, her eyes were wide . . . it was like she couldn't even see me. Later, after she was gone, my father explained to me that my mom hadn't just run off—she'd had a nervous breakdown. He said that she'd always had mental health issues, but when I turned ten, she became manic and even dangerous. He said that she had been in and out of hospitals for the past three years."

"When you say dangerous . . . ?"

"I don't know what he meant," Rachel said too quickly. "Dad said she was out of control. He said he had to get a court order to get her treatment. I was so confused. I was angry and scared and sad. I mean, it made sense, in a way . . ." She shook her head. "It doesn't matter. I just thought, well, my mother is crazy. My father, he tries, I guess, but he's distant. It didn't matter. I had my friends and school."

Rachel finally looked away from the bloodstain.

"Two weeks ago, my mom was let out again. By this time there were all kinds of court orders against her to stay away from us. She couldn't visit me without a social worker present, stuff like that. But I wanted to see her. So when she called, we met up in secret. I didn't tell my dad. I didn't tell anyone." Rachel looked up and a small smile came to her lips. "When we first met up, Mom hugged me and, I don't know, this will sound weird, but I flashed back to being a happy kid again. Do you know what I mean?"

I thought about the way my own mother hugged me. "Yes."

"I realized something—no one hugged me anymore. Isn't that weird? My dad, well, it got awkward as I got older, and boys never just wanted to hug like that, if you know what I mean."

I wished that I didn't. I nodded, feeling a lump in my throat. I thought about Troy Taylor and realized how incredibly selfish that was, so I made myself stop.

"So it was nice," I said, "seeing your mother."

"For a few days, it was great. And then something went wrong."

"What?"

"Mom started ranting again, saying what an evil man my father was, how he lied about her and poisoned her and told everyone she was crazy just to protect himself. She became paranoid and started asking me if Dad knew that we were meeting. I tried to reassure her, but she just kept saying he'd kill her if he found out."

Silence.

"What did you do?"

Rachel shrugged. "I tried to calm her down. I asked about her meds. In a way, I mean, I wasn't surprised. I had seen her like this before. Maybe I blamed myself too."

"Why?"

"It's like, if I had been a better daughter, maybe—"

"You know that isn't the case."

"I do know. I mean, my dad explained it to me a hundred times. She was sick. It wasn't my fault, it wasn't his fault—and it wasn't her fault. Like Cynthia Cooper's mother has cancer, my mom had a disease that attacked the brain. She couldn't help it."

I thought about my own mother, in a rehab clinic. They told me the same thing, about how her drug addiction was an illness. It wasn't a question of willpower and I shouldn't take it personally, the experts said, but still, no matter how much you told yourself that, no matter how much I still loved her and was sympathetic to what had happened to her, a part of me always felt that in the end my mother chose drugs over her son.

"So I'm looking at this woman who had raised me, the last person to show me genuine warmth, and suddenly I started to wonder something strange—something I hadn't really considered before."

"What?" I asked.

Rachel turned and suddenly her eyes were dry and clear. "What if my mother wasn't crazy? What if she was telling the truth?"

I said nothing.

"What if my dad *did* do something to her?"

"Like what?"

"I don't know. She kept going on about how she knew something bad about him. What if she was telling the truth? I mean, my father didn't just get her committed to a mental hospital—he also divorced her and remarried. He explained it to me—how they had fallen out of love years ago and how he deserved his own happiness and all that. But still. Did he really have to lock her up? Couldn't he have found another way? This was my mother—the only woman who ever loved me. Shouldn't I give her at least a little benefit of the doubt? If I don't believe her, who else will?"

"So what did you do?"

Now a tear escaped her eye. "I started looking a little harder at my father."

"What do you mean?"

She shook her head. "It doesn't matter."

"What?"

"The police say it was an intruder—maybe two of them. Burglars or something. See, my father was supposed to be away for the night, so I had my mom stay at the house with me. He would have been furious if he knew. I was in my bedroom. Mom was down here, watching television. It was late. I was on the phone with you when I heard voices. I thought maybe my father had come home. So I came down the stairs. I turned the corner . . ."

"And then?"

Rachel shrugged. "I don't remember anything else. I woke up in the hospital."

"You said you heard voices?"

"Yes."

"As in, more than one?"

"Yes."

"Male, female?"

"Both. One was my mother."

"And the others?"

"I told the police that I didn't recognize them."

"But?"

"I don't know. I thought maybe one of them . . . it may have been my father."

Silence.

"But your father would never shoot you," I said.

She didn't reply.

"Rachel?"

"Of course he wouldn't."

"You said you started to check into your father—to see if your mother might be telling the truth. Did you find something?"

"That doesn't matter. The police say it was an intruder. I probably just imagined my father's voice."

But I could hear the evasiveness now in her tone. "Hold up a second. At the hospital, why did Chief Taylor say not to say anything to Investigator Dunleavy?"

"I don't know."

I started to press her. "And why was that butterfly on the door?"

"Why do you think?"

I just looked at her. "You're working for Abeona."

She said nothing.

"How could I have been so stupid?" I almost slapped myself in the head. "You didn't just happen to be the one to help Ashley—you knew why she was hiding in our school, didn't you?"

Again she didn't answer.

"Rachel, after all we've been through, you still don't trust me?"

"I trust you," she said with a sharp edge, "like you trust me."

"What's that supposed to mean?"

"Are you going to tell me that you've told me everything? Are you going to claim that you trust me as much as you trust Ema?"

"Ema? What does she have to do with it?"

"Who do you trust more, Mickey? Me or Ema?"

"It's not a contest."

"Sure," she said, her voice dripping with sarcasm. "Right." Rachel shook her head. "Talk about being stupid. I shouldn't have told you anything."

"Rachel, listen to me." I put my hands on her shoulders and turned her to face me. "I want to help you."

"I don't want your help."

She pulled away.

"But—"

"What's going on here?"

I looked over my shoulder. A man in a business suit stood there, his fist clenched.

Rachel said, "Dad?"

As I turned toward him to introduce myself, Rachel's

father reached into his jacket and pulled out a gun. He aimed it straight at my chest.

Whoa.

"Who are you?"

My knees went rubbery. I put my hands up. Rachel slid in front of me and said, "What are you doing? He's a friend of mine!"

"Who is he?"

"I told you. He's a friend. Put that away!"

Her father and that gun stared me down. I didn't know what to do. I stood there with my hands in the air and tried not to shake. Rachel was right in front of me, blocking my path. Through all the panic, I felt cowardly. I wanted to move her out of the way, but I was also worried about making any sudden moves.

Finally Mr. Caldwell lowered the gun. "Sorry, I . . . I guess I'm still on edge."

"Since when do you carry a gun?" Rachel asked.

"Since my daughter and ex-wife got shot in my own home." Mr. Caldwell looked at me. "I'm sorry . . ." He stopped as though searching for my name.

"Mickey," I said. "Mickey Bolitar."

"Rachel, I don't remember you mentioning anyone named Mickey."

"He's a new friend," Rachel said, and I thought I heard an edge in her tone. Mr. Caldwell heard it too. I thought that maybe he wanted to ask something more, but he turned back to me instead.

"Mickey, I'm really sorry about the gun. As Rachel may have told you, we had something of an incident here."

He waited for me to respond, but I gave him nothing. Was Rachel supposed to tell me? I didn't know, so I neither confirmed nor denied that I knew about the murder.

"Someone broke into our home and shot my daughter and her mother," he said. "Rachel was just released from the hospital, and I specifically told her not to let anyone in the house, so when I saw you two arguing . . ."

"I understand," I said, not sure whether I did or I didn't. The man was carrying a gun. He had whipped it out and aimed it at me. I was having trouble gathering my thoughts.

"You should probably leave now," Rachel said to me. "I know you have basketball."

I nodded, but I didn't like the idea of leaving her alone with her . . . her dad? I searched her face, but she turned away and started for the door. As I passed Mr. Caldwell, he reached out his hand. I shook it. His grip was firm.

"Nice to meet you, Mickey."

Yeah, I thought, nothing like pulling a gun on someone during your first encounter. Some "nice to meet you."

"You too," I said.

Rachel opened the door. She didn't say good-bye. She didn't say we'd talk later. She closed the door behind me, leaving her alone inside with her father.

I had started down the road, lost in my thoughts, when I heard a souped-up car slow as it approached me. I looked up and saw two scary-looking guys staring daggers at me. The guy in the passenger seat wore a bandana and had a long scar running down his right cheek. The driver had aviator sunglasses hiding his eyes. Talk about a danger vibe. I swallowed and hurried my step. The car picked up speed and kept pace with me.

I was about to veer off the sidewalk when the guy with the scar rolled down his window.

"That the Caldwell house?" he asked.

He pointed at it. I didn't know what to say, but I figured that it would be okay to say yes because there was a security gate. I nodded.

The guy with the scar didn't bother saying thanks. The souped-up car drove up to the gate. I stood and watched, but then Scarface turned around and glared at me again. "What are you looking at?"

I started to walk away. They wouldn't get past the gate anyway.

I risked a look behind me and saw the gate open. Scarface and his friend drove through it.

I didn't like this. I didn't like it all.

The car stopped and the two men got out of the car. I had my phone out, ready to dial 911 or at least call Rachel. Warn her. But warn her about what exactly? The two men moved toward the door. Without conscious thought, I started running toward her house, but then the front door opened, and I saw Mr. Caldwell step outside. He smiled and greeted the men. They all clearly knew each other. There were lots of smiles and backslaps.

Then I saw Mr. Caldwell get into the car, and they all drove off together.

CHAPTER 30

Half an hour after I had a gun pointed at me, I was in the locker room getting changed to try out with varsity. I could hardly wait. Now more than ever, I needed the sweet escape I only found on the basketball court. As I laced up my high-tops, my stomach started to do flips.

I was nervous.

It wasn't as though I had any friends on the court yesterday, but I knew these guys on varsity actively hated me. From the other side of the locker room I could hear a bunch of guys, including Troy and Buck, laughing. The noise sounded alien in my ears. Would I ever be a part of that? Would I ever be welcomed?

It was hard to imagine.

I finished dressing and took a deep breath. To stall, I texted Rachel and again made sure she was okay. She said she was fine and wished me luck at the tryouts. I was about to put away my phone when it buzzed again. I figured that it was one more text from Rachel, but I was wrong. It was Ema saying good luck.

I smiled. **Thanks.** Then I added: **Guess what?**

Ema: **what?**

Me: **The old Nazi photograph. It was Photoshopped. That wasn't the butcher.**

Ema: **NO WAY!**

A whistle sounded in the distance. I quickly explained via text, then I put away the phone. It was time to head out on the court. When I opened up the door to the gym, it was like one of those scenes in a movie when the guy walks into a bar and everything goes quiet. All balls stopped bouncing. No one took a shot. I felt as if all eyes were on me. My face turned red.

With my head down, I jogged toward the free basket in the corner.

The balls started bouncing again, and shots started clanking off the rim. This was what I'd always longed for—to be part of a school team—and I don't think I'd ever felt so out of place. I took a few shots, got my own rebounds, took a few more. I had to wonder how Troy and Buck were reacting to my being there. I risked a glance toward them.

Troy was grinning at me in a way I didn't like.

"Well, that's weird," someone behind me said.

I spun toward the voice. It was Brandon Foley, team

captain. There weren't many people in this school I had to look up to, but Brandon, at six foot eight, was one of them.

"What's that?" I said.

"Troy looks happy," Brandon said. "I figured he'd be furious to see you here."

I didn't know what to say to that. Brandon stuck his hand out. "I'm Brandon Foley."

"Yeah, I know. I'm Mickey Bolitar."

"Welcome."

"Thanks."

"Troy isn't so bad."

I figured that once again it would be best not to reply. Brandon took a shot. It swished through the basket, so I threw the ball back to him. We got into a nice rhythm and kept shooting. We didn't talk much. We didn't have to.

"Mickey?"

It was Coach Stashower.

"Coach Grady wants to see you in his office."

He vanished. I looked at Brandon. Brandon shrugged. "Coach probably wants to introduce you to the team or something."

"Yeah," I said, hoping he was right. "Thanks for shooting around with me."

"No problem."

As I left the court, I saw Troy out of the corner of my eye. The grin looked even bigger.

I hurried to Coach Grady's office.

"You wanted to see me, Coach?"

"Yes, Mickey, come in and close the door. Have a seat."

I did as he asked. Coach Grady was wearing gray sweatpants and a polo shirt with the Kasselton Camel mascot as a logo. For a few moments, he said nothing. He had his head down, his eyes on the desk.

"Have you read this, Mickey?"

"Read what, Coach?"

With a heavy sigh, Coach Grady rose from his chair. He walked over to me and handed me the Kasselton High School student manual. I looked at it and then up at him.

"Have you read it?" he asked again.

"I've skimmed it, I guess."

He moved back behind his desk and sat down. "How about the part on conduct?"

"I think so."

"Last year, two seniors on the football team were caught drinking beers by the field. They were suspended for six games. One kid on the hockey team got into a fight at a movie theater—off school grounds. It didn't matter. He was thrown off the team. We have a zero-tolerance policy. Do you understand?"

I nodded numbly. I thought about Troy's grin. I thought that maybe now I understood its meaning.

"You were arrested last night, weren't you, Mickey?"

"But I didn't do it."

"This isn't a court of law. Those boys who got caught

drinking—they weren't put on trial. All charges were dropped on the hockey player who got in the fight. It didn't matter. You understand that, right?"

"But the arrest was all a misunderstanding."

"And your little tussle with Troy Taylor last week?"

I felt my heart sink. "We talked about that already," I said, hearing the panic in my own voice.

"Correct, and I was able to give you the benefit of the doubt. But I spoke to Chief Taylor today. He told me that in the past week you've been involved in several incidents. He said you drove a car when you aren't old enough to have a license. He said you used a fake ID to get into a club. Any of these things alone would get you thrown off the team."

I felt the panic in my chest. "Please, Coach Grady, I can explain it all."

"Did you do those things," Coach Grady asked, "or is Chief Taylor lying?"

"It's not that simple," I said.

"I'm sorry, Mickey, but my hands are tied here."

"Coach." I could hear the begging in my voice. "Please don't—"

"You're off the team."

I swallowed. "For how long?"

"For the season, son. I'm sorry."

CHAPTER 31

I had to pass through the gym in order to get to the locker room. Troy was still grinning like an idiot, and it took all my willpower not to run up and clock him. I felt numb. How could this have happened? Basketball was my life. My parents quit the Abeona Shelter and returned to the United States just so I could have a chance to play high school basketball.

Now that, along with everything else in my life, was gone.

I heard a laugh and then Troy called out in a mocking tone, "See ya, Mickey."

"Yeah," Buck added, "see ya, Mickey."

I felt my anger rise up, but I knew pummeling those two buffoons wouldn't help. Right now I just needed to get as far away from here as possible. I quickly threw on my street clothes and sprinted toward the exit.

I welcomed the outside. I squeezed my eyes shut and gulped down the fresh air. I dropped to my knees. I felt as though I was drowning and lost. I know, I know—it's just a sport. But basketball was more than that to me. It was my center, my core. It didn't define me, but it was what I wanted to do more than anything else. To have it snatched away like that—the grounding constant still in my life—it made my world teeter one more time.

"You're early."

I looked up and saw Ema. When she saw my face, her eyes widened with concern.

"What's wrong?"

"I was just thrown off the team."

As I told her what happened, Ema sat next to me and watched me. When I looked at her eyes—and yes, I know how this will sound—I saw kindness and goodness. They were almost . . . angelic. I looked into them and saw so many things. I drew strength from them.

Earlier, Rachel accused me of not trusting her as much as I do Ema. The truth is somewhat more complex: I trust no one as much as I trust Ema. I didn't hide how I felt from her. I didn't pretend that I wasn't angry and bitter and devastated. I didn't care what I looked like or sounded like. I just ranted, and Ema just listened.

"You try to do the right thing," Ema said, "and this is the thanks you get? It's so wrong."

She just gets it. Simple as that. Here was something else

remarkable about Ema: She was able, even now, to make me feel better. I flashed back to that horrible moment at the nightclub, when I was sure that Ema was going to die. There had been a knife against her throat, and I had never felt so helpless or known such fear.

Tears came to my eyes. Seeing them, Ema said, "It'll be okay. We'll figure something out. There has to be a way to get you back on the team—"

Without thought, I reached out and hugged her hard. For a moment she stiffened, but then her arms slid around and she gripped me too. We just stayed that way, her head against my chest, neither of us moving, almost as though we were afraid of what would come after we let go.

"Uh, what are you two doing?"

It was Spoon. Ema and I quickly released each other.

"Nothing," I said.

Spoon looked at me, then at Ema, then somewhere between the two of us. "Studies have shown that hugging can cure depression, reduce stress, and boost the body's immune system."

Spoon spread his arms. "So how about a group hug?"

"Don't make me punch you," Ema said.

Spoon just stayed there, arms spread. "This is for all our health." Ema looked at me. I looked at her. We both shrugged and gave Spoon a hug at the same time. He relished it, and I wondered about how starved for physical contact we all suddenly seemed.

"I do this with my parents all the time," Spoon said. "It's great, right?"

We all took this as a cue to let go. We sat down on a curb.

"How come you're not at tryouts?" Spoon asked.

Ema shushed him, but I quickly explained. First I told him about the photograph of the Butcher of Lodz being Photoshopped. Spoon's reaction:

"Well, duh. I mean, did we really think he was some weird Nazi who never aged?"

Then I told him about getting thrown off the team. Spoon's reaction to this news was interesting. Rather than commiserating, Spoon just got red-faced angry at the injustice of it all. It was like the sweet, naïve kid was suddenly going to a dark place. Ema changed subjects.

"So did you visit Rachel?" Ema asked.

"Yes."

"Is she okay?" Spoon asked.

"The wounds were only superficial. She has a bandage on her head."

"But not on her face?" Spoon looked relieved. "Thank goodness."

Ema punched him in the arm. Then we got serious. I told them all about my visit with Rachel, every detail. When I finished, Ema asked, "So what do you make of it?"

"I'm not sure. Here her mother makes these crazy accusations against her father . . ."

"And she ends up dead," Spoon said.

Silence.

Ema stood and started pacing. "You said that Rachel started to believe her mother—about her father, I mean?"

I thought about that. "I don't know if it was that strong. I think at some point Rachel decided that if she wasn't on her mother's side, who would be?"

"Okay, so let's follow that. Rachel's mom says the dad is a horrible man who locked her up because she knew bad stuff about him or whatever. Right?"

"I guess."

Ema kept pacing. "Then Rachel wants to give her mother the benefit of the doubt. So what would she naturally do?"

"Look into her mother's accusation," I said.

"How?"

"By looking into her father . . ."

My voice faded. And that was when I saw it.

Both Ema and Spoon spotted the look on my face. "What?"

I tried to sort through the thoughts even as I spoke. "Rachel had the Abeona butterfly on her hospital door," I said.

"So?"

"So she was working with them somehow."

"Okay," Ema said. "We sort of knew that. What's the big deal?"

"When that guy with the shaved head came by the morning after Rachel was shot, the first thing he asked me was so weird."

"What was it?"

"He said that he knew that Rachel and I had gotten close . . ."

Ema squirmed a little when I said that.

"But right away, he started asking if Rachel had given me anything."

"Like what?" Spoon said.

"That's what I asked. Like what. He said like a gift or package. I mean, here Rachel has just been shot. Her mother is dead. I've just finished talking to the police—and the first thing Shaved Head asks about is if Rachel gave me a gift or package? Don't you think that's weird?"

We all agreed that it was.

"So what's your theory?" Ema asked.

"Suppose Rachel found something," I said. "I don't know what. Something that proves her mother was telling the truth. Suppose she found something bad about her father and then she wrapped it up in a package or something—and maybe she was supposed to pass it on to the Abeona Shelter."

"But she ends up shot before she can," Ema added.

"And her mother, the woman who first made the accusation, ends up dead," Spoon finished for us.

Silence.

"We may be reaching," Ema said. "On one level, this all makes sense. On another, it doesn't. Rachel is still alive. Even if she doesn't still have this gift or package, I mean, she has to know what it was."

"Which may mean she's still in danger," Spoon added.

I thought about it. "We are missing something," I said.

"What?"

"I don't know. But something. Her father wouldn't shoot her. I mean, come on. He just wouldn't, even to protect himself."

We mulled that over for a few seconds.

"Maybe it was an accident," Ema said.

"How?"

"Maybe he shot at the mother and accidentally hit Rachel."

That made more sense, I guess, but it still didn't feel right. We were missing something. I just couldn't put my finger on what. We talked some more as the skies started to darken. At some point, I realized that tryouts would be coming to an end and all the varsity guys would be walking out the door. I didn't want to be here for that. I suggested that we break this up for the night.

Spoon glanced at his watch. "My dad will be done with work in another half an hour. I think I'll hang with him and catch a ride."

Ema and I walked alone down Kasselton Avenue. Behind us, the gym's heavy doors slammed open as the varsity players started pouring out. They were laughing and smiling and had wet hair from showering and they walked a little stooped, happily tired from the workout. Seeing them made the pit in my stomach grow tenfold.

Ema said, "Come on, let's hurry up."

We did. I let her lead the way. She took a right and then a left, and I knew where she was headed. A few minutes later, we were at the end of Bat Lady's street. The house was gone, burned to the ground. Only a few beams remained upright. After all these years, after all the stories to frighten children, the legendary haunted abode of the Bat Lady had been reduced to ashes. Fire marshals stood in the front yard, jotting notes on clipboards. I thought about that old record player, the old vinyls by the Who and HorsePower and the Beatles. I thought about all those photographs—the ones of Bat Lady as a hippie in the sixties, of Ashley at Kasselton High, of the sad-eyed boy with the curly hair, of all the rest of those rescued children.

All gone up in flames.

So where was Lizzy Sobek, aka the Bat Lady? Where was Shaved Head, aka I Have No Idea What His Name Is? For that matter, where was the phony Butcher of Lodz, aka the San Diego Paramedic/Arsonist?

Ema stood next to me. "Do you think it's over?"

"What?"

"The Abeona Shelter. Did the Butcher destroy it?"

I thought about that. "I don't know. I don't think it's that easy to destroy a group that's been around so long." I moved a little to the left, so that I could look into the woods in the back.

"What are you doing?" Ema asked.

"The garage in the back. Remember?"

"Oh, right," she said. "That's how Shaved Head would enter."

"And that's how he brought me into the house to see her—through a tunnel running underground. There were corridors and other doors."

The woods were too thick to see the garage, especially from this distance. That, I had figured, was intentional. It was supposed to be hidden.

"We need to check it out," I said.

"What? The garage and the tunnels?"

I nodded. "We obviously can't do it now. Maybe tonight—when the fire marshal isn't here and no one can see us."

I looked at her and again something started to bother me.

"What?" she asked.

"There's something different about you."

I spotted a dark smudge on her arm. She saw me staring and pulled down her sleeve.

"What was that?" I asked.

"Nothing."

But I kept thinking about the rumors Spoon had told me, about her living in the woods, about her father being a possible abuser. "Was that . . . was that a bruise?"

"What? No." She stepped away, grabbing at her sleeve again. "I gotta go."

"Don't do this again, Ema."

"I'm fine, Mickey. Really."

"Then how come you never invite me over?"

Her eyes, usually meeting mine, found a tree in the distance. "My parents aren't big on company."

"I don't even know where you live."

"What difference does it make? Look, really, I have to get home. Let's text later. If we can both get out, we can come back here and try to find those tunnels."

Ema started to hurry away. When she reached the edge of the woods, she looked behind her, as though making sure that I wasn't following her. Then she vanished into the thick. I wasn't sure what to do, so, as was my way, I did nothing. I just stood there like a dope. Something kept nagging my subconscious. I started combing through my mind, through recent memories, trying to figure out what it was, when I realized something.

Have you ever seen those games where you have two seemingly identical pictures and you have to find six differences? It worked a little like that. I closed my eyes. I pictured Ema from a few days ago. I pictured her from today. What was different—and why was it bothering me?

Difference One: The possible bruise on her arm.

Did I really need a Difference Two?

I stood there. Ema had been pretty clear. I should mind my own business. But that didn't mean I had to listen. Ema, despite her young age, seemed to get out a lot late at night. So did I, but my situation was pretty grim. She also had a lot of tattoos. What parent allows that at such a young age? Sure, that wasn't proof of anything. It was barely suspicious.

But then you add in the secrecy, the woods, the possible bruise, the rumors . . .

Sometimes the loudest cries for help are silent.

I decided to follow her. Now.

Ema would have a head start, but she wouldn't be running. If I kept my cool and moved quickly, I would be able to catch up. I tried to guess what direction she had gone in, but there really was no point. I wasn't a tracker. Instead I ran straight ahead, looking for any signs of . . . what?

Ema, I guess.

That six-difference picture game came back to me as I moved through the thickening brush. I thought about the tattoo on the back of her neck. I remembered that there had been the tail of a snake in that area. The snake had been green . . . and now, wait, is that even possible . . . today it was more like purple.

Huh?

I kept running. Could that be it? I started to think about her tattoos and realized that they had somehow . . . changed?

But so what?

A few days ago, we had gone to Tattoos While U Wait and met with Agent, her tattoo artist. He was offbeat, sure, but I liked him. He had helped us too. So maybe she had gone back for some touch-up work.

But didn't that usually require bandages and time to heal?

I was just mulling that over, hurrying through the brush, when I heard a sound up ahead. I ducked behind a tree and peered out. There, in a small clearing maybe fifty yards ahead of me, was Ema.

I'd found her.

She had found a small path in the woods and was following it in what I thought was a western direction. I didn't have a compass and I wasn't much of a Boy Scout and, really, who cared what cardinal point she was heading toward?

I stayed as far back as I could while keeping her in sight. This wooded area was actually part of the Kasselton reservoir. There were signs that you weren't supposed to be here, but the woods were also pretty huge and unpatrolled. Because Uncle Myron can't help but share, he told me how every fifth-grader in his day, including, of course, my father, had to collect wildflowers, identify them, and press them in a book. Most of the students found the flowers in these very woods. For some reason, Myron thought that I would find this fascinating.

Then again, why was I thinking about it now?

At first, I expected that Ema would eventually arrive at some kind of rusted sheet-metal shack hidden deep in this brush, but now I realized that probably didn't add up. Yes, I had never seen these woods patrolled, but that didn't mean that they weren't. This was a reservoir area. There was no way you could really build a house in here, even a dilapidated one. You'd have to move around. You'd have to maybe live in tents and keep a lookout or something.

None of this made any sense.

The sky began to darken. I thought again about not having a compass. We were getting deeper into the woods and while I could probably retrace my steps, I wasn't sure that I could do so by the light of my mobile phone. Thinking I better not lose her, I hurried my step.

Ema turned to the left and started up a steeper hill. I stopped and watched. If I started up the hill too, she would spot me for sure. I waited until she was pretty much out of sight before I followed. Now, of course, I was getting nervous again about losing her. I scampered up the hill, keeping low.

A twang of guilt strummed through my chest. I was secretly tailing my best friend. That didn't feel right, even if it was for her own good. For her own good. How often had that been used to justify dumb actions? Like this one.

I should stop and go home.

I debated that for a moment. I was seconds away from reconsidering my actions and turning around when I reached the top of the hill. There, blocking my way, was a chain-link fence.

No sign of Ema.

I looked right and then I looked left. The fence seemed to run as far as the eye could see. Every ten yards or so, there was a NO TRESPASSING sign, warning traveling woodsmen, I guessed, that they'd be prosecuted to the full extent of the law if they entered.

Where had Ema gone?

I moved right up against the chain-link fence and looked

through it. There were more woods, but up ahead, maybe twenty or thirty yards, I thought I saw a clearing. Still I wasn't sure how that helped. There was no gate or door in the fence. Could Ema have doubled back around as I climbed up? I guessed it was possible, but it seemed doubtful. Maybe she had spotted me. Maybe Ema was hiding behind a tree.

Frustrated, I reached out and grabbed the chain-link fence. I gave it a shake . . . and the fence gave way.

What the . . . ?

I looked closer. Someone had cut the wires where this part of the fence met up with the metal stake. You wouldn't notice it by just looking, but if you leaned against the chain link, the fence swung in almost like a door. I did that now. I pushed against it. A second later, ignoring the warning signs, I was on the other side of the fence.

Well, I had already been thrown off the basketball team for a host of indiscretions. I might as well add trespassing to the list.

Now what?

I kept moving forward until, finally, I could see a clearing. For a moment I slowed my step. Once I was out of the trees, I'd be exposed. I had no idea what would be in front of me, but it wouldn't be wise to just blunder forward. At the same time, Ema probably had a pretty good lead on me by now, so I couldn't dawdle either.

I got to the end of the tree line. When I looked into the clearing, I gasped.

The first thing I saw was a huge garden of some sort. There wasn't much in bloom, but there were bushes carved in the shapes of animals. Topiaries. That was what they were called. There was a swan, a lion, a giraffe, an elephant— all life-size, made from green bushes. There were also white statues that looked like something from ancient Rome or Greece. I spotted a swimming pool and a gazebo, but what stunned me was the house that stood behind all this.

The house, even from the back, still looked like a dark castle out of a Disney nightmare. I had just been here, though I had come up the long front drive rather than from the back.

Uncle Myron had brought me here to meet Angelica Wyatt.

Huh?

I stood there for a moment or two, completely dumbfounded. The most obvious answer was that Ema used this stretch as a cut through. Maybe there was another opening in a fence on another part of the estate and that would lead to the dingy shack I kept picturing in my head. But that answer suddenly wasn't fully computing.

I moved forward, closer to the house. It was so wide-open that the only way to do this and keep somewhat hidden was to sprint from hiding place to hiding place. So first I sprinted for the elephant topiary and stayed low behind its thick legs. Then I ran across the helipad and ducked behind a white statue of a woman wearing what looked like a toga and carrying a spear in one hand and a platter in the other. From there I made the big sprint to the side of the house.

I pressed my back against it and slowly slid forward. Mickey Bolitar, Super Spy. I wasn't sure where I was going anymore or even what I was doing. I thought about texting Ema and simply asking where she was at this moment, but I had gone this far. I couldn't go back.

When I made the turn around the corner, I stopped short. Ema stood in the middle of the courtyard. She frowned at me, her arms crossed.

"Uh, hi," I said.

Once again, my quick-witted tongue gets me out of trouble.

"We have cameras all over this place, hotshot," Ema said. "You're lucky security didn't shoot you."

I didn't know what to say, so I went with, "Sorry. I was just worried about you."

She turned and started for the door. I didn't move.

"Come on inside," Ema said. "You might as well learn the truth."

CHAPTER 32

Still reeling, I followed Ema into the dark mansion and then down to a finished basement. There was a sleek theater room with big comfortable chairs and a giant screen. A popcorn machine, like the kind you see at a theater, sat in one corner. On the walls were movie posters featuring Angelica Wyatt.

I looked at the posters and then at Ema. She lowered her head and took a step back, wringing her hands. I looked again at the posters. I looked again at Ema. "I should have seen it," I said.

"What?"

"The eyes."

Ema said nothing.

"When I met Angelica Wyatt, I kept thinking how warm and comforting her eyes were. Like I could just talk to her

224

forever. I couldn't figure out why I felt that way, but now I know."

Ema looked up at me.

"Is Angelica Wyatt your mother?" I asked.

"Yes."

"I don't understand. All those rumors . . ."

"About my living in a shack and my father being a dangerous man who beat me or whatever?"

I nodded.

"I started them," Ema said. "It was a way to throw people off the scent."

I waited for her to say more. When she didn't, I said, "But why?"

"You're kidding, right?"

"No."

"Do you hear the way the boys in school talk about how hot Angelica Wyatt is? Imagine if they found out she was my mother."

"I guess that could be weird."

"Could be?"

"Okay, I guess it would be."

"And now imagine those mean girls who won't give me the time of day—imagine how they'd treat me if they knew my mother was a world-famous movie star."

"They'd probably treat you like gold," I said.

"And you think I want that—those horrible phonies inviting me to their parties and having to sit with them at lunch?

How could I ever trust anyone, if they knew? How could I ever think anyone would like me for me?" Ema turned away. Her shoulders slumped.

"What?" I said.

"When I first heard that your uncle was watching my mother, do you know what I thought?"

"No," I said.

"I thought that maybe you knew the truth. That you knew all along I was Angelica Wyatt's daughter and that's why you started being nice to me."

"I didn't know," I said.

She kept her back to me.

"Ema, look at me."

She turned back toward me slowly.

"I didn't know," I said. "It doesn't matter to me."

"Okay," she said softly. "So why did we become friends?"

"I don't know. I guess I'm drawn to total pains in the butt."

Ema let herself smile. "Me too. But do you see what I mean?"

"Yes," I said, my head still spinning. "But it seems a little extreme. And how do you get away with it? How does the school not know?"

"My official name now is Emma Beaumont, not Emma Wyatt. The house is in my grandmother's maiden name. My mother sort of leads a secret double life. One, the glamorous movie star. Two, the normal mom. We are very careful about how we meet up. This house is secluded. She can come by car or directly by helicopter."

I said nothing, but something must have shown on my face.

Ema moved closer to me. "Tell me what you're thinking."

"You want the truth?"

"Yes."

I sort of shrugged, stopped, and said, "Why didn't you tell me? I mean, I get the Troy and Buck argument. But I trust you with everything. After all we've been through, everything I've told you . . ."

"It feels as if I betrayed you," Ema said.

"Yes."

"Would it help if I told you that I was going to?"

I didn't reply.

"Or that I was trying to find the right time? Would it help if I told you how hard it is for me to trust anyone?"

"I understand all that," I said.

"But not fully," Ema said.

"It's okay."

Ema looked away. I saw tears in her eyes.

"It's okay," I said again.

"I want to show you something . . . maybe that will help explain it." Ema opened up a closet. She looked back at me. "You're a lot taller than me. Do you mind getting that shoe box down? The one on the far left."

"This isn't necessary," I said.

"Please just do it, Mickey, before I lose my nerve."

I walked over to the closet, plucked down the shoe box from the top shelf, and handed it to her. In the center of the room was a couch. She sat on it and invited me to join her.

Ema opened the box and pulled out a clipping. It was from a tabloid and read: ANGELICA WYATT'S SECRET BABY SHOCKER.

She pulled out another: WHO'S ANGELICA'S REAL BABY DADDY? Then another: ANGELICA'S SECRET LOVE NEST IN FRANCE. Another: EXCLUSIVE! FIRST PICS OF ANGELICA'S BABY! One said that Ema's father was Angelica's costar in her current movie. Another claimed it was the British prime minister.

"This is hard to talk about," Ema said.

"Then don't."

"No, I want to tell you. I want you to understand why Mom and I did what we did."

"Okay," I said.

She held the clippings in her hands. "They never left us alone. My whole life, the tabloids followed us around. We'd go to the park, the paparazzi would be with us. I'd go with my mom on set, even closed ones, and then someone with a high-powered lens would snap my picture. It was . . . suffocating, to say the least. I started having nightmares. I saw a shrink. My mom even quit the business for a little while. She retired to watch me, but that just led to more rumors about her. And the truth is, she loves being an actress. Even as a kid I got that. I didn't want to take that away from her, you know what I mean?"

"Sure," I said.

"It was a hard decision, but eventually we decided to live, well, like this. Mom started a rumor that I was living at a boarding school overseas."

"So who lives with you here?"

"My grandparents. And, uh . . ." She looked a little embarrassed.

"Uh what?"

"I guess he's an assistant of sorts. He helps out too. His name is Niles."

I remembered him from my previous visit—Niles the butler. We fell into silence. I was thumbing through the articles, not sure how to raise the next question. "Should I ask you the obvious?"

There was a hint of a smile on Ema's face. "You're wondering about my father."

"If it isn't my business . . ."

"I don't know who my father is. My mom hasn't told me."

Again with nothing to say, I went with, "Oh."

"I know. She said she'll tell me one day—when it's right. But not now. We've had plenty of battles about it, believe me. I want to know, but Mom freaks out when I ask her. Like she's really scared for me to know."

"What would she be scared of?"

"I don't know," Ema said, as if considering it for the first time. "But for now, well, I've let it go. I mean, what can I do?"

"Right. I understand." Another thought occurred to me. "When you found out that information about the San Diego paramedics, you didn't want to tell me your source. Was it . . . ?"

Ema nodded. "Yup. When you use Angelica Wyatt's name, it is amazing what doors open."

It made sense, I guess. I was still looking through the articles, especially the ones that featured pictures of young Ema. "I can definitely see you in these pictures," I said.

"But I look different, right?"

"I guess."

"You can say it, Mickey."

"Say what?"

"I looked thinner," Ema said. "I looked more . . . normal."

I didn't reply.

"That was part of all this for me," she said.

"What was?"

"Dressing all in black. Dyeing my hair black. The jewelry, the tattoos. Maybe even putting on weight. I didn't want to be that kid who got ambushed. I wanted to be someone different. So maybe it started as a disguise, but I like the way I look now. It's somehow more me, you know? So now I don't know if I do it as a disguise or maybe I just dress like I always wanted to."

I held up one of the old clippings. "You haven't changed that much," I said. "And you're leaving something out."

"What?"

"The tattoos. That was the first real clue something was weird. I thought I saw a bruise on your arm. But it was a smudge. I couldn't figure out what about you was different, but then it came to me. Your tattoos. They changed. And your mom—she wouldn't let you mark up your body with a bunch of tattoos. Not at your age. So they're temporary, right?"

Ema looked almost pleased. "Wow, I can't believe you noticed."

"You know what's weird?" I said.

"Uh, everything about this?"

"Well, yeah, I know, but one other thing: Our mothers knew each other when they were teenagers."

"Right, when they were, like, our age. That is weird. Oh, and why is your uncle suddenly bodyguarding my mom?"

"I don't get that either. He said a close friend asked him to do it. I know Uncle Myron is more than just an agent or manager or whatever. I think he's, like, a secret private eye or security guy or something."

"So he's helping guard Mom while she's in the area?"

"I guess. Why don't you ask your mom?"

"I did. She just said she needed extra security, and Myron was an old friend."

"So maybe that's it then," I said.

"Maybe."

Neither one of us bought it.

"Bat Lady said I shouldn't tell Myron about Abeona," I said. "Not ever. And my father never told him either."

"I haven't told my mom. I mean, it just feels like something we should keep to ourselves, you know?"

I did.

"There's one other thing I need to tell you," Ema said.

"What?"

"You're right about the tattoos. Agent at Tattoos While U Wait . . . he puts them on for me. They're all temporary. Except, well . . ." She slid her shirt off her shoulder. For a moment, my eyes just popped open, like maybe this was a prelude to a striptease or something. Ema must have seen the look on my face, because she rolled her eyes and said, "Cut it out."

"What?"

"Just . . . never mind." Ema turned around and showed me her back. "Here, take a look. Agent says he doesn't know how this happened, but somehow, this tattoo never comes off."

I didn't even have to look because I knew which tattoo she meant. The image never quite escapes me. Or, I guess, us.

It was a tattoo of a butterfly with animal eyes on the wings.

CHAPTER 33

Ema and I talked a bit more. I suggested that we should try to meet up at Bat Lady's house later and see if we could find a way into the garage and the tunnels. Ema wasn't sure that she could make it.

"When my mom's not around, it's pretty easy to sneak out. But when she's around, like now . . ."

"I get it."

"Mickey?"

"Yeah?"

"I'm really sorry about this thing with the basketball team."

"Thanks."

It was funny how the mind takes weird, circuitous routes sometimes. Do you ever start thinking of something odd and try to trace back to what started your thought process and really, your mind is going all over the place? That was what was happening, so here was the trail my brain took: When Ema mentioned basketball, I tried to push the thought away, but the one thing that would help me escape the pain of getting thrown off the basketball team would be . . . well, playing basketball. That made me think of the last time I played basketball, which made me think about playing yesterday in Newark, which made me think about Tyrell Waters and what he might be doing, which made me think about his father, Detective Waters, which made me think about the ride home, which made me think about two things about Detective Waters:

One, he was working on busting a drug ring in Kasselton.

Two, he had known that Mr. Caldwell's first name was Henry.

How would he know that—and were those two things related?

In fact, Detective Waters had asked me a bunch of questions about the Caldwells, trying very hard to sound casual. At the time I figured that he was just naturally curious about the shootings. But now I remembered what Tyrell had said—that his father probably would have been the one investigating the Caldwell shooting except he was busy "working on this big drug ring in your hometown."

"What is it?" Ema asked.

I quickly explained about Detective Waters. Ema, as always, got it immediately.

"You have to ask him more about it."

I agreed, but it was getting late. I texted Tyrell to see if he was at the courts. He wrote back that he wasn't because his high school team, Weequahic High, had started practice today. Then Tyrell added: **Can you get down here quick? We need people to scrimmage.**

Damn, there wouldn't be time. Even if I ran to the bus stop, it wouldn't leave for another half hour and then the ride down . . . no way. I was showing the message to Ema when suddenly I heard footsteps coming down the stairs toward us. Ema stiffened. For a moment I thought that she was going to tell me to hide, but as the footsteps got closer, her face softened.

"Miss Emma?"

I recognized the British accent. It was Niles the butler.

"I'm here, Niles."

Niles entered the room. He was one of those guys who probably never showed emotion on his face—stiff upper lip and all that—but he stared at me as though an elephant doing handstands had suddenly materialized in the basement.

"Niles, this is my friend Mickey."

"We've met," I said, standing up.

Once the surprise was off Niles's face, he couldn't have looked more pleased. "A visitor!"

Ema frowned. "Yes, Niles."

"How marvelous. We don't get many visitors, do we, Miss Emma?"

"You don't have to look that shocked, Niles."

"This isn't shock, Miss Emma. This is delight. Will our guest be staying for dinner?"

"No," Ema said. "In fact, Niles, can I ask you a really big favor?"

"Of course."

"Can you drive us to Newark?"

CHAPTER 34

When Niles pulled to the front of the driveway in a lime-green Volkswagen Beetle, I felt relief. I was afraid that maybe we'd be driving down in that stretch limousine and I could just imagine the ribbing I'd deservedly take if I showed up to play basketball in that. Still, the lime green was a tad conspicuous and I asked Niles to drop me off two blocks away so I could walk.

"Why are we here again?" Niles asked.

"Mickey has a big basketball game."

"And he came to your abode looking for a ride?"

"I'll explain later." Ema turned to me. "Have fun at your game. Niles and I will wait here."

Niles said, "We will?"

"You don't have to," I said. "I can get a ride back."

"No, no, we wouldn't dream of it," Niles said, his voice

thick with sarcasm. "Miss Emma can entertain me by telling me how you two know each other."

Ema rolled her eyes. I got out of the car and jogged toward the school. Tyrell greeted me at the door. He wore a white basketball uniform with the word *Weequahic* across the chest. "You guys are red," he said, tossing me a red pinny to throw over my shirt.

The scrimmage between Weequahic High and whatever stragglers they could find was already in the final quarter. I quickly checked the stands. Yep, Mr. Waters was there. I gave him a little wave and he nodded back. During the next time-out, I entered the game. I saw Tyrell laughing it up with his teammates and felt my face start to burn. Tyrell's team put their hands in as one and shouted, "Defense!" and then broke. They were teammates. Tyrell liked playing with me in pickup games, but this was different. This was his school team. This mattered.

How could I have blown my chance?

I still had my junior and senior years, but they seemed so far away, impossible to imagine now. Maybe Mom would get better and we could move someplace else and I could start again—but she couldn't leave rehab for another six weeks. Maybe Dad . . .

Maybe Dad what?

I had trouble concentrating on basketball. I kept thinking about my father, supposedly in that grave out in Los Angeles, and I wondered whether I'd ever get the chance to know for certain. Usually I forget all that while I play. But not today.

I didn't play well. We stragglers got crushed and for the first time in my overly competitive playing life, I didn't care. I just wanted to get to Mr. Waters and ask him about Henry Caldwell. The sound of the final buzzer was merciful. I got in line and shook hands with the other team. When I reached Tyrell, he said, "What's wrong?"

"Nothing."

Tyrell frowned at me. "Then why aren't you at tryouts today?"

"I got kicked off the team."

"What?"

"It's a long story."

"Oh man, Mickey, I'm sorry."

"I'll be fine," I lied.

"Hey, Tyrell." It was one of his teammates. "Coach wants a quick meet."

Tyrell looked at me warily. "We'll talk about this in a few minutes, okay?"

He jogged away with his teammate. I started to wonder about how to approach Mr. Waters and what exactly to say to him, but there was no need. As soon as Tyrell was out of sight, he hurried over to me.

"How are you, Mickey?"

"I'm good, thanks."

"How is your friend Rachel?"

No beating around the bush this time.

"She's better."

"I heard they released her."

"Yes, I saw her earlier today. I even met her father."

That piqued his interest. "How is he handling all this?"

Should I tell him about Mr. Caldwell pulling a gun on me? I wasn't sure, so I decided to keep it simpler. "He seemed very much on edge."

"On edge how?"

"Jumpy."

"Jumpy how?"

"I don't know," I said. "Easily startled. Maybe a little scared. You can't blame him, I guess. His ex-wife was just murdered. His daughter was just shot." I tilted my head. "Mr. Waters, can I ask you a question?"

He didn't say yes but he didn't say no either.

"How do you know Henry Caldwell?"

Waters didn't seem to like that. "Who said I know him?"

"When you drove me home yesterday, you asked me how Henry was doing. How did you know his first name?"

His eyes hardened.

"Mr. Waters?"

"It's not important, Mickey."

"Are you investigating him?"

"That isn't your business."

"Rachel is my friend."

"And what? You're going to find who shot her?" He arched an eyebrow. "This isn't a game, Mickey. These people play for keeps."

"What people?"

He shook his head and suddenly he wasn't the nice father anymore—he was the tough cop. "I'll ask the questions. When you were at the Caldwells' house, did you see anybody else?"

"Like who?"

"Just answer the question."

"No, there was just Rachel and . . ." Then I remembered it. "Wait, there were two creepy guys talking to Mr. Caldwell right after I left."

"What did they look like?"

"Like, I don't know, street punks. One had a bandana on his head and a scar on his cheek."

Mr. Waters swallowed when I said that. He grabbed his smartphone and started pressing some buttons. "Is this the man you saw?"

He showed me the picture on the phone. No doubt about it. It was Scarface. "Yeah, that's the guy. Who is he?"

Mr. Waters's face fell. "He's a very bad man, Mickey."

"But who is he?"

"I want you to stay far away from him, you hear? You wouldn't believe the evil he's capable of."

If Mr. Waters was trying to scare me, it was working. "Did he have something to do with what happened to Rachel?"

But Mr. Waters was having none of that. "You stay out of this, Mickey." There was anger in his voice. "I'm not going to tell you again. Stop playing around or someone is going to get hurt."

CHAPTER 35

I didn't wait around for Tyrell because I didn't want to get into the whole getting-kicked-off-the-team mess. Mr. Waters remained firm with me. "If you see or hear anything, you call me. Here's my number."

He started to hand me his card again, but I took out my wallet and showed him that I still had the last card he'd given me. "I also plugged your number into my phone contacts," I said.

"Put it on speed dial," Mr. Waters warned me for the second time now.

I hurried back down the block. The lime-green Volkswagen Beetle stuck out like, well, like a lime-green Volkswagen Beetle. When I slid into the backseat, Ema said, "How was your game?"

I gave her a curious look as my cell phone buzzed. Ema

made a big production of staring hard at my eyes, then at my phone, and I got the message, so to speak. I picked up the mobile and saw that I had text from her: **don't say anything about shooting in front of Niles. he'll worry. let's talk later and try to sneak out to Bat Lady's tunnel tonight. just talk dumb stuff now, like you're a typical boy obsessed with sports.**

I frowned at her. She shrugged.

"Yes," Niles said, pulling away, "how did your important basketball game go?"

"Great, thanks."

"It was a very short game, wasn't it?"

"Uh, yeah," I said.

"And I had no idea Miss Emma was into helping facilitate your basketball prowess by having me drive down here."

"Yeah," I said. "She's a big, uh, facilitator."

"Miss Emma is just full of surprises today," Niles said, turning onto Route 280. "And I guess I'm supposed to just believe every word she says."

"Niles," Ema said.

"No, no, Miss Emma, I am merely a servant. You owe me no explanation."

I texted Ema: **Niles isn't buying it.**

"Ya think?" Ema said to me, not even bothering with the text.

In the driver's seat, Niles smiled.

We stayed silent for the ride home. Niles dropped me off

at Uncle Myron's house. I sat in the kitchen and tried to sort through the last day. Nothing came to me. I grabbed the phone and dialed my mother's rehabilitation center. I asked for my mother's room. "Please hold."

Two rings, a pickup, and a heavy sigh. "You know you can't talk to her, Mickey."

I did know. Mom had had a "relapse"—in short, she had taken drugs again within hours of her earlier release—and was now being isolated. The woman on the other end of line was Christine Shippee, the head of the rehab center. "I just want to hear her voice," I said.

"You know I can't do that."

I did. But I missed her, especially now when it felt as though everything was caving in on me again. Before my dad died, Mom had been so vibrant, so wise and wonderful—I'd have called her the perfect mother, but many of us think that, don't we?

"How is she?"

"You know I can't answer that either."

"What can you answer?"

"I'm pretty good at math."

"No, you're not."

"Yeah, that's true," Christine Shippee said. "How are you, Mickey?"

"How do you think I am?"

"You don't sound good."

245

"I'll be fine."

"Your uncle."

I frowned. "What about him?"

"I know you blame him for a lot, but he's not a bad guy."

"Thanks."

"Cute too."

"Well, that changes everything," I said.

"Talk to him, Mickey."

Christine Shippee hung up then. I stared at the phone and frowned. I tried not to think about what my mother might now be going through. I had tried to be there for her. I had gotten a job and supported us. I had dragged her home from bars, motels, and trailers. I had cleaned her off. I had made her shower and dress and get out of the house, all in the hopes that she would pull out of her nosedive. But that just wasn't happening. I was, according to Christine Shippee, an enabler. I wasn't so sure, but I decided to listen to the supposed expert. So now, much as it went against every innate tendency in my body, I let her be.

Except, well, when I weakened and called. Like this.

The front door opened. "Hello?" Myron shouted. "Mickey?"

"In the kitchen," I said.

Uncle Myron hurried in with an expectant smile on his face. "So how was basketball?"

My gut reaction, I'm not proud to say, was to lie. I didn't want to get into it. I didn't want to have Uncle Myron lecturing me about all the wrong I'd done or, worse, looking at me with pity. But I didn't have the strength to lie and he'd know soon enough.

"I got thrown off the team."

The look was closer to shock than pity. "What? What happened?"

So I sketched it out for him, awaiting the inevitable I-told-you-so, you-knew-the-rules, what-did-you-expect—but that didn't happen. Uncle Myron's muscles began to tighten. When I mentioned Chief Taylor's involvement, I saw the vein in his neck start to throb in anger.

Once I finished, there was silence. I was okay with silence. Uncle Myron wasn't. He was one of those guys who couldn't stand quiet, who constantly had to interrupt it because quiet made him feel uncomfortable. But right now, he stayed silent, unmoving, and for the first time, I could see what must have made him such a great basketball player. There was a fury in him now, one that made even me want to step back. His eyes had gone dark, and he had a look on his face that not only challenged the world but knew he could whip it.

"Ed Taylor," Uncle Myron finally said between clenched teeth.

"It's okay," I replied, which was dumb to say on several levels, not the lowest being that it was totally untrue.

"I'll talk to him."

"Who? Wait, with Chief Taylor?"

He didn't reply.

"Please don't," I said. "This is my battle."

"With Taylor?" He shook his head. "No, it's mine. You're just an innocent bystander caught in the line of fire."

"It won't make a difference. I broke the rules. Coach Grady made the call, not Taylor."

Uncle Myron didn't reply.

"Myron?"

"Do you remember what you asked me yesterday?" Myron asked.

For a second I was confused by the shift in topic. But then I remembered. "About exhuming my dad's body?"

"Yes. Why do you want to do that?"

"I told you."

"For closure."

"Right."

Uncle Myron shook his head. "You can't just exhume a body for reasons like that. There are strict regulations. That particular cemetery doesn't grant any exhumations. Even if they did, we'd need to get the permission of the next of kin. That would be your mother. Do you want to ask her to sign a certificate like that right now?"

I could feel my hope deflate. "No."

"So let me ask you again. Why do you want to exhume your father's body?"

I shrugged. "What difference does it make now?"

Myron seemed to be weighing his words on a hand scale. "Because there is a chance I can get it done."

"How?"

"I have this friend. This very well-connected friend . . ."

"Angelica Wyatt?"

"No."

I almost asked him whether he knew about Ema, about Angelica Wyatt having a daughter, but I knew that there was some secrecy regarding her identity, and I didn't want to say anything I shouldn't.

"So who?"

"You don't know him. He's the friend who asked me to watch Angelica."

"He can get Dad's body exhumed?"

"If I really push it, yes, he can do it. But I need to know your real reason, Mickey. I would go out on a limb for you for no reason. I can't ask my friend to. You get that, don't you?"

I nodded. We sat at the kitchen table. It had been updated within the last five years, but again, this was the kitchen of my father's childhood. Dad had spent countless hours here with his family. It was a simple thought and yet, for a moment, it overwhelmed me.

"I'm not sure Dad is in that grave."

Uncle Myron opened his mouth, closed it, opened it again. "I don't understand."

249

"I know it sounds crazy," I said, "but I need to know for certain that Dad is in that coffin."

Myron blinked twice. "Do you have reason to believe he's not in there?"

I wasn't sure how to respond. I couldn't go into the sandy-blond paramedic. For one thing, Myron would never believe me, but even if he did, both Bat Lady and Shaved Head had warned me not to tell Myron. I also knew that my father never told Myron about Abeona. There had to be a reason, right?

"Mickey?"

I met his eye and held it. "Yes," I said. "I have a reason."

Then Myron caught me off guard with his next question. "Does this have something to do with the fire at Bat Lady's house?"

"What makes you think that?" I asked.

"I told you. Your father visited that house. It changed him. Now suddenly you're drawn to it too." Myron leaned a little closer to me. "Have you met the Bat Lady?"

"Yes," I said before I could stop myself.

"What did she say to you?"

I shook my head, remembering the warnings. "Please, Myron. Please ask your friend to help us."

"I need to know more."

"Can't you just trust me on this?"

"That's not the issue. You know that."

I wasn't sure what to say to that, but Myron's cell phone buzzed. He checked a text message and sighed. "It's Angelica. I have to go. We aren't done with this, okay?"

"Okay."

He rose and looked at me as though he were seeing me for the first time. "Mickey?"

"Yes."

"I'll talk to my friend. I'll try my best to help you."

CHAPTER 36

I could smell the charred remains of the Bat Lady's house.

It was eight P.M.—not too late. Night had fallen. I had a flashlight, but for now, standing on the sidewalk, the streetlight gave me enough illumination. A few wooden beams from the house remained upright, stretching up into the darkness like fingers on a giant hand.

"Hey."

I turned. It was Ema. "Hey. How did you get past Niles?"

"Are you kidding? He's so happy I have a friend, he practically shoved me out the door."

I smiled. I thought about how wonderful the hug we shared earlier had been and tried to sort through my feelings about it. Ema was my friend. My very best friend. That was where that overwhelming sense of warmth came from, right?

252

We slowly approached the house. I kept my flashlight off because I didn't want the neighbors to see. We stopped at the crime-scene tape. Ema turned to me, shrugged, and ducked under it. I followed her up those front porch steps and inside the house. There was debris all over the floor.

"This was the living room," I said to her.

The light was getting pretty dim now. I still didn't want to use the flashlight, but I figured that maybe the light of my mobile phone would do the trick. Ema did the same.

"What's this?" she asked.

The frame was shattered, but I recognized it right away—the faded color photograph of the five hippies.

"Is that . . . ?" Ema pointed to the attractive woman in the tight T-shirt in the middle. Across her chest was the Abeona butterfly.

"Yep," I said. "I think it's Bat Lady."

"Wow. She was kind of hot."

"Subject change," I said, and Ema smiled. I tried to pick up the frame from the sides, but it pretty much fell apart. I slid the picture out and slipped it into my pocket. I figured that it might come in handy at some point.

The old record player had been damaged. There was no vinyl on the turntable, but I did manage to find the Beatles, the Beach Boys, and the Who albums. I doubted that they were in working condition anymore. I looked for the album that Bat Lady seemed to always play—*Aspect of Juno* by Horse-Power—but it had either been burned completely or . . .

Or what?

"Should we head to the garage?" Ema asked.

I shook my head. That had been the original plan. We would go to the garage, try to break in, see if we could find the tunnel. But the tunnel I had gone through had led from the garage to the basement below us, to a door that no longer existed between the kitchen and this living room. With the garage locked, wouldn't it be simpler and probably more productive to simply go in reverse—to start in the living room, go down to the basement, see where it led?

Okay, the basement door was gone. So was most of the kitchen. I tried to picture the house's layout as it had been before the fire. I moved closer to where I thought the basement door would be. The remnants of the second floor and roof had collapsed over it. I started to pull up the plywood, trying to dig through the rubble. Ema joined me.

We worked in silence, removing debris, carefully moving it to the side. When I stopped and thought about it, we were, in fact, tainting a crime scene. I was already in plenty of trouble, but what about Ema?

"We should stop," I said.

"Huh?"

"We're tainting a crime scene."

"You're kidding, right?"

Ema kept on digging.

"Seriously," I said, "this was a mistake."

"You didn't tell me what happened with Detective Waters."

Ema was trying to distract me, but that was okay. "He got pretty annoyed with me."

"Annoyed how?"

"Annoyed like he wants me to stay away from it all."

"Annoyed like we got it right about Rachel's father?" Ema asked.

"Yes."

"Whoa."

"Remember I told you about those two hoodlums talking to Mr. Caldwell right after I left?"

"What about them?"

"Detective Waters had a picture of the guy with the scar. He said he was dangerous."

"So they have to be drug dealers."

"Or at least bad guys."

"And you saw Rachel's dad being all friendly with them."

"Yes," I said.

"So then we still believe that Rachel found something incriminating about her dad—some kind of package that backed what her mom had said about him?"

"Yes," I said, back on the floor, moving debris. I tried to make sense of it. What had Rachel done with the package? Had her father gone ballistic when he found it missing?

Had Scarface?

Ema stopped digging. "Mickey?"

I shook away the thoughts and looked toward her voice. The debris was gone now. I could see steps leading down into the basement. I bent low, took out my flashlight, shined it down into the hole.

Nothing much to see.

"I'm going down," I said, "alone."

"It's cute when you get all macho bossy on me," Ema said, "but no. I'm going too."

"The floor up here may be weak. It could collapse."

Ema looked as though someone—me, I guess—had punched her in the stomach. "You think I'm going to break the floor?"

"What? No. Listen, I need you to be my lookout."

She wasn't appeased. "Excuse me?"

"Someone might come. Be my lookout." I grabbed her shoulders and made her look up at me. "Please. Just this once. For me?"

"Just this once what?"

"Don't be a pain in the butt. I don't want you to get hurt. That's all."

The tears in her eyes broke my heart, but she nodded through them. "All right, go. I'll be your"—she wiped her eyes and wiggled her fingers at me—"lookout."

I didn't wait for her to change her mind. I quickly started down the steps into the black hole. Now that I was pretty much out of view, I turned on the flashlight. I descended slowly.

"What do you see?" Ema called down in a whisper.

"Give me a second."

The basement was, as you might expect, dingy and dusty and, well, old. There were rusted pipes and broken glass and old cardboard boxes filled with who knew what. There were spiderwebs in the corner and mud on the floor. The mud could have been wet soot from the fire, but I suspected the origin was somewhat older. Okay, the garage would be behind me and to the left, ergo, that was probably where the door to that tunnel would be.

Found it.

"Mickey?"

"I found the door to the tunnel."

"Wait for me."

"No. Hold up."

The door was made of some kind of reinforced steel. I remembered that from my previous visit with Shaved Head. There were other doors and corridors too, but he wouldn't let me go down them. I grabbed the door handle. Locked. I grabbed it again and shook.

"It's locked," I said.

"So now what?" Ema asked. "Oh, enough. I'm coming down too."

Ema started down the stairs. I swung my flashlight in her direction—and that was when I saw it. I stopped, retraced the beam back to the spot on the floor, and stared. Ema came up behind me.

"What is it?"

I said nothing.

"Wait," Ema said. "Is that a picture of Ashley?"

I nodded. Ashley. The girl we—Rachel, Spoon, Ema, and I—had risked our lives to rescue.

"That's the portrait you saw upstairs?" Ema asked.

I nodded numbly.

"So somehow her picture survived the fire."

"No," I said.

"What do you mean, no? You said you saw it upstairs with, like, thousands of others, right?"

"Right."

"So now it's down here—somehow it survived the fire," Ema said.

"No."

"Why do you keep saying that?"

"There were thousands of pictures up there. Yet only one managed to float down to the basement, make it all the way through the debris, and end up on the floor right in front of the door to the tunnel?"

Now Ema looked skeptical.

"Forget the odds of any photograph making that voyage," I said. "What are the odds that the one that does happens to be the girl we rescued?"

Ema swallowed and said, "You have a better explanation?"

"Sure," I said.

"What?"

I felt a chill even as I thought it. "Someone left it for us."

"Why would someone do that?"

I picked up the photograph of Ashley. I turned it over. On the back, there was a butterfly with two animal eyes on the wings. The Abeona butterfly. It looked like the other butterflies I had seen—and yet the coloring was just slightly different.

The eyes were purple. Like the one on Rachel's hospital door.

It hit me like a surprise wave on the beach. "Oh my God," I said.

"What?"

"I think I know where Rachel hid the package."

CHAPTER 37

Here was how Spoon answered the phone: "Spoon Central."

"What are you up to?" I asked.

"Dad and I are watching the season-three *Glee* season finale. For the fourth time. Have you seen it?"

"No."

"It's very moving."

"I'm sure."

"Don't worry. I have it on DVD. You can borrow it. Did you know that Lea Michele was the original Wendla in *Spring Awakening*?"

"Yeah, that's great. Listen, Spoon, can you get out?"

"Get out? You mean, like, out of this house?"

"Yes."

"And do you mean, like, now?"

I sighed. Ema stood next to me. We were back on the street, heading toward Kasselton High. "Yes, I mean now."

"I'm still grounded, remember? Why, what's up?"

"I need to get into Ashley's locker," I said.

"Ah," Spoon said, "I knew something was wrong with that."

"With what?"

"With Ashley's locker. See, there was a Sevier combination lock on it."

"So?"

"So the school only issues Master Lock. If a new student had taken over Ashley's locker, that would be what they used. A Master Lock. The school would never permit a Sevier."

It just confirmed what I now realized when I looked at the photograph. Bat Lady or Shaved Head or someone high up in the Abeona Shelter had left it on the basement floor so the message would be loud and clear:

Help Rachel.

That was our current assignment. Forget the fire. Forget finding Bat Lady or Shaved Head. Our first assignment had been to save Ashley. Now we needed to save Rachel.

"When the episode ends, it'll be my bedtime anyway," Spoon said. "I'll get my warm cup of milk, climb into bed, turn out the lights, and then I'll climb out the window. What do you think?"

"Sounds good," I said.

"Maybe I'll stick a couple of pillows under the blanket

HARLAN COBEN

so it looks like I'm still in there. Do you think that's a good idea?"

"Your choice, Spoon."

"Okay, the show is almost over. I'll meet you by that same door as last time."

Then another thought struck me. "Wait," I said.

"What?"

Ema looked at me, confused. How could I explain this? Spoon was just a kid. Yeah, we all were, but he seemed younger. He was home innocently watching *Glee* with his father. I couldn't ask him to come down here and illegally break into the school again.

I was about to tell Spoon to forget it—to stay in his nice cozy bed and drink his warm milk—but then I remembered something else. Spoon was his own person, and he could make his own decisions. Hadn't he told me that he'd even been arrested once? Maybe he wasn't such an innocent, and maybe I shouldn't act like I was his overprotective big brother.

Plus, last time Spoon broke the rules, he had saved Ema's life.

"Something wrong, Mickey?" Spoon asked.

My grip on the phone tightened. I wasn't sure what to do. I didn't want to get him in any more trouble, but we needed him. "Nope, nothing. We'll see you soon."

I hung up. Ema and I huddled by the school's side door. There are few places more empty and lifeless than a school at night. It was after nine P.M. by the time Spoon joined us.

"Put these on," Spoon said. "To hide our faces."

He handed Ema and me masks. He kept one for himself. But these weren't, say, ski masks, like you might expect.

"Are these . . . ?" I began.

"Yup, *Lion King* masks," Spoon said. "Ema, I gave you Mufasa. I was going to give you Pumbaa, but he's a warthog and, well, I figured you'd kill me."

Frowning at the mask in her hand, Ema said, "You figured right."

"So, Mickey, you'll be Pumbaa, and I'll be"—he slipped on the mask—"Timon. See? Timon and Pumbaa? *Hakuna matata*. Come on, put yours on. It will be practical yet fun."

I didn't move.

Spoon lifted his up and frowned. "There are surveillance cameras inside. If something goes wrong, we don't want anyone recognizing us."

I looked at Ema. She shrugged. He had a point.

Spoon slipped the mask back into place so that he was now a smiling meerkat. "Mickey, with your height you should also hunch over. In fact, we should all alter our gait. Ema, maybe instead of your usual angry strut, you could twirl or something."

"Twirl?"

"Or something. So they can't identify you."

"I'm not twirling," Ema said.

"Or something."

"I'm not or something-ing either."

"I think the masks will be enough," I said.

Spoon shrugged. "Suit yourself."

We moved toward the school door. Spoon swiped his card key. I heard a click, and the door opened. I looked over at Ema for assurance, but instead of her face, I saw Mufasa's. Well, Mufasa looked pretty resolute, so I followed Spoon inside.

"There's no audio recording in here," Spoon said. He used his regular voice, no stage whisper or even "indoor" voice. The sound was loud in this still corridor, jarring and echoing. "There are cameras in every hallway. They are shot from above, but since we have masks on, this doesn't matter much."

He made a right turn. We followed.

"That's Mrs. Nelson's classroom. Do you know what Dad told me? She keeps her old underwear and socks underneath her desk. And not the sexy kind. I mean, have you seen Mrs. Nelson? Shudder, right? But Dad says she has an amazing sock collection. All different colors and styles. Do you want to see her sock collection?"

"No," I said.

"It's okay. The classroom doors are never locked. Fire hazard or something. Oh, unless there's a lockdown. Do you know what that is? See, every classroom has a panic button under the teacher's desk. In case of a school shooting or some kind of emergency, it sets off an alarm and the school goes into lockdown. Cool, right?"

Mercifully we arrived in front of Ashley's locker. Spoon examined the lock. "Yep, just as I suspected. A Sevier combination lock." He shook his head. "Pitiful, really."

"You have a key to open it?"

Timon looked at me. It was so weird to look at your friend and see someone else's smiling face. "No, of course not. It isn't regulation."

"So what should we do?" Ema asked.

Spoon took out a tire iron, slid it through the lock's loop, and turned it hard. The lock snapped open as if it were made of porcelain.

"Voilà," Spoon said.

That was when I heard a noise. I froze. "Did you hear that?" I whispered.

"Hear what?" Spoon/Timon said.

I looked over at Ema/Mufasa. I stared at her mask as though I could read her face that way. "Ema?"

"Let's just hurry."

Spoon cleared away the leftover lock debris. When he was done, he stepped back and gestured for me to take over. I reached forward, grabbed the metallic latch, and lifted it up. I opened the locker and peered inside.

There was a gym bag.

I pulled it out and dropped it on the floor. The three of us surrounded it and peered down through our masks. I bent down, took hold of the zipper, and pulled it open. The sound echoed through the still hallways, sounding like a giant rip. For a moment, no one spoke. We just stared down.

Then Spoon said, "O. M. G."

The first thing I noticed was the money—bundles and bundles of cash, wrapped up in rubber bands. It was impossible to say how much. Ema reached down and picked one up. She started fingering through the bills of Ben Franklin.

"They're all hundred-dollar bills," Ema said.

"Did you know," Spoon said, "that Benjamin Franklin was an expert swimmer?"

"Not now, Spoon."

Ema moved a few packs of bills to the side, and that was when we saw the plastic bags loaded with white powder.

"Do you think those are drugs?" Spoon asked.

"I don't think they're baby powder," I replied.

"We need to get this to the police," Ema said.

Spoon stood back up. "You're kidding, right?"

"No."

"We just illegally broke into the school," Spoon said, with a tinge of agitation in his voice. "We illegally broke into this locker. Do you know how much trouble we'll get in?"

"He has a point," I said.

"And who's going to believe that we just found it?" Spoon continued, raising both arms in the air excitedly. "Suppose they think we're the drug dealers. I've already got a rep, you know. They'll send me to the big house."

"The big house?" Ema repeated.

"The slammer, the joint, the pen, up the river, juvie, the clink—"

"Okay, Spoon," I said.

"We can't tell anyone we found this," Spoon insisted. "Don't you see? Imagine a tasty morsel like me in a prison."

"Relax," I said. "No one is going to prison."

"And suppose they do believe us?" Spoon continued. "Suppose we tell the truth and they believe us and it all traces back to Rachel. How is she going to explain this?"

Silence. Even Ema knew that he was making sense.

"We need to think," I said.

"Quickly," Spoon added.

"We can't just let it go either," Ema said. "We know what happened now. Rachel's mom goes on a rant about how evil her father is. Rachel investigates. She finds this bag. She hides it and contacts the Abeona Shelter, right?"

I nodded, remembering my conversation with Shaved Head. He had thought that maybe Rachel had given me the package. She hadn't. I wondered why Rachel hadn't told me about it, but now I understood. Her mother was killed over this package. Rachel herself was shot. If she told me where it was, well, she'd be putting me in danger too.

"Meanwhile," Ema continued, "Rachel's dad or those bad guys are wondering what happened to the bag. They figured out that Rachel must have taken it . . ."

"No," I said. "They probably figured that Rachel's mom had taken it."

"Right. So they went after her, and, well, we know what happened next."

"She ended up dead."

Spoon said, "We gotta go. Let's just put the bag back in the locker and try to think it out."

"That won't work either," I said. "The lock is broken. We can't leave it in an unlocked locker."

"So what do we do?" Ema asked.

"You give it to us."

I spun toward the rough voice. The two men I spotted in the souped-up car at Rachel's house were there. Both men were carrying guns. Scarface, the one Detective Waters had warned me about, said, "Nobody move. Put your hands up."

"But if we're not supposed to move," Spoon began, "how can we put our hands up?"

Scarface pointed his gun at Spoon's chest. "You being a smart mouth with me?"

"No, no, it's okay," I said in the calmest voice I could muster. "We're all doing exactly what you tell us. You're in charge here."

"Bet your butt I'm in charge," Scarface said, turning his attention back to me. "Now take off those stupid masks."

Spoon: "But if we're not supposed to move—"

"Spoon," I interrupted. I shook my head at him to shut him up. We all took off our masks and dropped them on the floor.

Scarface pocketed his gun, but his partner was still at the ready. The partner was a huge guy. He wore his sunglasses indoors in the dark and sported the blankest expression I had ever seen on his face. He looked like a bored, cold killer, like he would just as soon shoot us as not, no biggie. I didn't know what to do or say, so for now, I just stayed silent.

Scarface walked over to the gym bag. He bent down and looked inside.

"It all there?" Sunglasses asked.

"Seems to be," Scarface said. He stood and grinned at me. "Thanks for finding our stuff for us, Mickey."

"How do you know my name?" I asked.

"Simple really. We figured that either Rachel or Mommy stole our little package from Daddy. So we got a hold of her cell phone records. Seems she called you right before the big bang-bang, so we figured, hey, maybe you, her boyfriend, helped her hide it. So we started following you. Easy-peasy, right?"

The baby talk, to put it mildly, was unnerving.

"Right," I said. "You got your stuff. You can go now."

Scarface grinned at Sunglasses. The corner of Sunglasses's lips twitched. I didn't like that twitch.

Scarface zippered the bag back up. "When we followed you to that burned-up old house, well, for a second I thought maybe she hid the stuff there and it got burned up. That would have been very, very bad."

HARLAN COBEN

"But that wasn't the case," I said, trying to stand a little taller. "Your stuff was here the whole time. Now it's yours again."

"Yep," Scarface said. "I see that. Only one problem."

I swallowed. The small stone of fear in my chest started expanding, making it hard to breathe. "What's that?"

"You guys. I mean, you saw our faces."

"We won't say a word," Ema said.

Scarface turned his attention to her now. As he moved closer to Ema, I tried to slip between them, but he stopped me with a glare. I didn't like the look in his eyes. They were cruel eyes, the kind that enjoyed hurting others—the kind, I realized with mounting horror, that would never listen to reason.

"You expect me to just trust you, sweet cheeks?" Scarface asked. His face was mere inches away from Ema's now. She looked as though she was about to cry. "You expect us to just, what, let you go?"

"My arms are getting tired," Spoon said. "Can I put them down?"

Scarface spun toward him. "I told you not to move."

"Well, yes, you did, but then you had us move twice— once to put our hands up, once to take off our masks." Spoon slid toward the right. "So that whole 'don't move' thing? It seems more like a guideline than a hard, fast rule, you know what I mean? So I was hoping, seeing how my arms are getting really tired—"

SECONDS AWAY

And then Spoon did the unthinkable.

With all attention on the inanity of what he was saying, Spoon suddenly leapt at Sunglasses. The move surprised everyone, me included.

Next thing I knew, the gun went off. And Spoon fell to the ground, bleeding.

271

CHAPTER 38

For the briefest of moments, no one moved.

I say the briefest of moments because in reality, it was more like a flash—a whirlwind mix that will forever be frozen in my mind. Have you ever had a moment like that, a moment that is shorter than a snap and yet stays with you forever? It was as though time had truly stopped. I remember it all. I remember the sound of the gunshot. I remember Spoon falling back. I remember Ema screaming. I remember Spoon on the ground, the red stain on his shirt spreading, his face losing color, his eyes closed.

I will never forget any of that.

But even in that flash, the one that couldn't have lasted more than half a second, I could feel the sickening guilt wash over me.

I had done this to him. I had gotten Spoon shot.

But while part of me was devastated and panicked, another part of me relied on my martial arts training. Somewhere in my center I was suddenly calm. I could not let Spoon's sacrifice go to waste. Spoon, for all his outward immaturity, had understood the truth. These two men were going to kill us. Someone, he realized, had to make a move. Someone had to do something even if it meant sacrificing himself.

Spoon had distracted them. I could stand here and cry.

Or I could take advantage of the opening.

The rest was a quick fury. It seemed as though a hundred things happened over a long period of time, but when I looked back on it, I knew that it had only taken a few seconds from the time Spoon was shot until the time it was over.

First, we all moved at once. It was as if someone suddenly released us from this pause into a frenzied tornado. I was the first to react. I started toward Sunglasses and his gun, though Scarface was in the way. Ema dropped to the floor to take care of Spoon. Scarface turned toward me. And Sunglasses swerved his gun in my direction.

I was too far away from him.

I was fast; I had gotten a jump on them. But I was still too many yards away to reach Sunglasses before he pulled the trigger again. I tried to calculate the odds. I could hope that he missed, but the chances were remote. I was simply too easy a target.

So what to do?

Make myself a less consistent target, for one. As Sunglasses began to pull the trigger, I jumped suddenly to the left and tackled Scarface. The bullet whizzed past me. I made sure now to keep Scarface's body between the gun's trajectory and, well, me. Scarface hadn't been expecting that attack. As we toppled backward, I moved my forearm into his throat. When we landed on the floor, my forearm jammed deep into neck. His eyes bulged, and he made a choking sound.

I had him just where I wanted him.

Of course, if that had been all, if my only concern was Scarface, I'd be a pretty happy guy right now. But it wasn't. He wasn't even my biggest worry. My biggest worry was Sunglasses. He had quickly recovered from my surprise move and was now heading toward us with his gun raised.

I could only hide behind Scarface's body for so long—and by "so long," I meant "maybe another second."

Sunglasses stood over us. He pointed his gun down at me. From my spot on the ground, I unleashed a kick that landed on his shin. He cursed, shook it off, took a step back, and once again took aim.

This was it, I realized. I was out of moves. It was over.

Scarface was rolling away, coughing, trying to regain his breath. It would take a while, but that didn't really matter. I'd be dead by then. Sunglasses altered his aim slightly so that the barrel was at my chest. I was going to raise my arms in surrender, but I knew that would do no good. I was staring at that smile-twitch again, the last sight I'd ever see, when I heard a shriek.

It was Ema.

She leapt on Sunglasses's back, her momentum knocking him forward. He managed to keep on his feet but just barely. Ema's arms snaked around his neck and squeezed for all she was worth. Without hesitation, I rolled toward Scarface and threw another blow at his throat. It landed but not flush.

Sunglasses tried using his free hand to pry Ema's arm off, but she was a lot stronger than he expected. He lifted the gun hand toward her, as though hoping to shoot her off his back. Ema was ready for it. She took her right arm off his neck and chopped down on his gun hand.

The gun dropped to ground.

Now was my chance!

I dived for the gun, but Sunglasses wasn't through yet. He kicked the gun with his right foot just before I got to it. The gun skittered all the way down the recently waxed floor of the hallway. No time to go for it. Scarface was starting to recover. He, too, had a gun.

Sunglasses reeled back, trying to get Ema off him, but she wouldn't budge. Then he stumbled backward and slammed her into the wall of lockers. He did it again, harder this time, head-butting her in the face with the back of his head. It worked. Ema's grip went slack. She slumped to the ground, dazed. Sunglasses turned toward her, but when I shouted, he turned back to me. Ema used the distraction to roll into a classroom and out of harm's way.

Meanwhile, Scarface was stirring again—and he still had a gun.

I leapt back toward him, but this time he was ready. Scarface rolled onto his back and kicked his foot out. It landed in my solar plexus. The air whooshed out of me. As I fell to the ground, I threw a flailing elbow strike. It struck pay dirt—Scarface's nose. I heard a crunching sound and knew that it was broken.

But before I could get back up, Sunglasses was on me too. He kicked me hard in the ribs. I fell flat. He threw another kick. I grunted. The third kick made my head start to swim. I thought I might throw up. I lay there, defenseless.

The next kick sapped me of whatever strength I had left.

I was losing consciousness, almost ready to surrender, when my eyes traveled past Scarface and landed on Spoon. His eyes were still closed. His face was pure white. The blood poured from an open wound. I didn't know if he was dead or alive, but I'd be damned if I would let him bleed out.

I had to do something, and the answer was suddenly obvious.

Scarface's gun.

It was in his back pocket. If I could just reach . . .

Sunglasses saw what I was going to do. He smiled down at me and lined up for another kick, one that would probably finish me off, but suddenly the air was shattered by the sound of an alarm.

"Lockdown!" a voice over the loudspeaker intoned. "Lockdown . . . Lockdown!"

Ema! That was why she had rolled into the classroom—to hit the panic button Spoon had told us about. The distraction was all I needed. With one last grunt I reached over and grabbed the gun from Scarface's back pocket. I pulled for it, but it wouldn't come out. Sunglasses looked back over at me. He reeled back for another kick, but it wasn't in time.

I freed the gun and pointed it at him. "Freeze!"

Sunglasses stopped and slowly put his hands above his head. I crawled away, keeping the gun on him, making sure I was far enough from Scarface too.

The loudspeaker kept going: "Lockdown . . . Lockdown . . ."

Ema ran back out into the hallway and knelt down next to Spoon.

"Spoon? Arthur?" Her voice was a tearful plea. She cradled his head. "Talk to me, okay? Please?"

She was crying. I was crying. But Spoon didn't move.

I could hear sirens approaching in the distance. I turned and looked at Scarface and Sunglasses. Part of me hoped that they would make a move, because I wanted to shoot them for what they'd done.

They must have seen my face and knew. Neither moved.

I looked over at Ema. "Is he . . . ?"

"I don't know, Mickey. I don't know."

CHAPTER 39

I don't know how many hours passed.

When the cops showed, they surrounded me and told me to put down the gun. I did. The rest was just a murky haze. Sunglasses and Scarface were cuffed. Paramedics rushed over to Spoon. Ema sat, cradling his head, trying to stop the flow of blood. I ran toward him too because for a moment, a very brief moment, I feared one of the paramedics would be the sandy-haired paramedic who took away my father. I feared that he would wheel Spoon out of there and I'd never see him again.

"Mickey, what have you done?"

That voice, I knew, came from deep inside of me. I had been warned, hadn't I? Detective Waters had told me in no uncertain terms not to get involved, but I hadn't listened. It would have been one thing to put my life at risk. But look what I had done to Spoon.

I don't think I will ever forgive myself.

I don't know how many cops showed up. I remember the flashing lights from a long line of emergency vehicles slicing through the still night air. For the next several hours—I cannot tell you how many—I answered questions. I kept asking only one in return, over and over:

How is he?

But they wouldn't tell me about Spoon's condition.

For the most part, I told the truth, but when they asked, "How did you guys get into the school?" I lied and said, "I forced open the door."

"Kid," the cop said to me in a grave voice, "breaking into the school is the least of your friend's problems."

Several officers came in and out, including Chief Taylor and even Detective Waters. The mood of the officers swung between pissed and pleased—pissed because we had been foolhardy and gotten Spoon shot; pleased because we had cracked the case of who shot Mrs. Caldwell and Rachel. Two hardened criminals had been apprehended and were going to jail for a long time. The surveillance cameras would see to that, plus the guns they used were Smith & Wesson .38s— the same kind used to shoot Mrs. Caldwell and Rachel.

At some point, Uncle Myron showed up. He took on the dual roles of panicked guardian and attorney. He immediately told me to stop talking to the police. But I waved him off. They needed to know. So instead Myron sat next to me and listened too.

The last person to interrogate me was Detective Waters. When he finished, I said, "Does this help your other case?"

"What case?"

"Mr. Caldwell. He's a drug dealer, right?"

Detective Waters glanced at Myron, then back at me. "That isn't your concern."

"Are you going to arrest him?"

"On what charge?"

I stared at him. "I just told you. The stuff in that gym bag—"

"What about it?"

"It came from his house."

"Do you have any proof? How are we going to prove any of that stuff belonged to Henry Caldwell? Maybe if you'd left it there and told us about it, maybe something could have been done. But now?"

He shook his head and walked out the door.

By the time Ema and I met up in the hospital waiting room, the sun was up. Uncle Myron and Angelica Wyatt had wanted to take us home, but we were not about to abandon Spoon. We sat in the waiting room. Ema and I were in one corner. Angelica Wyatt, decked out in sunglasses and a head scarf for disguise, and Myron kept their distance.

"Wow," Ema said to me.

"Yeah."

Her eyes were tinged with red from tears and exhaustion. I imagined that I looked the same.

"He's going to be fine," I said.

"He better be," Ema said, "or I'm going to kill him."

A few minutes later, I saw a thin black woman wander into the waiting room zombielike, looking worse than we ever could. It was Spoon's mother. We had never met, but I had seen her hug her son when I dropped him at his house. The devastation was written all over her face. Her eyes had that thousand-yard stare you sometimes see in war documentaries.

I looked at Ema. Ema took a deep breath and nodded. We rose together and started toward Spoon's mother. It seemed to take forever to reach her, like the more we walked, the farther she moved away from us.

When we finally arrived in front of her, Mrs. Spindel had her head down. We didn't know what to say, so we just stood there, waiting. A few seconds later, she looked up at me and when she saw who it was, a shadow fell across her face.

"You're Mickey," she said. "And you're Ema."

We both nodded.

"What are you doing here?"

"We just wanted to know how Spoon—I mean, Arthur— is doing."

She looked at Ema and then back to me. "He's . . . he's not good."

It was like my heart was on the top of a long staircase and someone shoved it off.

"He's out of surgery, but the doctors . . . they don't know."

"Is there anything . . . ?" I tried, but I couldn't finish. Tears started brimming in my eyes.

Spoon's mom said, "I don't understand why you were all at the school so late."

"It was my fault," I said through the tears.

Ema was about to add something, but I gave her arm a nudge.

I saw the shadow cross Mrs. Spindel's face again and then she said something I didn't expect but completely deserved. "Oh, I know it's your fault."

I squeezed my eyes shut, her words landing like punches.

"I never heard of you a week ago. Now you're all Arthur talks about. He wanted everyone to start calling him Spoon. He said his new friend gave him that nickname."

My heart crashed to the bottom step, and now a foot with a heavy boot stomped on it.

"You were Arthur's friend," she went on. "Maybe the first real one since the fourth grade. You probably don't get how much you meant to my son. He looked up to you. He worshipped you—and how did you repay him? You used him. You used him to break into some stupid locker and now look." She turned away in disgust. "I hope whatever was in there was worth it to you."

I opened my mouth, closed it, tried again. But what could I say?

"I think," Mrs. Spindel said, "that you should both leave."

"No."

I turned toward the voice and recognized Mr. Spindel, Spoon's father.

She looked up at her husband and waited.

"Arthur just woke up," Mr. Spindel said, turning and meeting my eyes. "And he's insisting that he speak to Mickey."

CHAPTER 40

There were tubes and machines and beeping noises.
There were curtains and antiseptic smells and monitors
with green lights. I saw none of it. All I saw as I entered the
room was my friend lying in the middle of all this horrible
gadgetry.

Spoon looked so small in that bed. He looked small and
as fragile as an injured bird.

Mrs. Spindel's voice—*Oh, I know it's your fault*—still
echoed in my ears.

The doctor, a tall woman with her hair pulled back, put
a hand on my shoulder. "Normally I would never allow it,
but he's so agitated. I need you to make this short and keep
him calm."

I nodded and slowly walked toward his bed. My legs
felt rubbery. I stopped at one point because the tears were

starting to come. I turned around, bit down hard on my lip, and gained enough composure. It wouldn't help Spoon if he saw me hysterical. To keep him calm, I knew that I needed to be calm.

When I got to the bed, I wanted to pick him up and take him home and make it somehow yesterday. It was all so wrong, my friend lying here in this hospital.

"Mickey?"

Spoon seemed suddenly to be straining to move. He looked distressed. I bent down low, close to him. "I'm right here."

He lifted his hand and I took it in mine. He was struggling to talk.

"Shh," I said. "Just get better, okay?"

He shook his head weakly. I bent my ear to be closer to his mouth. It took him a few seconds but eventually he said, "Rachel is still in danger."

"No, Spoon. You saved us all. It's over."

Spoon's face tightened. "No, it isn't. You can't sit here doing nothing. You have to save her. You can't stop until we find the truth."

"Calm down, okay? Those two guys shot her. They're in jail."

I saw a tear escape his eye. "They didn't do it."

"Of course they did."

"No, listen to me. Get out of here and help her. Promise me."

Spoon was getting more agitated. The doctor rushed over and said to me, "I think that's enough. You should go wait in the other room."

She started to add something into his intravenous tube, a sedative, I guessed. I tried to let go of Spoon's hand, but his grip grew tighter.

"It's going to be okay, Spoon."

Nurses came to the bedside too. They tried to hold him down and pull me away.

"She was shot in her house," Spoon managed to say.

"I know, Spoon. It's okay. Calm down."

But he suddenly had new strength in his arm. He pulled me close, desperate. "You said they asked you which house was Rachel's. Remember? When you saw them that first time on the street?"

"Right, so?"

The doctor finished injecting the medication. The effect was immediate. Spoon's grip grew slack. I was about to pull away but now—

That the Caldwell house?

—Scarface's voice came back to me. Spoon looked up at me and managed to ask me the same question I was suddenly asking myself:

"So if those two guys had already been at the house, why would they ask you where it was?"

CHAPTER 41

Spoon was right.

I was hustled out of the room. Mr. and Mrs. Spindel were in the corridor. They rushed past me into the room. It took a few minutes, but Spoon was stable again. I thought I heard one of the nurses say something about his legs not moving, but I immediately shut that out. I couldn't deal with that. Not now.

When I got back to the waiting room, I grabbed Ema and pulled her to the side. We found a quiet corner away from the television.

"What happened?" Ema asked. "Is he okay?"

I quickly explained about what Spoon had said—if Sunglasses and Scarface had already been at Rachel's house when they killed her mother, why would they ask me which house it was?

HARLAN COBEN

"Maybe they were just, I don't know, playing with you," Ema said.

I frowned. "Playing with me?"

"Like a prank."

"'That the Caldwell house?'" I said, mimicking Scarface. "Does that sound like a prank?"

"I don't know. Maybe when they came the first time, it was dark."

"So?"

"So maybe they weren't sure where the house was during the day."

I frowned even harder.

"Lame, right?" she said.

"Very," I said. "There's a gate around that house. If you had managed to break in and shoot two people earlier, don't you think you'd remember where the house was?"

Ema nodded slowly, seeing it now. "And come to think of it, why would you break in and shoot them in the first place? Let's assume these two guys wanted the gym bag back. Wouldn't they, I don't know, try to beat the information out of them? What good would just shooting them do?"

"Exactly," I added, "and if you went there to get the package back, wouldn't you toss the place? They clearly wanted their money and drugs back. Why not search for it? Why just shoot the two people who could tell you?"

The official conclusion wasn't making sense anymore.

"There's more," I said.

"Like?"

"Like how come Mr. Caldwell was all chummy with them when I saw them at the house? I mean, he'd have to know they just shot his ex-wife and daughter, right?"

"Right." She shook her head. "We have to consider another possibility."

"What?"

"Let's just go back over this, okay? Rachel's father is a drug dealer. He was willing to keep his ex-wife locked up for years to protect himself. Now she comes back. Rachel gives her mom the benefit of the doubt and steals his cash and drugs."

Ema stopped. I stopped. It was right there in front of us, but neither one of us wanted to say it.

"He wouldn't shoot his own daughter," I said.

"Are you sure?"

"I just don't believe it."

"The man drew a gun on you."

"To protect her. Because he was worried about her."

We pondered that for a few moments.

"It could have been an accident," Ema said.

"How so?"

"Think about the whole scenario. Rachel's dad finds out his money and drugs are missing. He comes home and finds, to his surprise, that his ex-wife is there. They argue. He pulls out a gun, maybe they struggle. Rachel surprises them. Maybe he shoots Rachel accidentally."

It added up. And yet . . . "There's one more thing," I said. "What?"

"What's up with Chief Taylor?" I asked. "Why has he been hanging around Henry Caldwell? Why does he keep worrying about what Rachel will say about the shooting? Is it just a coincidence he was first on the scene?"

"Wait," Ema said, showing me her palms in a double stop. "I mean, okay, I know we have our problems with him and Troy, but you're not suggesting . . . ?"

"I don't know what I'm suggesting. But Spoon is right. We have to get out of here. We are all in danger until we figure out who shot Rachel."

CHAPTER 42

Uncle Myron was quiet during the ride home. I expected a lot of questions and a long lecture, but because he sat with me throughout the interrogations, maybe he'd concluded that there was little more to ask.

I hadn't slept now in more than twenty-four hours. Fatigue was setting in, making my bones feel heavy. Uncle Myron pulled the car to a stop and said, "You were trying to help a friend."

It seemed more a statement than a question, so I didn't say anything.

"I get it," Myron continued. "The need to rescue people. I guess it's genetic."

I didn't know if he meant it came from him or my father. Or both.

"You think you're doing good. I get that too. But when you upset the balance . . ."

I waited. Then I said, "So you think, what, people should step back and just let things take their course?"

"No."

"So what's your point?"

"Maybe nothing," Uncle Myron said. "Or maybe I need you to understand that what you're trying to do isn't easy. It isn't black and white." He shifted in his seat. "Pretend there are a bunch of figurines on a shaky shelf."

I arched an eyebrow. "Figurines?"

"Just go with me, okay? If one of the figurines tips over and starts to fall, you should reach for it and try to catch it. But if you try too hard or dive after it too clumsily, you might knock down more figurines. You may save the first figurine but ultimately break more."

He looked at me. I looked at him. Then I said, "I have a question, though."

Myron grew serious. "Yes?"

"When you say figurines, do you mean like bobble-heads or those weird little Hummel kids that Grandma loves so much?"

He sighed. "I guess I was asking for that, wasn't I?"

"Because I don't think I'd want to save any of those," I said. "They creep me out."

Myron laughed. "All right, all right."

"Don't tell Grandma, okay?"

"Wise guy."

We got out of the car and went inside. I started heading down to the basement when Myron asked me one last question. "Does all this have something to do with Bat Lady or your wanting to exhume your dad's grave?"

It was a good question, and he had earned a truthful answer. "I don't know."

Down in the basement, I collapsed onto the bed. I had to block out Spoon. If I kept thinking about him lying in the hospital, I'd freeze up. Spoon had pushed through the pain and asked to see me for one reason. He didn't want us to quit. He wanted us to find out who shot Rachel. Much as I wanted right now to just curl up in a ball and give up, I had to honor that request.

So what was the next step?

My cell phone rang. When I saw on the caller ID that it was Rachel, I sat up, hit the green answer button, and put the phone to my ear. Her voice was distraught and angry. "How could you do that to me?"

"Rachel?"

"There are cops all over my house."

"Are they asking you questions about the gym bag?"

"They tried to, but my father won't let them talk to me. Why did you do this, Mickey? Why couldn't you just leave it alone?"

"We were trying to help. We were trying to—"

"You know what?" she snapped. "I don't want to hear it. I just called because I wanted to know how Spoon was."

I thought again about the look on Spoon's mom's face. Would I ever forget that? "I don't know. He's in critical condition."

"That poor kid."

"We were just trying to help find the shooters."

"Who asked you to do that?"

But I'd had enough of being on the defensive. "You know the answer to that, Rachel."

She did. The Abeona Shelter.

"We are all linked in this together. You could have trusted us. You could have told us about believing your mom and hiding that gym bag."

"I was trying to protect you," she said.

"And I was trying to protect you," I said, remembering Myron's dumb figurine metaphor. "Look where that got us."

Silence.

"You went to Abeona for help, didn't you?" I said.

"Yes. But Bat Lady told me to leave it alone," Rachel replied. "Like I could. Like I could just forget what my father had done to my mother—locking her away in a loony bin for all those years. So I hid the gym bag in the locker. Just until I could convince them that this was important to me or, I don't know, to buy some time. But I messed up, Mickey. I messed up and those two men came after my mother."

"No," I said.

"No what?"

"They didn't kill your mother."

"What are you talking about? Chief Taylor is here. He says the case against them is open and shut."

Chief Taylor again.

"What else did he say?"

"He told us they had the murder weapon. He said the ballistics test will show a match."

"*Will* show?" I said.

"Yes."

"How does he know what a test *will* show?"

"Because it's obvious?"

"They didn't do it, Rachel. Spoon figured it out. Whoever killed your mother is still free."

"That's impossible."

I started explaining all the things wrong with the official scenario. She listened in silence. When I was done, Rachel asked in a surprisingly calm voice, "Do you think my father shot us?"

"I don't know. I mean, it could have been an accident."

"I don't see how. Someone shot at me from across the room, but my mother was shot with the gun pressed against her head. How could that be an accident?"

"Maybe," I ventured slowly, remembering Ema's theory, "your mother was shot on purpose, but you were hit accidentally."

We fell into silence, but something was bothering me. Rachel was hit from across the room while her mother was shot in the head from very close. That made sense, of course. The shooter would have been right near Rachel's mom . . .

So why was something niggling at the back of my brain?

"Mickey?"

"Yes?"

"I love my father."

"I know."

"He would never hurt me, but . . ."

"But what?"

"But he and Chief Taylor are good friends," she said. "And they've both been acting so suspiciously."

I gripped the phone a little tighter. Mr. Caldwell and Chief Taylor were friends—and somehow Taylor ends up being the first cop on the scene. That was some coincidence.

I was liking this less and less.

"I think we should talk to the police."

"And tell them what?" Rachel said. "We're just kids. We don't have any proof at all. The first thing any cop will do is tell Chief Taylor."

She had a point. "I still think it's our best option."

"No, it's not," Rachel said, her voice coming alive. It was like a switch had been flicked. "Mickey?"

"Yes?"

"Are you up for getting in more trouble?" she asked. "Because I have an idea."

CHAPTER 43

When I got off the phone with Rachel, I called Ema and filled her in on the plan. I wanted to get an update on Spoon, but, one, I didn't know who to call, and, two, I didn't want to be distracted. Spoon had made it clear: There was nothing I could do for him. I had to concentrate on finding the truth.

I had eight hours before we enacted Rachel's idea—serious downtime that I desperately needed. My body was torn between sleep and food, and as usual, food won. As I headed up to the kitchen, Uncle Myron was watching the news on TV.

"Can I make you a sandwich or something?" he asked.

"No, I got it."

I opened the fridge. Uncle Myron had recently purchased turkey, Swiss, lettuce, tomato, and submarine rolls. Awesome. I made the sandwich in maybe forty seconds. I grabbed an ice water and started heading back to the basement when something on the television made me freeze in midstep.

Myron saw it. "Mickey?"

I ignored him, keeping my eyes on the screen. Myron fell quiet.

The anchorman with the too-green tie was using his best "gravely serious" voice: "A sad anniversary coming up. Tomorrow morning, there will be a memorial service for Dylan Shaykes, marking twenty-five years since little Dylan, then age nine, was kidnapped from his school playground and never seen again."

I looked at the picture on the screen. Oh no, I thought. It can't be . . .

"The story of little Dylan made huge international headlines. His photograph was plastered on milk cartons. There were sightings everywhere from coast to coast and even in Europe. The police seriously questioned his father at the time, but William Shaykes was never arrested for the crime. Young Dylan's blood was found in a nearby patch of woods, but all these years later, a body has never been found. So the mystery remains."

The television screen continued to show the photograph of nine-year-old Dylan Shaykes. Little Dylan had curly hair and sad eyes. I had seen his picture—this exact snapshot, as a matter of fact—in the Bat Lady's upstairs hallway. There had been another picture of Dylan, taken sometime later, sometime *after* his disappearance, on the Bat Lady's nightstand.

On the screen, the female coanchor shook her head and said, "Sad story, Ken."

"Sure is, Diane. And with no new clues after all these years, we will probably never know what happened to little Dylan Shaykes."

But he was wrong. Because now, looking at the photograph again, I knew.

CHAPTER 44

So much for sleep.

The sad-eyed, curly-haired boy haunted my dreams. Dylan Shaykes. He had been on milk cartons and news reports. I remembered thinking when I first saw that photograph in Bat Lady's hallway that his face was familiar. It may have been from seeing missing-children stories over the years. But I doubted it.

I checked out the news stories about what happened to us online. Maybe because we were all minors, there were very few. On our local news website, the Kasselton Patch, there was a video of a press conference with Chief Taylor announcing the arrests of Brian Tart and Emile Romero, two well-known drug dealers with prior convictions for assault and armed robbery, for the murder of Nora Caldwell and the shooting of her daughter. The chief made it clear that they now had "physical evidence that shows without a doubt" that Sunglasses and Scarface were guilty. The murder case, Chief Taylor emphasized, was officially closed.

I made a face. Chief Taylor seemed awfully anxious to put the matter to rest, didn't he?

At six P.M., Rachel, Ema, and I met up on Coventry Road near the mall. I didn't think that any of us would be able to sneak out, nonetheless all, but it worked out. Angelica Wyatt was filming a major scene today, and putting it off even a day would have cost the studios half a million dollars. That got rid of Angelica and Uncle Myron. As for Rachel, once her father declared that she would not speak to the authorities, they pretty much left her alone.

I had a feeling that there wasn't much supervision at Rachel's house.

"Okay," Rachel said, "do we need to go over the plan again?"

"I don't think so," Ema said. "We wait by the back door until you open it. Then we sneak in. Simple, right, Mickey?"

They both looked at me. I was frowning. "I don't like it."

Rachel said, "Why not? It's perfect."

A funny look crossed Ema's face. She got it, and in this case, it wasn't a good thing. "Yeah, Mickey, what's the problem?"

"I don't want anyone else to get hurt," I said.

That reasoning sounded hollow in my own ears and judging by the looks on both Rachel's and Ema's faces, it wasn't exactly ringing in theirs either.

Here was Rachel's plan: From her days dating Troy Taylor—first ugh—she had learned that Chief Taylor kept copies of all the important police files in his home. There weren't many. Kasselton isn't a town with a lot of mayhem—at least, it wasn't until recently. But Rachel knew that he kept all his files in his home office off the kitchen. Troy the Dumbwad had explained to her early in their "relationship"—second ugh—that his dad's office was strictly off limits to everyone, including family members.

The plan? Simple. Rachel had already called Troy and asked if she could stop by his house. Troy was anxious for a "reconciliation"—third ugh—though Rachel stressed repeatedly that their relationship had really been "nothing much" and "very minor league."

"If it was very minor league," I had said when she revealed this, "how do you know the layout of his house so well?"

Ema stomped on my foot at this point. I couldn't tell whether she wanted to shut me up or whether she was annoyed with me for caring. I think both.

Anyway, back to the plan. Rachel would go into the house to "talk things out"—do I need to bother with the ughs anymore?—with Troy. She would ask to use the bathroom, slip into the kitchen, and unlock the back door for us. Ema and I would sneak into Chief Taylor's office. From there, it'd be up to us to rifle through his files and see what we could find about the Caldwell shooting while Rachel kept Troy "occupied."

Okay, one last ugh. "What do you mean by 'occupied'?" I'd asked, which earned me another foot stomp from Ema.

So what exactly were we going to look for in Chief Taylor's files? Beats me.

Ten minutes later we watched Rachel approach the front door. She rang the Taylors' doorbell and then did that thing with her hair that some might call "fix," but it always made my mouth go a little dry. Next to me I heard Ema sigh.

Troy opened the front door, leading with his chest, like a preening rooster. My hands, working on their own, formed two fists. Troy invited Rachel in and the door shut behind them.

"Let's go," Ema whispered.

We headed to the back via the house next door and then cut over into the Taylors' yard. The truth was, I loved this idea. I loved the idea of getting into Chief Taylor's files and figuring out what he was up to because I knew, *knew*, that he was covering up something.

I just didn't like the idea of Rachel in there alone with Troy.

Ema and I ducked behind a bush by the back door. I knew that we were both thinking about Spoon, but we both also knew that we didn't need that distraction right now. There was nothing we could do for him, other than figuring out who'd shot Rachel.

So that was what we would do.

I thought again about the twenty-fifth anniversary of Dylan Shaykes's disappearance. I didn't tell Ema about it because with everything else going on, it could wait. But the Abeona Shelter was growing murkier and murkier. First, there had been the touched-up photograph of the Butcher of Lodz. Now I had the photograph of that sad-eyed little boy to consider.

No time for that now, though. There was a sound coming from the back door—a slide bolt sliding open.

"You ready?" Ema said.

I nodded. We had agreed that we would not speak or even whisper once we were inside unless there was an emergency. Ema would stand by the office door and let me know if Troy started toward us or if anyone else came home. I would be the one to go through Chief Taylor's desk.

When my hand hit the doorknob, a new thought hit me: fingerprints. I should have worn gloves. There was not much I could do about that now, and besides, who was going to dust for fingerprints? We didn't plan to steal anything and if we got caught in the act somehow, no one would need to check for additional physical evidence.

I turned the knob and pushed the door. It opened with too loud a creak that made me stop. Then I heard Rachel make a horrid giggling noise.

"Oh Troy!" Rachel exclaimed in a too loud, too sickeningly sweet voice. "That's sooo funny!"

I made a face like I'd just gotten a whiff of something that really reeked.

Rachel giggled some more. Not laughed. Giggled with a tee-hee. I confess that suddenly Rachel seemed less attractive. Then I remembered that this was just an act, an ingenious one to cover up my clumsy entrance, and she became mega-hot all over again.

Ema and I slipped inside and closed the door behind us. Rachel had already informed us that Chief Taylor's office was to the left after we entered. I tiptoed in that direction. Ema followed. The office door was wide-open, so I just stepped inside. Ema turned around and pressed her back against the kitchen wall. From there, she could see the back door, the office door, and the corridor leading to the den where Rachel was currently tee-heeing with Troy Taylor.

Chief Taylor's office was loaded up with trophies and plaques and citations, all involving law enforcement. Two of the trophies, featuring bronzed guns, were for marksmanship. Terrific. There were also tons of photographs of various teams Chief Taylor had coached in baseball, basketball, and football. On the far wall, there were certificates and citations from his own sporting days, including being named All State in football and . . .

Hello.

I couldn't help it. I moved over to take a closer look. It was a "State Champions" photograph of the Kasselton High School basketball team from twenty-five years ago. There, in the front row holding a basketball, were the team cocaptains,

Eddie Taylor and Myron Bolitar. Yep, Uncle Myron. The two now-nemeses looked chummy in the picture, and I wondered what went wrong.

But that wasn't my concern right now.

I sat at Chief Taylor's desk and worried for another second or two about fingerprints. No time. I saw a basket full of files. As I reached for one, I heard Rachel's voice from the other room say, "Troy, don't do that."

There was a quick flash of rage. I got ready to stand up and go out there, but then I stopped. What was I going to do, bust in on them? Besides, Rachel seemed pretty much in control. If she needed me, she'd call for help, right?

I didn't like it, but this had been part of her plan. If I went out there now, she'd probably kill me. Time to get back to the task at hand.

The first folder I grabbed was fairly light. I checked the right tab. There were only three words written on it: NORA CALDWELL—HOMICIDE.

Bingo. I considered finding the file so easily a stroke of luck, but then again, the Caldwell murder was far and away the biggest case in the town. Why shouldn't it be front and center?

Ema looked in on me. I gave her a big thumbs-up and opened the file. Paper files—talk about old-school.

The top sheet of paper read: BALLISTICS TEST REPORT. It was dated today.

There were three columns, one for Gun A (the one that had shot Spoon), one for Gun B (the one being carried by

Scarface), and one for Gun C (the one used to shoot both Mrs. Caldwell and Rachel). There was a lot of scientific mumbo jumbo, terms like sample type, shot sequence, weapon type, projectile weight, cartridge/projectile type, impact velocity, impact energy, you get the idea. None of this would do me any good, so I skipped down to the finding: NEITHER GUN A NOR GUN B IS A MATCH FOR GUN C.

Whoa. If I was reading this right—and the conclusion did not seem all that difficult to understand—neither gun was a match for the murder of Mrs. Caldwell.

This was huge.

Or was it?

While it would have been excellent physical evidence against Sunglasses and Scarface, it certainly did not prove that they were innocent. Unless you've never watched a television show in your life, you'd know that if you committed a crime with a gun, it would be best to get rid of it. Wasn't that the most logical conclusion? Sunglasses or Scarface had simply replaced the murder weapon with a new one.

Except, of course, that Chief Taylor hadn't mentioned this finding in that press conference. In fact, he made it sound just the opposite. They had, he'd said, the physical evidence to lock these guys away for the murder of Nora Caldwell.

But if it wasn't a match on the bullets, well, what other "physical evidence" could there be? Or was he lying? And this report wasn't a copy. It was the original. Why would it be in Chief Taylor's private office?

From the den, I heard Troy say, "Let me get us something to drink."

I froze.

Rachel said, "That's okay. I'm not thirsty."

I could hear a creak from the couch, as if Troy was getting up. "I'll only be a second, babe."

Babe?

"Troy?" Rachel's voice sounded coquettish, and I'm not even sure what *coquettish* means.

"Yeah?"

"Please don't leave me right now."

Oh man. I had to hurry.

I paged through the next sheets until I reached one titled MEDICAL EXAMINER REPORT. The name on the top was NORA CALDWELL. There were two sketches of the human body—front and back. I skimmed it over, trying again to ignore the scientific mumbo jumbo. According to the findings, the death was due to massive injuries sustained by a bullet wound to the head. I already knew that. The medical examiner could tell by the "burn patterns" that it was a "contact shot"—that is, the barrel of the gun had been pressed against the victim's head. Rachel had told me that too, and something about that still bothered me.

But what?

I tried to run through the murder scenario in my head. The gunman slips into the Caldwell den. He places the barrel of the gun against Mrs. Caldwell's head and shoots her execution style. Hearing that sound, Rachel comes running into the room. The gunman raises his gun and aims it at her. . . .

Wait. Now I saw the problem.

Rachel hadn't told me that she heard a gun blast. She told me that she heard loud voices. That was what had made her come downstairs and check out the den. Not a gunshot. Voices.

I heard a noise outside and looked out the window. A police car had just pulled into the driveway.

Oh no.

I looked over at Ema. She was gesturing for me to hurry. I waved for her to head out. She nodded and vanished. I glanced out the window again. Chief Taylor was already out of the car and starting up the front walk. He looked upset.

I heard Troy say, "Dang. My old man is home."

As I quickly stood, I took one last look at the file. That was when I saw the words *hand powder residue* highlighted in yellow. Whoa. I risked one more glance out the window, and as I did, Chief Taylor veered off the front walk and started for . . .

. . . for the back door!

Oh man, I was trapped.

I looked for a place in his office to hide, but there was nowhere. I kept low and looked out the window. Chief Taylor was nearly rounding the back. There'd be no chance of getting out of here. Maybe I could roll out the window as he entered. I tried to open it, but it was stuck.

I'd have to bolt. What else could I do?

With all hope lost, the front door of house opened. "Chief Taylor?"

It was Rachel.

"Chief Taylor? Hi, it's me."

Rachel did the tee-hee again. The noise was ridiculously grating. But Chief Taylor stopped and turned toward her. "Hi, Rachel."

"Can I, uh, talk to you for a second?"

She stepped out into the front yard. Taylor looked unsure. He glanced toward the walk to the back, sighed, and then started toward her.

"What is it?" Taylor asked.

I didn't wait.

I turned and hurried through the kitchen and out the back door. I ran hard toward the woods in the yard. Ema had planned a meeting place. She was there waiting for me.

I was just upon her when I realized two things.

One, I now knew who killed Mrs. Caldwell and shot Rachel.

Two, I left the murder file open on Chief Taylor's desk.

CHAPTER 45

We didn't wait for Rachel to extricate herself from the Taylor household. She was a big girl. She'd figure that one out on her own. Besides, I had things to do before I met up with her.

"Well?" Ema said. "What did you find?"

"I have to think this through."

Ema shook her head. "Seriously, do you know how annoying it is when you say stuff like that?"

"Yeah," I said, "I guess I do."

"So think it through while talking to me."

I didn't really want to, so I told her what I'd seen in the plainest "just the facts" language. Her mobile phone buzzed. Ema looked down at the screen. "It's my mom."

Still felt so weird—her "mom" being one of the most glamorous women in the world.

Ema picked up the phone with a sigh and spoke with lots of "I'm fine, Mom"s before hanging up and turning to me. "Your uncle is with her. They both want us to go home pronto."

That was okay by me. I wanted to be alone for a bit. I wanted to sort through this and consider my next step closely. Most of all, though, I wanted Ema to be someplace safe and away from me. I had already gotten one friend shot. I did not relish the idea of putting another in jeopardy.

So Ema and I went our separate ways. I got home, still lost in my thoughts. I had figured out what had happened in the Caldwell household. Most of it, anyway. I was having trouble making all the pieces fit. There was, I knew, only one way to get the answers I needed. It was going to involve putting myself in more peril. I didn't relish that either. There was a fine line between being daringly brave and foolishly suicidal. I wasn't in the mood to find out just how fine.

But what choice did I have?

When I got home, I headed into the basement and texted

Rachel: **Are you out of there?**

Rachel: **Just leaving Troy's now.**

Good. I didn't even bother to reply. Knowing she wouldn't be there, I quickly dialed Rachel's home phone. As I did, the front door opened, and Myron entered. "Mickey?"

I put my hand over the phone. "One sec," I called back.

On the third ring a man picked up and said, "Hello?"

"Mr. Caldwell, this is Mickey Bolitar."

"Oh, hello, Mickey. Rachel isn't here right now."

"I wasn't calling for her."

"Oh?"

"I know what happened to your ex-wife and daughter."

There was an odd tightness in his voice now. "Then you should tell the police at once."

"You mean, like Chief Taylor?"

"Yes, of course."

"Well, sure, I guess I could tell him, but we both know he'd just cover it up."

There was a pause. I could hear Mr. Caldwell's breath through the phone.

"What are you trying to say here, Mickey?"

"You and I need to meet," I said.

"Come by the house then."

"I'd rather meet somewhere else. Do you play basketball, Mr. Caldwell?"

"That's an odd question."

"I'll meet you by the outdoor courts in the center of town," I said. "Oh, and wear basketball clothes. Shorts and a T-shirt."

"Why?"

"Because this time," I said, "I want to make sure you aren't armed."

313

CHAPTER 46

Rachel kept buzzing my phone. I kept ignoring it.

From a tree about a hundred yards away, I saw Mr. Caldwell pull up in his BMW. The court lights were on, but no one was playing right now. He came out of his car carrying a basketball. I guess that was meant to give me comfort. He wore, per my request, basketball shorts and a T-shirt. It might be possible to hide a gun somewhere, but I doubted it.

We met up at half court. Henry Caldwell looked exhausted. There was enough baggage under his eyes to qualify for an airline surcharge. His hair had a wispy quality to it, as though a strong wind could blow it off his head.

"What do you want, Mickey?"

I was standing on the diving board now. Might as well just jump right in. "You were there when your ex-wife was murdered. I want to know what happened."

He looked at the basketball in his hands. "How do you know I was there?"

"Rachel said she heard voices, both male and female. One was you. One was your ex-wife."

There we stood, center court, him holding a basketball. I probably had four or five inches on him. He looked up at me with his dark eyes. "Are you wearing a wire, Mickey?"

"A wire?"

"Yes. Is anyone else listening in on this? Are you recording it? Lift up your shirt."

I lifted it so he could see that I didn't have a microphone or recording device.

"How about your cell phone?" he asked.

Uh-oh. "What about it?"

"Some people leave it on so others can hear on the other end of the phone."

I took my cell phone out of my pocket, secretly pressing the end button as I did, and then I handed it to him. Mr. Caldwell glanced at the screen. I wondered whether he saw all the texts and missed calls from his daughter. If he did, he didn't say anything. All he did was take the back off my phone, pry out the battery, and hand it back to me.

"Start talking," he said.

"Look, Mr. Caldwell, I saw the police report."

"How did you see it?"

"That's not really important."

"Did you break into Chief Taylor's house?"

"Mr. Caldwell . . ."

"Answer me."

"Your ex-wife had gun residue on her hand," I said.

"Excuse me?"

"Gun residue. That means she pulled the trigger."

His face lost color.

"What? Are you out of your mind?" His voice was full of bluster. Not rage, not anger—bluster. It sounded phony, like lines he was reading off a script. "Those two goons fired the shots."

I shook my head. "No, sir, your ex-wife did."

He opened his mouth to say more, but nothing came out. His shoulders slumped; his eyelids looked heavy.

"Your ex-wife committed suicide," I said.

Tears started to fill his eyes. When he lowered his head, I saw the police car slowly cruise up behind him. My pulse started speeding up.

"Is that Chief Taylor?" I asked.

"Yes."

"You called him?"

"You left the file open on his desk. He put it together himself."

My mouth felt dry.

"You forgot something, Mickey."

"What's that?"

"If Rachel's mother shot herself, who shot Rachel?"

So now we were down to it. I knew because in the end

only one answer made sense. Our eyes met. I saw the pain there. No doubt in my mind anymore—Mr. Caldwell had been there. He had seen his own daughter shot.

But he hadn't been the one to do it.

"Your ex-wife," I said, my voice barely a whisper. "Your ex-wife shot your daughter."

He didn't say anything. He didn't have to.

"I don't know exactly how it played out. Rachel finds your gym bag and hides it. She tells her mother that she knows the truth now—that she believes her. You come home later. You find your bag is missing. You're angry. You confront your ex-wife. That's what Rachel hears—you two arguing. Your ex-wife whips out a gun. Rachel comes charging in the room. That was one of the things that bothered me. If Rachel was shot first, your ex-wife would never have stood still for the killer to press the gun against her head and fire like that."

"So maybe Nora was shot first," he said, but there was no conviction behind his voice.

"No, sir. Rachel was clear. She didn't hear gunfire. She heard voices and came down the stairs. She burst into the room. Your ex-wife is holding the gun. I don't know what happens exactly. She panics, I guess. Or maybe she tries to shoot you, but her aim is off. Whatever, she hits her own daughter. Rachel falls to the floor. Your ex-wife can't believe what she's done. She's distraught. The gun is still in her hands . . ."

317

I stopped. Chief Taylor parked the car, but so far, he hadn't gotten out.

"Do I have it right?" I asked.

"Close," he said. He took a few breaths. "Nora didn't shoot and miss me. Yes, she had the gun out. Yes, she had it pointed in my direction. But when Rachel came in, she just . . . she just turned and fired. Just like that. I saw the blood spurt. I saw Rachel fall to the ground." He closed his eyes, tried to gather himself. "I ran toward my daughter and tried to stop the bleeding. I didn't even look at Nora. Then I heard the gun go off again. I turned and . . . I guess in hindsight I wasn't surprised. Nora was deeply disturbed with suicidal tendencies anyway. Now she had shot her own daughter. In her mind, I'm sure she thought Rachel was dead."

Chief Taylor got out of the car and started toward us.

I debated cutting my losses and breaking into a sprint right now. I knew enough. I knew now who shot Rachel. How would Chief Taylor react to my knowing the truth?

"People know where I am," I said. "They know the story."

"I don't think that's true, Mickey. I don't think you had time to tell anyone the story. It doesn't matter anyway." Mr. Caldwell looked up at me through wet eyes. "Are we done here?"

"Just about," I said. "Your daughter was injured. Your wife had killed yourself. You didn't call nine-one-one at first, did you?"

"No," he said. "I didn't."

"You called Chief Taylor."

"Yes."

"So he'd be first on the scene. So you could cover up the truth and try to pin it on a random break-in."

I didn't expect him to admit this, but Mr. Caldwell took a deep breath and then said, "Yes."

"You were afraid people would learn the truth about you. That you were a drug dealer."

"No."

Chief Taylor arrived. "Hello, Mickey," he said.

I ignored him and kept my eyes on Mr. Caldwell. "What do you mean, no?"

"I mean, you're wrong. I wasn't worried about what people would learn about me. If it was all to protect me, why do you think Chief Taylor agreed to help?"

"He's on your payroll," I said.

I saw the anger flash in Chief Taylor's eyes, but I didn't step back. "You think I'm a crook?"

"Take it easy, Ed," Caldwell said.

"Did you just hear what he said?"

"It's understandable from his perspective. Just calm down. He doesn't get it yet."

Taylor glared at me.

He was right. I didn't get it. "What are you two talking about?"

"I'm not a drug dealer, Mickey."

"And I'm not a cop on the take," Taylor added.

Then, with the three of us standing there, I saw the truth. In fact, when I stopped and thought about it, maybe I had known the truth before we all arrived here. There was a reason I set up this meeting without telling Rachel or responding to her constant texts. Subconsciously—or maybe not so subconsciously—I didn't want her to know the truth yet either.

"You covered it up," I said, "to protect Rachel."

Taylor kept his head down. "I don't like the way you put that. Covered it up."

"Mickey," Mr. Caldwell said, stepping in front of Taylor, "have you ever noticed the burn mark on Rachel's arm?"

"Yes."

"Do you know how she got it?"

I shook my head.

"Her mother did that to her with a clothing iron."

I didn't know what to say. I looked over at Chief Taylor. His head was back up now.

"That was the final straw really. Rachel's mother was unbalanced for years. I tried to hold on to her as long as I could." He blinked hard. "I loved Nora. When we first met . . ." His voice faded away. "But the illness robbed her of all that. You have heart disease, people understand. When the brain gets sick, well, it's almost impossible to comprehend. I lived in denial a long time. Friends warned me. Heck, Ed here warned me. They could see Nora was coming apart—that she wasn't right. I tried to get her help, but she got worse and worse, and then one day, Nora thought she saw little bugs attacking her little girl. So she went after them with a steam iron set on high."

I swallowed. "Does Rachel remember?"

"Maybe. I don't know. She may have blocked on it. Anyway, I couldn't risk it anymore. So I finally sent Nora away. She didn't want to go, but we had a judge commit her. It was the hardest decision of my life. I talked to a lot of doctors. They all agreed. She was a danger to herself and to our child."

I felt my heart start coming up to my throat. Poor Rachel.

Mr. Caldwell smiled at me but there was no joy in it. "I tried to tell Rachel. I tried to explain. But she was too young. Maybe she still is. Sometimes she got it. Sometimes she didn't. I probably should have spent more time with her. I shouldn't have remarried so fast. Maybe that would have helped, I don't know. It doesn't matter now. The years passed. Rachel started to need someone. A hero. Someone who would love her unconditionally."

"Enter her mother?" I said.

"Yes."

"And Rachel wanted now to believe her mother was okay?"

"Naturally," Mr. Caldwell said.

"So Rachel helps her mother get out of the hospital. She helps get her off her medications. She brings her home. She helps convince her mother that she isn't sick."

"But the irony is, she is," Mr. Caldwell said. "Nora was very sick. Don't you see what would happen if Rachel knew the truth—that her mother shot her and then shot herself? Can you imagine the guilt Rachel would feel? For bringing her home? For helping her off the meds? She'd never get over it. She'd blame herself."

I did see.

"But wait," I said. "Rachel did find drugs you were hiding. She did find that money."

"Yes."

"So maybe that was what caused the illness or at least exacerbated it. You were a drug dealer."

"No," Mr. Caldwell said.

Taylor sighed. "He works for us. Well, more for someone you know in the county office."

I thought about it and the answer was so clear now. "Detective Waters?"

"It was a sting operation," Mr. Caldwell said. "I was working undercover. Those drugs were supposed to be used to bring down Brian Tart and Emile Romero."

In the distance I heard the town's emergency whistle blow.

"I have to go," Chief Taylor said. He looked over at me. "Are you going to tell?"

I didn't reply. I had thought that Taylor was a creep of biblical proportions. Now I could see the truth. He had done what he had done—he had covered up the truth—to protect Rachel.

The fire whistle sounded again. Taylor looked at me again. I nodded at him. He nodded back. An unspoken understanding passed between us.

Mr. Caldwell moved closer to me. "I know you and the chief don't get along, but Ed did what he did for Rachel and me. He risked his own career to help us out. Do you see that?"

I looked at him. "Are you going to tell Rachel the truth?"

"About my working for the police? Yes. I'm going to tell her soon."

I shook my head. "Not about that. About what really happened in that den."

"No."

I said nothing.

"Listen to me, Mickey. I'm her father. I want what's best for her. You get that, right?"

I still didn't know what to say.

He put down the basketball and rested his hands on my shoulders. He leaned in close and made sure I was looking him straight in the eyes. "It would kill her," Mr. Caldwell said, his voice a plea. "Rachel did mess up. She messed up so big, her own mother shot her. It wasn't the contents of that gym bag that got her mother killed. It was the illness, yes, but Rachel isn't going to see that. Rachel is going to see that if she had left well enough alone, her mother would be alive right now. She is going to see that she helped facilitate her mother's delusions. She is going to see that she brought her mother here and that her actions led to her mother's death. She's going to realize that because of what she did, her mother shot her own daughter and was so pained by that, so tortured by that last vision, she ended her own life. Do you see, Mickey? I'm a father. My job is to protect my daughter. Do you see how I couldn't let Rachel spend the rest of her life with that kind of guilt?"

"Because she is to blame," I said, my voice sounding far away in my own ears. "There may have been excuses. It may have been understandable. But in the end, what happened was Rachel's fault."

"Yes," Mr. Caldwell said softly. "Which is all the more reason for those of us who love her to keep this quiet."

It felt like someone had scooped out my insides. "So you just let Brian Tart and Emile Romero take the fall?"

"They have so many counts against them, those two won't matter. The prosecutor could never prove it anyway. It'll be one of those cases where everyone knows who did it but there won't be a need to try it. The police won't look too hard because they don't want the truth out. I'm still a valuable commodity working undercover. If this became public, it would ruin that. A lot of criminals would go free."

I felt a fresh pang of sadness. "So we all stay quiet."

"For Rachel's sake. Can you do that, Mickey?"

But I didn't feel like answering that right now. I turned and walked away, toward a tree in the distance.

"Mickey?"

I didn't turn around. I just kept walking. Eventually Mr. Caldwell started back for his car. I stopped and waited for him to drive off. Then I finished my walk to the big tree.

Uncle Myron was standing behind it. "I got scared when he asked to see your cell phone."

"I hung up before I handed it to him," I said.

"I was going to move in, but, well, you never gave me the distress signal."

"I was fine," I said, heading with Uncle Myron back toward his car, "but I felt better having you here as backup."

CHAPTER 47

I had to start answering Rachel's texts.

When I got home, I told her that I'd found nothing significant in Chief Taylor's files. In short, I lied. Or at least, I bought more time because I didn't know what to do. Ema also wanted to know what was up. I wasn't sure what to do, but in the end, this was Rachel's private business, not mine, so I again kept it to myself.

The doorbell rang.

Myron was on the phone. "It's the pizza guy. You mind? The money's on the kitchen table."

I grabbed the money, gave it to the guy at the door, took the pizza. I dropped the pie on the kitchen table, filled two water glasses, and waited for Uncle Myron. He came in and sat down next to me.

Uncle Myron opened the box. The wonderful aroma

wafted out as though conjured up by the gods we studied in mythology class. He gave me a slice first, then he took one for himself. He bit into it and said, "Heaven."

"Pretty much," I agreed.

He swallowed. "You still don't want to tell me what that was all about?"

"I appreciate you backing me up," I said.

"But?"

It was getting late. I was tired and confused. "Do you believe it's okay to lie sometimes?"

Myron put down the slice and wiped his hands on a napkin. "Sure."

"Just like that?"

"Just like that. It's the eternal question—do the ends justify the means?"

"And do they?"

Myron smiled. "If anyone has a sure answer to that one, be wary. Anyone who answers definitely yes or definitely no is someone who isn't thinking things through."

"So the answer is sometimes?"

"If it was always or never, life would be far simpler. But life isn't simple."

"So sometimes it's okay to lie."

"Of course. Are you dating yet?"

"No."

"Well, here's an example. If your future girlfriend asks you if a certain dress makes her look fat, say no."

"That's not what I mean."

"Oh?"

"I mean something big. Is it okay to lie about something big if the truth will really hurt the person?"

Myron thought about that. "I wish I could give you a definitive answer, Mickey. It depends."

"How about if a parent asks you to lie to their child? For their own good? I mean, you can't just go against the parent's wishes, can you?"

"Wow," he said. "You're in a mess."

I said nothing.

"I lied to my father once," Uncle Myron said. "It cost me my relationship with your father. I sometimes wonder, if I had told the truth . . ." He stopped and looked away. Tears filled his eyes and ran down his cheek. His head dropped. I could feel the anger starting to rise in me now. Yes, Uncle Myron, maybe if you'd told the truth, maybe if you'd been more understanding and kind, my father would be alive and my mother would be out of rehab and I would be nowhere near you.

I almost stormed out right then and there, but Uncle Myron, as if sensing what I was about to do, put his hand on my forearm.

"Here's what you need to know, Mickey. There's always a price you pay when you lie. Once you introduce a lie into a relationship, even for the best of intentions, it is always there. Whenever you're with that person again, that lie is in the room too. It sits on your shoulder. Good lie or bad lie, it's in the room with you forever now. It's your constant companion. Do you understand?"

"I do," I said. I pushed his hand off my forearm and stared down at the pizza. "But suppose the truth will devastate the person."

"Then maybe you should lie," Uncle Myron said. "But you need to understand the price. You need to ask yourself if you're ready to pay it."

Was I?

We had both finished the first slice in silence and were reaching for our seconds when Myron said, "It's all arranged."

I stopped. "What is?"

"The exhumation of your father's grave. We fly out to Los Angeles tomorrow afternoon. The county officer said we can bring up his coffin the next day."

I just sat there, stunned.

"Are you sure you still want to go through with it?" Uncle Myron asked.

"Yes, definitely." And then—maybe because I wanted to reach out a little or maybe because he really seemed to need it—I said, "Thank you, Myron."

CHAPTER 48

The next morning I woke up early and put on one of Myron's old suits. It was a little big in the chest and waist, but it did the job. Uncle Myron's tie closet was jam-packed with bright pink-and-green ties from some friend's clothing company, but I managed to find a darker, somber one that would fit the occasion.

My cell phone rang. The caller ID said: KASSELTON HIGH SCHOOL.

"Hello?"

"Mickey, it's Coach Grady."

"Oh." I sat down. "What can I do for you?"

"I just got off the phone with Chief Taylor," he said. "He said all the charges against you have been dropped. In fact, he thinks you've gotten a pretty raw deal."

I could feel my grip on the phone tighten.

"Mickey?"

"I'm listening, Coach."

"Well, when I'm wrong, I'm wrong. You're no longer suspended from the team. We will see you at practice Monday afternoon."

I nearly leapt in the air with joy, but then I remembered where I was and what was happening today and so I stopped, thanked Coach Grady for calling, and finished tying my tie.

"Do you want a ride?" Uncle Myron asked.

"I'd rather walk."

"I'm not sure I understand why you're going. I mean, this is really sad and all, but this boy vanished twenty-five years ago. You obviously didn't know him."

I didn't bother correcting him.

"Mickey?"

"Yeah?"

"Whether you knew this kid or not, I mean, you look kinda happy for a guy heading to a memorial service."

I decided to tell him. "Coach just called. I'm back on the team."

Without warning, Myron threw his arms around me and pulled me close. My body went rigid at first, but then I softened. We both got this—what the game meant to us. Not even Ema could understand like Myron could. I wouldn't say I hugged him back or anything, but I stayed there and let him hug me and then I thought about how much Spoon loved hugs and I gently pushed him away.

I ran most of the way to the memorial service, ran that stupid thrill out of me, so by the time I slowed down, I remembered why I was here. I thought about the Photo-shopped picture of the Butcher. I thought about the Bat Lady and where she might be. I thought about Ema wanting to know who her father was, and I thought about finding out the truth about my own father. I thought about Spoon and when I did, I could feel a stab of pain go so deep in my heart I could barely breathe. And mostly, I thought about Rachel and her father's desire to protect her and what, if anything, I should do about it.

The church bell rang. The sun shone bright off the church spire as if it were making fun of the sadness. There was a blown-up photograph of Dylan Shaykes on an easel board in front of the church door. It was the same picture of the sad-eyed, curly-haired boy I had seen in Bat Lady's hallway.

The church was maybe three-quarters full. The organist played something appropriately sad. The people communi-cated via "church whispers," though today they were even quieter and more respectful than normal. I sat in a pew near the back and checked out my surroundings. The same pho-tograph of Dylan Shaykes was up on the altar.

I looked around for a familiar face, but so far, he had not shown up.

The organ music stopped at exactly nine A.M. The whis-pering faded into silence. The service began. Dylan Shaykes's mother had passed away, but his father, the man the authorities suspected at first, sat front and center. He had a shock of white-gray hair and wore a tweed jacket.

The first person to speak was a boyhood friend of Dylan's. The contrast was startling. We looked at a picture of a nine-year-old missing boy and now this man in his thirties was talking about him—about how Dylan liked kickball and collected baseball cards, about how he liked to walk through the woods and study butterflies.

One in particular, I bet.

The room fell extra-silent now, as though the very building were holding its breath. It was hard to fathom. Twenty-five years ago today, a little boy had been snatched from a school yard. Then, as if on cue, that little boy entered the church from the back.

I froze.

He stood for a moment in the back, all grown up now, before he found a seat in the last pew. He wore sunglasses. Nobody but me had seen him come in. Nobody but me knew who he really was.

When the first friend stopped speaking, I made my move. I slowly slid out of my pew and headed toward the back. I could see the surprise on his face when he spotted me. He rose and started for the exit. I followed. He burst through the door and into the warm sun. I followed.

Ahead of him, I could see the familiar black car.

"Stop," I said to him.

Shaved Head slowly turned around. He took off his

sunglasses and headed back toward me. You wouldn't see it if you just looked at him. The curly hair was obviously gone now. The kid in the photograph had been a scrawny scarecrow while this man was tall and well built. The only thing that might give it away, when the sunglasses were off, were the eyes. They were still somehow sad.

"So now you know," Shaved Head said to me.

"I know," I said, "but I don't understand."

A small smile came to his lips.

"If you're alive," I went on, "why haven't you told anyone? What happened to you?"

He didn't answer.

"Did the Abeona Shelter rescue you?"

"I guess you could say that," he said.

"Where is Bat Lady anyway? I don't understand any of this. That picture she gave me was Photoshopped. It wasn't the Butcher."

He cocked an eyebrow. "Are you sure?"

"What do you mean?"

"The man in the picture is the Butcher."

"But—"

"He's your Butcher, Mickey. That's what she wanted you to see." Then Shaved Head, aka Dylan Shaykes, stepped back up to the church's glass door and looked at his father sitting in the front row. "We all have our Butcher."

I could feel my whole body begin to quake. I remembered

his words after Rachel was shot. I had asked him why had we—Spoon, Ema, Rachel, and I—been chosen. "Why you?" he had said, and then, looking devastated, he'd added, "Why me?"

I swallowed. "Were you kidnapped or were you rescued?"

Still staring at his father, he said, "Sometimes even I don't know."

"Dylan?"

He closed his eyes. "Don't call me that."

"Is my father still alive?"

He didn't reply.

"I'm flying out to Los Angeles. We are going to dig up my father's grave."

He turned toward me now.

"What will we find?" I asked him.

He put his hands on my shoulders and smiled. "The truth." He let me go and started down the walk toward the black car. "Good luck, Mickey."

"Where is Bat Lady?"

"She's fine. She'll be back soon with another assignment for you guys."

"My friend was shot."

"I know."

"How is he?"

"He's not good, but . . ."

"But what?"

Dylan Shaykes stopped and came back over to me. "There is one thing you should know about us—about all of us who are chosen for the Abeona Shelter."

I stood there. "What's that?"

The church doors opened behind us as the parishioners started to file out. "We are all stronger than we realize," Dylan Shaykes said as he slid into the back of the black car. "And no matter where it leads, we must always seek the truth."

CHAPTER 49

There was enough time before we caught the plane to Los Angeles for one final, important stop.

Even as Rachel buzzed me in through the gate, I wasn't sure exactly what I would do. I thought about what Mr. Caldwell had said. He wanted to protect his daughter. That was his right as a father, wasn't it? I thought about my own father and the way he had sheltered me from harm. Who was I to interfere with that? Why force Rachel to live with the guilt that her mother was dead because of her? A father had thought this through and made a decision about what would be best for his daughter.

Who was I to contradict that?

I was seconds away from turning and heading home when Rachel appeared. She spotted my face and said, "Mickey? What is it? What's wrong?"

Seconds away.

"Mickey?"

But then in those seconds, I thought about what Uncle Myron had said, about how the lie never leaves you. I thought about the Abeona Shelter and my friends and what Dylan Shaykes had said. Yes, Ema, Spoon, Rachel, and I had originally joined forces to save Ashley, but what kept us together, what really gave us our unbreakable bond, was our need to know the truth.

I looked at Rachel and felt her strength. The truth could hurt her, sure, but not like a lifetime lie could. And forget Dylan Shaykes—Spoon had said it all as he fought through the pain on the hospital bed:

You can't stop until we find the truth.

"Mickey?" Rachel said. "What is it? You're scaring me."

It wasn't an easy decision for me. Uncle Myron had warned me that life was rarely simple. But in the end I had promised Spoon we wouldn't stop until we found the truth. You don't do that—you don't make those sacrifices—just to let your friend live a happy lie.

"I have to tell you something," I said to Rachel, taking her hand in mine.

She looked in my eyes. "Is it that bad?"

"Yes."

Rachel swallowed and stood tall. "I'm listening."

And then I told her the truth.